How to Be Human

HOW TO BE
HUMAN

A NOVEL

PAULA COCOZZA

METROPOLITAN BOOKS

Henry Holt and Company   New York

Metropolitan Books
Henry Holt and Company
Publishers since 1866
175 Fifth Avenue
New York, New York 10010
www.henryholt.com

Metropolitan Books® and m® are registered trademarks of
Macmillan Publishing Group, LLC.
Copyright © 2017 by Paula Cocozza
All rights reserved.

Library of Congress Cataloging-in-Publication Data

Names: Cocozza, Paula, author.
Title: How to be human : a novel / Paula Cocozza.
Description: First edition. | New York : Metropolitan Books, 2017.
Identifiers: LCCN 2016039491| ISBN 9781250129253 (hardback) |
ISBN 9781250129260 (electronic book)
Subjects: LCSH: Marriage—Fiction. | Domestic fiction. | BISAC: FICTION / Literary.
Classification: LCC PR6103.O348 H69 2017 | DDC 823/.92—dc23
LC record available at https://lccn.loc.gov/2016039491

ISBN: 978-1-250-12925-3

Our books may be purchased in bulk for promotional, educational, or business use. Please contact your local bookseller or the Macmillan Corporate and Premium Sales Department at (800) 221-7945, extension 5442, or by e-mail at MacmillanSpecialMarkets@macmillan.com.

First Edition 2017

Designed by Kelly S. Too

Printed in the United States of America

1 3 5 7 9 10 8 6 4 2

This is a work of fiction. All of the characters, organizations, and events portrayed in this novel either are products of the author's imagination or are used fictitiously.

How to Be Human

CHAPTER ONE

There was a baby on the back step. A white bundle, downward sloping, spilling two arms and a head, the head looking at the edge of
the step precariously. Not really looking. The eyes were shut. One
hand lay beside an ear, fingers stiffened into a fist that might have
held something or lost something. Such a beautiful hand: its sliver
of palm was streaked with shimmers of purple and blue, veins
rubbed with moonlight.

The surprise came not from seeing the baby, but from seeing
what was around her. A baby on the back step. It was the step that
was wrong. She was meant—Mary turned to check that she was
alone before she finished the thought. She was meant to take the
child into the house.

She stared down at the . . . parcel, she thought, studying but not
touching the sheath of white seersucker that lay between her feet and
her door. She was thinking of the way it had been left to wait for
her, so carefully wrapped. She squinted into her dark garden, half
expecting someone to jump out and laugh at how she had fallen for
such an extravagant practical joke. She was unsure what kind of
person would play a trick like that. In any case, no one moved. The

bushes hunched secretively. From somewhere within the block of streets, the owl hooted again, on patrol from his warehouse. This was the first night she had heard him; now she had heard him twice.

Just the perfect baby on the step, her mouth open as if she had said something a while back. Wrapped in white, legs shrouded inside her bedtime ghost costume, lying incredibly on a slab. Mary crouched for a closer look. She ran her thumb over the marbled forehead and traced the thread of violet that wriggled across one eyelid. There should be a note, she thought, with a sender's name. *Dear Mary. Congratulations on your new arrival. From* —. Obviously she didn't expect a note. It was the bizarreness of the situation that made her imagination busy, made her unfurl a couple of rigid fingers just to see what they held. But all they let slip was a fistful of night.

A heavy warm breath slid down Mary's throat. So this was what it felt like to be trusted. The proof lay here, beneath the knee that gently dropped to prod an arm, warm but still. She sucked in another draught of night medicine. The air tasted clear and dry and tangy with green spice. The baby's face remained impervious, so she jabbed the arm again, hoping to surprise the eyes open—but the eyes stayed shut. Oh, Christ. She had assumed, but what if, what if the blood making the arm warm was not a sign of life but of life's residual warmth cooling?

"No, no, no! You mustn't do that," Mary whispered. She wished someone else were here, and she was very glad that someone else was not. With a hand hovering over the baby's chest, she cast around the empty garden again. She was looking for help and looking to see if anyone was watching. If she touched the baby, someone could witness her—what? It was not a crime to touch a baby. Though it might become one, if she were the last person to touch her alive. Mary cupped the head and carefully rolled it away from the drop. As she did so, the scalp popped softly at her fingers.

Her hand was slippery with sweat, so she wiped it on her jogging bottoms and shook the near shoulder, which made the head wheel back to face her with a stony roll. Mary pressed her cheek to the baby's chest, but it was her own brain she could hear, throbbing and whistling with fear. "Psssst!" she said into the little ear. "Are you OK? Please tell me you're OK."

No answer.

Mary picked up the near hand. The palm was so plump, the lines on it were like seams sewn into cushions. She flattened out the fat bits between her thumbs and rubbed wisps of silver fluff from the crevices. She kissed the baby's forehead. Still not a flutter. Then she clasped the little nose in a firm pinch, waiting for the mouth to wake. These maulings made her feel that she was mugging the child for a breath. She hung on to the nose, but she was flailing, a thief trying all the windows and doors, and still the mouth stayed shut. Mary let go of the nose and gently laid a finger on the purple vein, stroking it upward until she had prized open the eye. She held it like that, her fingertip pinning the lid to the brow. "Wake up!" she hissed at the pupil. It was deep gray-blue velvet, replete with color yet in denial of its color. In a few months, this eye would be brown. Could the eye see her? The iris rolled into the corner of its socket, looking back at her through misty glass from some far-off place, as distant and disinterested as a dead eye must be.

Several positional steps were necessary to lift the child. Concrete pared Mary's knuckle as she slipped a hand under the neck, forked another beneath the legs. How light the baby was! Moonlight tinted her face blue. With her long white robe, she looked like an infant just christened in time. Mary shook her gently, listening for the rattle as you might with a stopped watch, but the shake jolted the head forward, and the blue pallor deepened.

An outside door closed nearby, one of those sounds that hides whether it has come from left or right.

Mary waited, but the night was silent. There was nothing and no one to see. Only a snail in the corner of the patio broke out from his hiding place behind the plant pot and began to haul his short silvery string toward them. She drew the baby tightly to her chest. She had the baby, had taken possession of her by who knew what form of special delivery. Delivery, deliverance, she mused. Which was right? And what sort of damn brain did she have that in a moment of crisis it wanted to pick at the gaps between words? She brushed a leaf from the cap of dark hair and pressed her lips to the spot. The kiss produced a fluttering sensation in her stomach, then she realized the flutter was on the outside and that against her own stomach a tiny foot flexed. She swallowed down a silent scream, let it growl around her belly. Somewhere there, it must have tweaked the baby's foot, because the toes twitched again, curling into the scream, and Mary let her breath go. The air and the words rushed out in one heavy stream. "You're alive!"

She crossed her wrists over the little one's back and squeezed her closer. Chest to chest like this, the child's rib cage fitted exactly inside the cavity of Mary's own ribs. They were like two wicker baskets nested for convenience. The baby breathed inside her own breath, as if her own breath had consumed the baby's. Together their bodies rose and fell, their insides taking care of a conversation that neither of their tongues knew how to voice. If only the moment would hold them both still in their funny belonging. An air lock popped in Mary's stomach, a tiny bubble released, as if into the waters within her some new thing had stolen.

Amazing the way a baby could get inside you like that.

So here was an idea. Take her into the house. Just lie down on the bed, with the little one on top, pretty much as they were now, but horizontal. Standing out here with their bones snugly jammed, it made sense. Look at the sky beginning to lighten. Dawn was not far off. Who cared if she had no equipment, no nappies. The heat of her body, the stroke of her hand, were all the two of them needed.

It would be enough for Mary to watch the baby sleep, to mind the rise and fall of her chest, to lay a hand on her heart and collect the pulse. She herself needed rest. A truck shook its heavy chains down the main road, but the poppet in her arms slept on. Mary lifted her a moment, felt the weight of her, guessing her like a package she had signed for and promised to keep safe. It seemed obvious then that that was her job—to keep the baby safe. "Flora," she breathed into the sleeping ear.

All she needed to do was open the door and walk inside.

CHAPTER TWO

The beginning, when you looked back from the middle, had come four weeks earlier, one miserable Tuesday in June. Mary went to work, did her work, some of it anyway, came home from work. There was not yet anything to distinguish it from other Tuesdays of that time, which were themselves hard to distinguish from Wednesdays, Thursdays, Fridays, and Mondays. She walked into the lounge, shrugged her bag onto the mound of envelopes on the table, and glanced out the—

He was lying on the grass in the center of her garden. He had chosen an ostentatious spot for a doze. But she didn't believe he was sleeping because although his body presented itself as entirely still, his ears spiked sharply, ready to countermand his elegant sprawl.

Mary felt her way around the table to the window. At the corner of her eye, a stray hair bobbed and gleamed, large and knobbly as a hair under a microscope, but she resisted the urge to brush or blow it away. Now that she had him in her sights, the slightest move seemed a concession. It might unlock their standoff, and she wanted to keep him where she could see him, which meant she had to stay right where she was, pinned to the rear window. She stared at him, her gaze a kind of cage, throwing down bars to the lawn to keep him trapped. One moment of inattention, and he would be free.

The complacency of his posture struck Mary as a provocation. He gave the impression of both purpose and ease, as if relaxation were just a pose, and he might now, or now, or now, wake to quick feet. She understood his show of nonchalance was the disguise for an as yet unarticulated intention. He was curled loosely on the grass, but his head poked out from the bottom of the curve like an unfinished question mark.

What did he want?

He had come to her garden and no one else's. So he had chosen her, Mary, and he must have come for something. While she had chased from meeting to meeting, trying to nudge and soothe the large egos of her midsize, midlevel university's human resources, he had been idly sunbathing on her lawn. In a single visit he had acquired an air of permanence, as if he had been here yesterday and would be here again tomorrow. She tried to step out of her shoes, but in the heat her feet had swollen and the shoes stuck fast. She may as well have been caught in a glue trap.

His rudeness riled her. He had plonked himself smack in the garden in an obvious plea for attention, and now that he had it, he was making a big show of ignoring her. He was trespassing brazenly. His very presence, his solitary sit-in on her lawn, seemed to dispute something. Her right to be here. The supremacy of humans. The subordination of foxes. She began to speculate about where this might end, briefly pictured him barking orders at her for dinner from his place at the table while she scuttled around the garden foraging for toads.

She shook her head—just a little, so as not to unsettle her stare. There were other things she should be getting on with. She needed to eat. Or sit down. She imagined a nice, comfy chair sidling up behind her, a well-upholstered chest, a pair of firm arms outstretched.

But there were only three chairs left in the house and all were hard. "What the hell is he doing?" she said aloud. Silly question because he was doing nothing.

She bowed her head against the window frame, flaking a paint brittle, and trained her eyes on him through her favorite pane. The house had no other window like it; the fault was original. It was the fault that she loved. In this one segment, a broad wrinkle ran top to bottom, warped the glass, made the leaves look out of sequence with the branches, the picture jump like a scratch on a disc. Sometimes bits of garden life got lost within its folds. Sometimes, caught inside a magnifying seam, they grew. You could stand there and try out different ways to see what you saw. She frowned at the fox, who, despite her best efforts, was refusing to vanish into the kink. His eyes were sleepy slits; they gave the impression he had accidentally left the lids ajar. He had seen her. She supposed he had seen her. But it was impossible to be sure. And what if he had? What dull shape would she make behind the glass?

She straightened up and gave a little sway, watching his haunches hump and subside under the wrinkle as if she had run her hand over him.

The movement stirred the sun in the fox's lids, and daylight leaked into the crack of an eye.

Ah, now she had his attention. Mary rocked her head again and watched her prisoner's back ripple in muscular spasm. The pane seemed to buck his torso halfway to standing, then force him back down. He was caught in the crease of the glass, and as she bobbed and waved, she yanked him around like a puppet.

Time to open an eye.

He was looking at her. Half-looking at her. Thinking. One eye sufficed to contain her; let the other eye sleep. From her swaying, he'd say a breeze blew through her pen. Strange. No breeze out here. Swaying, swaying. No threat. Just shuffling shadows so. No problem there.

Her edges fuzzed in his drowse, blurred in a haze of lashes and whiskers. Tiny Female, locked up all alone and too far away to care. Darker, darker fuzz because. It was fine. To shut the eye.

Mary gawked, strained to see through the glass. Do it again, she thought. Go on! Once more. So I know for certain. But she knew what she had seen. He had opened an eye, stared right at her, then shut it in a funny slow-motion wink. That's exactly what it was. He had winked at her! From the way he was lying there now, with both eyes clamped shut in exaggerated denial, it seemed obvious that the wink had been deliberate. With one gesture, he had opened up a line of communication between them. As if he had heard this thought, the tip of his tail flicked on the lawn.

OH, MARK. WHAT would you do, if you were here now, and this beast was in the garden?

Actually, she knew what Mark would do, because Mark had done it lots of times. He would dart to the back door, dip a quick hand into his pot of stones, and run at the fox.

The fox tilted his head, though his eyes stayed shut.

Yes, life was better now. Better and worse.

Even as Mary eyed the twitch of a ginger ear, Mark loomed before her at the wrinkled window. It was where the house began for them. They knew they were going to buy it as soon as they stood here and saw . . . well, saw all that couldn't be seen. Not a building in sight. Not a chimney poked through. Even the high-rise blocks on Shepherds Bridge Walk were hidden behind a thick screen of vegetation. It was the only starter house on the market in their part of east London, right when the market slumped: a miracle they could afford it. Mark had reached round and squeezed her waist, in the way that she took to mean she needed to lose weight (she didn't) but which he swore meant nothing of the sort (it did). It was a work habit, he claimed. He was a quantity surveyor. Lean himself. While the real estate agent paced in the hall, Mark had whispered, "It's practically a forest!" and grabbed her lobe in his lips. She put the back of her hand to her ear and wiped off the saliva from five years ago. She had won that battle. It was her house now. Mary Green, 53 Hazel Grove, London E8.

On the other side of the glass, a spider ran along the guy rope of his web, legs blurring into a serif scrawl at the edge of her vision.

Her eyes stayed on the fox on the lawn.

Sleeping or not sleeping.

What the hell was she going to do with him? This one must have escaped from the woods that ran between the back gardens of this terrace and the houses on the road behind. "Woods," she said, still said. It was her and Mark's joke because if you looked from upstairs in winter, you could make out the shape of a bicycle under a heap of ivy, the arms of a wheelbarrow thrusting up through brambles like a final plea from the drowning. It was just a patch of wasteland, but magical for all that—an island of wilderness in the inner city, left to do its own thing while property prices soared and the council forgot it was even there. Trees were overlaid so densely on trees that the greens meshed and knotted, and perspective itself seemed made of leaves. Locked inside a rectangle of terraced streets, the woods kept their secret. They belonged only to those who could reach them.

Footsteps chimed on the pavement behind her, but Mary was not going to be tricked into distraction. She watched the fox. Her front garden was reflected in this window anyway. It hung over him like a garden within the garden, a phantom mid-ground in which the soft edges of her shrubs, the long fingers of her giant palm, lurked. Just then, the outline of a passerby with a stroller stepped into this ghostly oasis. A tiny hand waved from beneath its awning.

She liked it when that happened, but you had to catch them fast before they disappeared into the thick foliage of the laurel. After the stroller vanished in there, she heard its wheels bump up the step next door. It must have been Michelle.

Focus, Mary. Don't let him go now. So what if you're tired and hungry. So what if you've crawled to the end of another miserable day in a job you hate, and tomorrow will bring only more of the same, which will feel not the same but worse, and you can't sleep and can't eat, which means there's only waking and working, waking and working. And now *this*. What was she going to do?

She dropped her hip to pry off her shoes, one foot jabbing at the heel of the other, and that was when . . . he did. She saw it. He bent his ear to her. Just the one. His right. He really did. Tipped it forward, then pulled it back, showing her the darker hairs inside. First a wink, and now he had practically doffed his cap. Outrageous! She rapped hard on the glass. His fur filled the shape of the leaves and made them rust. The phantom garden vanished into the movement of his body. Each limb knew its duty. He regained his feet and changed direction in a single stroke. He didn't look back, didn't rush. She watched him over the wall, the white tip the last of him. Then she went to check that both doors were locked.

THE SOUND WAS a siren, a baby crying, a shriek that seemed to pass through a human pitch and turn animal. Mary opened her eyes. She reached for her clock, but her hand fell through unfurnished space. She had traveled in her sleep to the wrong side of the bed, the side that used to be someone else's. She sat up, unpeeling her back from the damp sheet, and kicked off the duvet.

The room was silent. Only the lull came in through the open window. That's how she thought of this special piece of night when the main road had fallen quiet and the birds had yet to sing—an overlapping of silences that meant it was around 3:45 a.m. Over the five months since Mark had left, Mary had come to know these hours well, but it still surprised her how quickly they passed. There was such a brief lapse from 3 a.m., when there was hope of sleep, to 6 a.m., when there was none. She got up.

Her room was at the front of the house, and the window frames bloomed amber from the street. The blinds, which had long since reneged on their promise of blackout, sagged and curled at the edges to reveal a wavy slice of road. She pulled back the fabric, and a fly buzzed against the glass in protest. "Sorry, Mr. Fly," she said. Then out of her sleepy eye something darted. A red smear of tail, a blur on the road, a moving speed mark, gone. She held her breath for further news, but all was still. Perhaps it was just the strange intimacy of seeing the street when no one else was seeing it, but Hazel Grove looked different.

THE NEXT MORNING Mary had her key in the front door when Eric called out. He was reversing down his path and nodded at the pram. "I hope she didn't wake you. We've got a bit of a sniffle."

Mary clocked the "we," and wondered as she turned the key, double-locking, why parents chose to live so much in their children's lives that they gate-crashed their first person. Eric and Michelle had moved in about a year after her and Mark. The four of them—and this was not something to be taken for granted with neighbors—had seen the insides of each other's houses. True, she thought of them as neighbors rather than friends, but they were friendly neighbors. Eric, especially. And then the children came. First one, then, not long ago, this tiny other.

"I didn't hear her," Mary said at last. These days, Mary herself made very little noise through the walls.

"I'm hoping she'll be better by next weekend. He glanced toward his top windows, where the curtains were closed, and lowered his voice. "I really want to get Michelle out."

Mary hadn't seen Michelle since the birth. It was Eric who had dropped by to show off the baby—Flora, had they called her? He had stood on the doorstep while Mary tried to sound appreciative. She looked again at the pram where Eric was stooped over the parasol. So this scrap was the source of all the noise. She had been born early, a pale slip in an enormous carry-cot.

"This is hopeless," Eric said, tilting the parasol. "You think you can burn at this time of day?"

"You could stick to the other side of the road. Run through the sun, slow through the shade. Would that work? Where's George this morning?" She had no interest in George, but the little boy heard his cue and roared out from behind the hedge with his familiar scowl. He looked such a little shit. "Ah, there you are!" she said. "Excellent hiding place!"

"Say hi to Mary, George," Eric said, his tone wavering between a command and a plea. He caught the boy under his arms and lifted him up. "Come on, Georgie, you can say hi, can't you? Mary's going to look after you next Saturday. We hope."

The child hid his face in his hands, turned his head, then, as his legs began to thrash, kicked his father in the groin.

"I should get going," Mary said. She was thinking of her meeting at ten. What had Dawn said? "Lateness non-optional." A formal hearing, the paperwork for which was stuffed unread in her bag. It was pretty dire for a member of the so-called People team to be on the receiving end of the procedures she was meant to implement. "Embarrassing," Dawn had said. In fact, that was the only upside, that the whole business, rumbling on for months, had exposed Dawn's managerial deficiencies. Mary had come down the path into the street and, unusually, was closing the gate behind her. "But sure, Saturd—"

Soft, the thing her foot found instead of the pavement. Her sandal slid moistly forward, and she lurched, her bag jumping off her shoulder, the strap unspooling quickly down her arm to her wrist. It was so hot that when the wetness touched her toes, she was grateful for its coolness, till she looked down and saw it. She had painted her nails blue the night before, and now, with her gold sandals, they seemed to mock her. "Shit!"

"Oh dear," Eric said, sniffing from a safe distance. "Fox."

"What?"

"That's how they mark their territory. You think this is your house. He thinks it's his."

Christ, she thought. I'm not going through that again. It is my house. My name on the mortgage. But she didn't stop to answer. She was already hobbling back up the path.

"You've got to let them know who's boss!" Eric called. "Find the hole. Mary . . ." He checked behind him and then said, softly, across her front garden, "Get some vet's poison. You can buy it online."

Mary flinched in understanding; the sensation was a small, interior nod. That was what Mark would have said too. The fox had entered her garden. He had laid a trap for her on the pavement. He was attacking her from the front and the back. He was there in the day, at night. She had no idea what he wanted, but she knew his incursions amounted to a sustained campaign against her. As soon as she got to her desk and Dawn stopped staring at her, she would go online.

"Shall we say seven next Saturday?" Eric said.

Indoors, Mary gripped the banister, hopped up the stairs and washed her foot over the bathroom sink. Why did he have to make her late today? The mess was so deliberately placed. He seemed to want to get her into even worse trouble at work. Of course he didn't want that. He was a fox! But at the same time, she believed, from the force with which he was imposing himself, that he had sensed her vulnerability. She splashed at the porcelain. The fox's smell curled around the basin but would not run out with the water. She dried off and in the bedroom sluiced her foot with Mark's old cologne. She had seen it in a box while he was packing, and now it lived on the shelf that used to be his. (He had put it up, and in that sense her shelf also felt like his.) There was little else left of him: a couple of shirts, a little wooden puzzle they had bought in the souvenir shop of some museum. She shut her eyes to the long streak of coffee that stained the wall.

This residual Mark was pretty good company. He gave Mary freedom and independence and never lost his temper. She had whittled him down to the perfect partner. Mark in a bottle, helpfully warding off the prospect of total solitude while kept in check by a heavy glass stopper. Today, though, she was letting him out. Whew. The cologne was potent. She slopped some on the other foot too. Show the fox who's boss. That was the name of it, Boss. The fox was hardly going to notice that the logic was erratic, that this was Mark's scent. You couldn't expect a fox to be reasonable.

Ten minutes later, she stood the clean sandals on a few sheets of the local paper outside the kitchen door. Water soaked into the print, making the eyes of the poor owl in the photograph transparent. "Tawny owl," she read, just as words from the other side of the page began to appear through his beak. Apparently they were nesting in one of the old factories by the canal. It would almost be worth losing sleep to catch a hoot, she thought, toeing a shoe clear of his feathers. She loitered by the step a moment. The sky was cloudless, and the sun brightened a small circle of lawn, like the floor of an amphitheater. What a waste. The disciplinary, an afternoon of conducting staff reviews while air-con froze her arms . . . She would leave as early as she could, come out here and make the most of it.

WHEN SHE REENTERED the house that evening, Mary could tell from the postmark that the envelope on the mat was from work, presumably containing belated confirmation of today's appointment. Her department was a shambles. She stepped over the letter and headed down the hall. It mystified her how Dawn had got that job, how she had the nerve to harass Mary for recurrent lateness and persistent failure to fulfill tasks, when she, as manager, couldn't even send out a letter on time. At the back door, Mary drew the bolts and cranked the handle up and down as clunkily as she could. The rattle was fear's emissary, sent out on reconnaissance while she hung back in its cover. If the fox was there, he would hear it and take off.

The noise filled the garden. Then she followed, and she was in the garden, and he was on his feet. Or perhaps he had already taken to his feet at the sound. She thought to shout or chase him off, but the sight of him so close sucked away her breath. His jaws slackened to liberate his tongue, and he licked his lips with her thoughts. As she hesitated, stalled by the sheer physical fact of him, the fox seemed to occupy more richly the space that her hesitation created. His fur thickened. And the next thing she saw, after his intrusion, the absolute wrongness of his being there, was how magnificent he looked.

In the sunlight, his coat was glossily auburn with lowlights, which she thought of (absurdly, she realized) as expensive. He was making an effort with his posture. Head up, back not slumping, haunches taut, as if he had instinctively adjusted his tension at the sight of her. He lifted his snout; she supposed he was sniffing the air. Most striking of all, he was holding out his tail unquiveringly straight behind him. He must have been six feet, nose to tip, and like those large dogs she tried to avoid in the park, he seemed taller than a subservient animal should. His legs were black, giving her the idea that he was a creature of two halves: bright and conspicuous above, below full of subterfuge. He shone with a predatory capability, to which she felt herself instinctively deferring.

At that moment, the patio darkened, and Mary glanced up. The sun had entered thick cloud, and even though the air was as warm as it had been a second before, and even though in a minute or two the sun would reappear, the effect was as chilling as a flame abruptly snuffed.

The dullness touched the top of the fox's head with a cool flutter. His ears twitched at the sensation, but his eyes watched the human Female's feet as they Beetled back, Beetled back, enough to say. Respect.

The garden began to brighten, and the sun, edging out from the cloud, warmed Mary's arms. "Not so sleepy today, then," she said under her breath. She tried to speak without moving her lips, because she felt sharply alert to the idea that any small movement from her might elicit a larger one from him. There was nothing to do but stare because stopping staring struck her as the greater act of communication. Without a window between them, she felt unable to rely on the balance of power which yesterday she had assumed. Was he still in a cage of her making? Would he obey again her command to leave? His poise today was a stillness with caveats: every hair bristled with his power to surprise. Her palm turned upward, moved of its own accord, as a magnet moves. But she did not otherwise stir; his eyes held her in place.

He yawned then, dropped his lower jaw like a drawbridge and let it hang. There was something careless about the way he so casually showed her his fangs—there was no other word for them—and it was unclear to Mary whether the carelessness implied harmlessness or its opposite. His pink tongue flicked up, a string of saliva impaled on one spiked tooth, and then he shut his mouth, turned, and headed for the back wall. Something about the way he did this— the way he kept his head up, held his brush aloft—suggested that he left out of choice, and on another day he might just as easily choose to stay. His exit, his magnanimous readiness to be the one to go, alarmed her, but she couldn't think why.

Mary hastened to the lounger to consolidate the territory she had regained. There was no sound from Eric and Michelle's garden, and she had no neighbor on the other side; the house had been empty since old Mrs. Farnworth died last year. Mary stepped out of her skirt, unbuttoned her shirt and slipped her bra straps from her shoulders.

Since yesterday she had been waiting for this moment, the chance to nourish herself with sun and rest, but now that she was alone, the garden felt unsettling: not so much empty as temporarily vacated. It reminded her of flat-sharing with Saba years ago. There must have been ten or twelve apartments in that mansion block; and the garden, which they could all access, never felt private, even when you were the only one in it. As she lay out here now in her underwear, the space felt uneasily communal, as if she mustn't inhabit it too fully or freely. The fox had gone. She had the place to herself. But for how long?

She wished she had remembered her book, but she knew if she went to fetch it, the fox would take her absence as permission to return. So she lay there thinking instead about what had just happened, and her mind kept returning to one thought. Since there was nobody to hear, she said it aloud. "He was as interested in me as I was in him." It was hard to dispel the idea that he had come back for a second look and that his repeated raids amounted to some sort of mission.

Perhaps because of this sensation, Mary heard every noise as a trespass. She jumped when a scorched leaf clacked across the patio. A shrub knocked against the fence, and each time she wondered who was at the door. Inside the clank of cranes where the old estate had been demolished, she heard the ringing of a telephone. Dawn had cited "entrenched lateness." And a "disappointing attitude." And other things Mary could no longer remember. Mary had been given every chance, but poor Dawn had been left with no choice . . . The disciplinary had ended as Mary knew it would, with a formal warning. Now every sound struck her as an attempt by some greater force to drive the threat home to her. If she lost the job, how long would it take to lose the house?

At some point, she must have dropped off because when she next looked the lounger was in shade, her skin cool. Mary dressed quickly and walked down the garden; she had the idea for some exploring of her own. Twice the fox had made his exit over her rear wall. Unlike her neighbors, she had no gate to the woods, and the wall bowed at the force of a huge lime tree which was bursting through her boundary. Seven bricks had already fallen, making a desultory gravestone on the other side.

Peering over the back, with the masonry chilling her forearms, Mary saw that although the light had gone from her garden, something of the day was still left out here. One perfect rectangle of the hazel tree blazed yellow, a bright window of leaves. It looked for all the world as if someone—and she knew who—had got home and put the light on. She marveled at the size of the fox's garden: all the woods and no mortgage! A picture flitted through her mind of him beneath the hazel, stretched out in front of the TV after another hard day sunbathing, and suddenly she grasped what she had been unable to grasp earlier. The distinctive manner of his exit—his ease over the wall, his readiness to oblige her by leaving—made it clear that his departure was not an expression of compliance but of hospitality. In her garden, he saw himself as proprietor and her as his guest.

MARY DIDN'T SEE the fox the next time he came. But she knew he had called because when she went outside the following morning to retrieve her sandals, they had gone, and a pair of blue boxers lay in their place. Torn and dusty, they were the sort of classic style that Mark used to wear. She wrinkled her nose in disgust. Now what was she going to do? She paced her garden, scouring the long grass for a telltale flash of metallic leather. When she walked back to the house, dirty as they were, the boxers seemed to mock her. Men's underwear had no place in her house at the moment.

She looked up at her neighbors' windows. God! Did they belong to Eric? "No," she said. It was bad enough the fox had stolen into her garden, but she refused to let him break into her imagination too. The fact was, she would have to spend another day in the wrong shoes. Always the wrong shoes, bought two years ago for the promotion she hadn't got. She was, now as then, joint second-in-command of a people department sub-team of four. She felt herself irresistibly stepping into the footprints of a long-term failure. It was a delusion to think that working in HR for a university was stimulating, that it to some extent kept alive her own hopes of a second degree. If you worked in HR, your business was nothing but people and their problems. The underpants, scooped into a carrier bag, went in the trash can as she clomped to the pavement.

Mary hurried across the park to the station, checking behind herself at every bend. The path snaked through the grass, and she had the impression she was being followed. Footsteps shadowed her, passed her, came at her. She kept looking over her shoulder, to the sides, and the bright grass rolled around like a green bowl turning in someone's hands.

FOR THE FIRST time that week, Mary returned home to an empty garden. The fox must have got the message, she thought. She leant over to brush lime dust from the lounger, and as she did so, a slither of gold leather caught her eye in the long grass. The sandal was hot from lying in the sun. She turned it over, looking for teeth marks or saliva trails, but there was no sign it had been touched. Just something about it felt different, as luggage feels different, handled, when it's collected from the carousel.

Mary slithered her foot inside. Perhaps this was going to turn out OK. With one foot shod, the other bare, she walked down the garden and crossed the line of shade thrown down by the lime. She found the second shoe beside the shed. Having made her decision with the first, she slipped it on without a sniff. One foot hot, one foot cold.

It was a bit of a scramble to get over the wall—she had to stand on a chair from the shed. But then she was in the woods, skirting a large nettle bed on her way to the hazel, sunlight dappling the floor. He had helped himself to her garden, so she was helping herself to his. The edge of the land disappeared into deep shade, and the bindweed that crept up the boundary had sprung its flat round blooms like torches. Mary felt conspicuous in their beams. She was making a lot of noise. Twigs broke under her feet. A nettle prickled her arm, and she cursed as it needled her in several discrete places, cursed again when her sandal scooped up leaf mulch. She hoped it was leaf mulch. She pushed a dead fern out of the way, and at last she was in a clearing barely six feet from the hazel. And this time she had the advantage: she had surprised him.

He was lying down, facing away from her, but she had not surprised him. He had heard her the moment she clattered the chair out of the shed, knocking over the shears. His ears tapered toward her, his nose lifted, riffling through his index of neighbors: the pungent tom, the stale tobacco of the mastiff. Long before she first saw him in her garden, he had known her by the particular crosshatch of flavors that made up her scent. She smelt of warmed milk—three canteen lattes a day—cut with rose soap. But the precise muskiness, its fractional composition of old and fresh sweat, fragrance-free detergent, antiaging serum, the digestive breakdown of lunch break's crayfish sandwich, associated gases on slow release within, and the dry-down chalkiness of another unused egg beginning its slow journey to waste, was something only he could grade.

She hadn't moved from the clearing, and he hadn't turned to look. It would take her ages to cover the ground from the burnt fern that was crackling to where he lay. He had time to move. If she set off. She would not set off.

He curled himself into a neat whirl like a breakfast pastry and tucked his brush under his snout; it was too hot for over.

Mary was surprised, and a little disappointed, by his inattention. She cast around and saw, as she had suspected, the hole under the hazel. She had found what she had come for. There was nothing else to do. He wasn't troubling her, and he wasn't in her garden. In any case, there was nothing to rap on.

He heard her leave with little interest but caught one new note. Overlaid on everything else, he could smell his own scent on her too.

His scent. Was very rich. An endless supply.
He drizzled it with his paws. He blew it
from a notch in his tail. He packed it in
his scats. His life in a footprint pressed
midair. Sniff and show respect!
Keeping the respect fresh was what he
did day, night. Wherever he went. Wait.
Wherever he went and wanted other
creatures to know he went. He sprayed,
wiped, released, squeezed, twisted,
dropped. Amazing smell cloud. Dark
made light. Wet made dry. Nothing like
on earth. Each puff was the inside of his
body turned outside in the world.
The scent told the news. Here he was.
Here he would come again.
Again, again, again.
Looping roads, crossing trails, scraping the
belows of fences, splaying stalks of
hedges, opening gaps. Under, over,
through. Garden to garden. Posting news
at all the stops. The mastiff's fence. The
egg tree. The dry hides humans peel off

their feet. Good for chewing, jaw
exercise. He could go on. He did go on.
This whole plot was built on scent.
Every day the edges needed rebuilding.
Patching over. He had to track and
re-track. Once the humans stayed in their
pens. Now they roamed the woods.
Males and Females. Messing with his
scent map. Making him work harder just
to own this place. But what a place!
This place was the best of both.
Wilderness in the middle. Human food
dens round the edge.
Strange fact. Humans never dig holes for
food. Every human has a special
stand-up knockdown store outside their
main den. Sometimes two! They make
them dark, improve the flavors. All the
best stuff buried / not buried in there.
Crazy. Just jump up. Forepaws on. Push
over. Flap flaps. Out it all comes.
Animal, fish, fruit, toys, bones. The sun
grows it hot and squelch.
This place could feed more than one. That
was proven. Beautiful, slow, tasty Beetles.
Did he mention the Beetles? Place was
crawling with them.
His land was growing. He was stretching out
the edges into all these fenced human
runs.
Blackberries soon. But blackberries were such
a sad thought.

CHAPTER THREE

Michelle stood at the door, beaming. Mary had assumed it would be Eric she saw first, but it was his wife who had raced to answer the bell and whose body now blocked the entrance, as if in two minds about whether to let Mary in. Michelle looked pale through her olive skin. Under her eyes were two gray half-moons, which shone a little limey from her dress: acid yellow and in need of a wash.

"Wow! Look at you!" Michelle said, closing her hands around Mary's forearms.

It was hard to judge whether the gesture was cordial or deterrent, especially as Mary's feet were still outside and Michelle's were in the hall. "Wow!" Michelle said again. "You look amazing!"

It was the first time they had seen each other in . . . however old Flora was. Three weeks? Four? Five? Mary tried to count back to that awful night when she had lain awake, listening to Michelle's screams. She was still lying there unable to sleep when blue light flooded the bedroom and she realized an ambulance had come to take Michelle to hospital, rendering her entire wakeful night pointless. Since then, it was Eric, now raising a silent hand to Mary from further back in the hall, who was usually front of house.

"Thanks!" Mary said to Michelle; she had finally released her arms. The navy dress did look good. In thirty-four years, this was the first time Mary had been asked to babysit, so she'd had no idea of the dress code. It had taken an hour to get ready, and all her discarded outfits lay heaped on the bed, waiting to be heaped on the floor. Michelle, on the other hand, looked awful. "I made an effort for the kids," Mary said brightly.

"They're both asleep. For God's sake, don't disturb them."

"OK. I made an effort for the TV then! By the way," Mary said, touching her own shoulder, "you've got a stain just here."

Michelle stared past Mary into the street, as if this information were of no consequence. "Hurry up and come inside. Eric saw a fox prowling out there earlier. They've moved into the wasteland over the back. Here," she said, looking at Mary's feet. "Just leave your shoes in the hall. No bag? Not going out after? We won't be late."

A hum was coming from the lounge. Mary slipped off her sandals and followed Michelle toward the noise. "I've got the fans on. Everything you need is here," Michelle said. Mary suppressed a cough. The room was stifling. Arranged on a coffee table were a bottle of red wine, a plate of biscuits, and a page of notes. They had been written in slanting block capitals, so that regardless of the words, the message was clear: *Written in haste by a very busy woman.*

"Flora's had her feed," Michelle continued. "She's in the little room upstairs."

"Tough love," Eric said, poking his head around the door. "Michelle likes them to sleep alone."

"We'll be home by ten, in time for the next feed," his wife said. "We've filled Tigger's bowl, but he'll come in when he's hungry. Anyhow, you've got my mobile. We're only going round the corner. Any problem, just ring."

"I will," Mary said. "Relax. Enjoy yourselves."

She heard Eric pulling back the front door latch. "See you later,

Mary," he called. She heard Michelle hushing him. She waited for the door to shut and realized that it had done so only when she heard the soft click of the key outside. There was a little rip of jagged metal as one of them whipped out the blade. Few species as fast as a parent with a babysitter, she thought. Thank God they had gone, and she could relax, alone in the house. Well—alone in their house, with two sleeping children.

It was strange, and a little thrilling, to be left unsupervised in her neighbor's lounge. The place felt intimately familiar yet vividly disorienting. A sort of halfway house between indoors and out because Mary had gone out, but only for a night in. Somewhere new, but much like home. She felt as if she had stepped behind the mirror in her own living room and found herself in a peculiar reflection.

She turned to get her bearings. Eric and Michelle's lounge remained divided from the dining room, but otherwise the layouts of their houses were broadly symmetrical. Eric and Michelle's sofa faced the wall of Mary's living room. Their TV backed almost exactly onto her own screen, two intersecting rectangles. But while her wall was painted duck-egg blue, Eric and Michelle had papered over theirs with an exuberant pattern of floral vines and woodland creatures, wildlife gone rampant up a feature wall. The theme extended to the soft furnishings. Hares ran over a throw on the set-tee, on top of which the cushions had been stacked. Despite the presence of a new baby, the whole place seemed spotless. Mary shifted the cushions and was just lowering herself to sit when she jumped: knitted into one was a giant red fox face. She went to inspect the shelves instead. A blue porcelain owl caught her eye, inviting her to lift it. There was no price label. She put it back.

Mary was as close to home as she could be without actually being home, but everything about the lounge unsettled her with its wrong-ness. She was barefoot, having obeyed Michelle's request to leave her sandals in the hall, and the rug sprouted with unnerving furriness between her toes. Tick, tick, tick went the fan, as if its revolutions were also counting seconds. It harassed her, this clickety whirring which seemed to tell both time and heat. She pulled out the plug and felt herself relax a little as the blades clacked to a stop. The place badly needed some air.

Mary began to unscrew the window lock. Wedging the heels of her hands under the sash, she thrust upward, inhaling as she did so a vaporous curl of Mark's old cologne. Its sandalwood riff was growing on her. Three days running she had unstopped the bottle, watched the neck imprint her wrist with its wet rim. It reminded her of an illustration in a fairy tale she'd loved as a child, of a genie unfurling in the vapor of a lamp. Scary, but helpful. Both things at once. That's what she liked about it. She pushed again at the window, but it wouldn't budge, and then she saw that a second lock was holding it shut. She began to wonder if opening windows was forbidden in this house. Disuse had made the sash unwieldy, and when she unscrewed the next lock it gave a dismayed clatter at being pried from the sill.

A siren sped down the main road in three swoops of sound. "That's fine. That's fine," a voice said from the pavement, and she followed it to a man with braids. He was leaning against a tree, legs sloping, feet crossed, talking loudly into his phone. Mary had barely begun to listen to his conversation, when she lost his voice in the rumble of a police helicopter. It took several minutes for the windows to stop rattling. "'Zactly," she heard the man with the braids say. It was soon after seven: too early for most. Or possibly too late. This afternoon, the park had been full of half-naked bodies. In this heat, they would still be there. Two girls stopped to perch on the front wall of the house opposite—Frank, was he called, the man who lived there? A magpie landed on one of the cables from the telephone pole, and Mary watched the cable bounce like a skipping rope. She made a mental note to close the window by half past nine, to be on the safe side.

On the table Mary found the remote control and Michelle's notes. She read them carefully, pleased to find that the children came with instructions. She flicked on the TV. Owing to stubbornness or tightness or intellectual superiority, Michelle and Eric appeared to have only five channels. There was no way she was going to watch a crappy talent show on a Saturday night: the ultimate humiliation of a single life. How she wished she had brought her book. Appraising the wall that joined their two houses, with its violently bulbous flowers, petals clasped against an imminent eruption, she calculated that it was approximately fifteen feet away—diagonally, as the crow flew. No, a crow couldn't fly through walls. As the mouse crept.

She knew that children should not be left alone in a house, and yet she could conceive of a reasonable argument in which there would be no harm in nipping home for a moment, since home was right next door. She felt herself unlikely to do this, but to test the feasibility of the idea, she slipped on her sandals and rummaged on the hall table for a set of house keys. When she found none, she returned to the lounge and slid her hand along the high marble mantelpiece, but discovered only a card that read *Thank you for being a wonderful daughter*, a button decorated with an anchor, and a triptych of photographs of Michelle and Eric on their wedding day. George, not yet old enough to walk, was wearing chinos, a waistcoat, and a white rose.

The house was so tidy, there was nowhere else to look.

"Let's just think about this sensibly for a moment," she said. Mary knew her book was beside her bed. She exchanged a look with the ceramic owl, silent witness. The round journey would take barely a minute. She would be no more absent than if she went to the toilet or than parents who lived in double-fronted houses must be every day of the week. There was one of those at the end of the road.

At the front door, she set the latch and, stepping outside, carefully pulled on the knocker until the door was as close to closed as possible without necessitating a key for readmission. From outside it was impossible to tell that it wasn't shut. She waited a moment in the shallow porch, felt the heat of the door on her back, which made her picture undressing later to find Eric and Michelle's house number seared between her shoulder blades. The girls opposite had gone. Frank's cat was in the window now, curtains hanging in folds behind him, as if he had sneaked out front after the auditorium had emptied.

Mary stood on the threshold of her decision. If she was going to do this, she thought, speed would be the answer. But before she could assess the thought and evaluate how much speed would be required to permit the action, she was already halfway down the path, then cornering Eric's hedge. Each time a foot struck the pavement, she counted. On six she was at her gate. She hit the door on ten. Quick with the key, and she was in. She left the house gaping behind her; it felt safer to keep two open doors between her and the children. She knew it was absurd to be so frantic. This was no different from watching telly downstairs while the children slept—or from lying in the garden, as she had once seen Michelle do through the gaps in the old fence, while George was indoors.

Upstairs Mary hunted for her paperback, which was not where she remembered. She pulled back the duvet and in panic turned upside down the pile of discarded clothes, listening for the thunk of discovery. She yanked open the drawer of her bedside table, sweeping its contents hopefully for the black-and-cream cover she knew so well, then slammed it shut, toppling over all the little bottles of lotion inside. Her cheek pressed the floor as she scanned the dust under the bed. Of course! Last night she had slept on Mark's side. She leapt onto the bed, grabbed the book, sped down the stairs, out of the house, along the pavement. She had stopped counting a while back, but she had the sensation that barely three minutes had passed.

Now that Eric and Michelle's front door was in sight, Mary felt safe. But when she reached it, whether owing to the heat or just the self-determination that objects can sometimes seem to exercise, it had flexed slightly and sprung a little further ajar than she had left it. She stepped into the hall with the uneasy conviction that danger itself had been ushered inside. The walls vibrated with a sense of equivocal emptiness. Mary felt her absence as firmly as if it had made an impression on the space in her shape and waited there for her to share the house with it.

"Hello?" she called, but of course there was no answer. Always jumping at things, she reproached herself. This was the life that awaited those who live alone. Paranoia, basically. After all, she had left her own door wide open while she ran to the bedroom, and that had been fine. She needed to get a grip. Michelle, bossily overseeing the removal of shoes in the hallway, came to mind, and Mary emulated the way she had closed the door. "Come in," she told herself. "Leave your shoes in the hall." It was calming to imitate someone else's sensible behavior. Mary took off her sandals and lined them up next to George's little trainers. Obviously she needed to check on the children. She was going to do that. In about one minute. Right after she checked the lounge.

The room appeared exactly as she had left it. Which was good. But the untouched wine struck her as an oversight. Mary tossed her book on the sofa and poured a large glass. She rested a hand on the mantelpiece. A couple of sips to steady herself, and she would go up.

Tonight was the first time she had been in this room since Eric and Michelle had decorated. When she and Mark had brought round a bottle of wine to welcome their new neighbors one spring evening four years ago, the wallpaper had been of an entirely different kind, and they had all laughed at the late Mrs. Brown's taste in interiors. They had stood, she remembered, in the way that people stand at a party, though there had been only four of them, upright and wooden like knitting dolls. They had found things in common: she and Eric were only children. Someone Michelle knew used to work for the same firm of surveyors as Mark. At the end they vowed to get together soon. Mary swilled another mouthful. Of course, they never had.

Most of all, what she remembered about that evening was a feeling of immense validation. She and Mark had enviable local knowledge. At thirty, they were already old hands. They had held their silence on the short walk home and, as soon as their own door was behind them, broken into giggles. They had chosen and bought an excellent house before Hackney was obviously excellent, and other young professional people like them were following suit, a whole year later, with prices a whole year higher. They would never have been able to afford it now. And also, though neither of them had said so, for all those reasons they felt more impressive as a couple, more together. It was as if they predated their new neighbors in every way. They were still in their blissful period then. Mary shut her eyes when the next memory came. Later that evening she had asked Mark if he thought Eric and Michelle would last. It was only when George was born that she realized Michelle must have already been pregnant.

Mary emptied her glass and put it on the table. What was she doing, standing around daydreaming when there was responsible babysitting to do? She had never been upstairs before, and she winced as each step creaked, the sound rising like the inflection of a question. *Is she allowed up here?* If there was a quiet path, she failed to find it. At the half-landing, she turned right and in her spare room found George, bare-chested in pajama shorts, the duvet kicked off. He was sleeping with his mouth open, and Mary realized that she had no idea what checking on a child entailed. Was it too sinister to make sure he was breathing? She cupped one hand close to his lips and after a moment felt her skin glow with heat, then fade, then glow again.

She was about to return along the landing toward Flora's when she noticed that the door to Eric and Michelle's bedroom stood ajar. She toed it open, and the edge of a single mattress came into view on the floor beside the bed. Was that for Eric? The sheets were mussed up, the room a total mess. Packets of nappies, used tissues, biscuit wrappers, a stew of clothes everywhere, odors thickening in the gloom of drawn curtains. She had lifted the lid on the tangled heart of the house, and it looked nothing like the immaculate lounge. She pulled the door to and took a deep lug of air.

At the other end of the landing, in her study, Mary found Flora, doll arms poking out of a long white sleeping bag. It was stuffy in here too, so Mary parted the curtains and gave the fanlight a sharp push. Liberating, to open windows in someone else's house. The side rail of the cot had been left in the lowered position, and when Mary tried to raise it, she realized it was broken. No matter. That made it easier to lean in. She placed her hand on Flora's head. It was surprisingly hard in its warmth, and the impression it made, above all else, was of persistence. The thrum of a pulse pushed at Mary's palm like bubbles rising to the surface. Next to Flora's young skin her hands looked so old. They were covered in a mesh of faint lines, as if someone had Spirographed over them, a pattern of aging to come.

In contrast, Flora's face was beautiful, her closed eyelids edged with straight, dark lashes. Mary touched the baby's cheek, and as if a button had been pressed, the lids pinged open and two deep-gray eyes looked up at a face that didn't belong. The child murmured, half asleep. Her little legs kicked inside her sleeping pouch, and she began to whimper. "Hussssshhh. Husssshhh," Mary said, in line with Michelle's instructions. She was meant to pat the baby's back at the same time, but the baby was lying on her back. So she placed her hand on the eyelids instead and held them fast. "Sleep time," she said, stroking the lids firmly shut. But each time she lifted her hand for a new stroke, the eyes reopened.

The whimper grew louder, lengthened, became a proper cry. Mary didn't want George to wake too, so she unpopped the shoulders of the sleeping bag and peeled back the envelope to reveal Flora's tiny legs. Eric and Michelle had said nothing about having to pick up the children, let alone how to do it. "One last chance to go quiet," Mary warned as she slid her hands under the baby, but Flora gave a loud wail, and Mary began to lift. Head, legs, arms . . . Everything rolled in different directions. Shifting her hands one way, then the other, as if at the wheel of a three-point turn, Mary managed to catch the head and get the baby vertical. Flora's body locked onto her own and instantly stilled. The cry faltered. Mary rubbed her nose on the baby's head. What a satisfying nuzzling of cartilage and bone. Its hardness was the comfort.

"There, there, there. I'm Mary from next door, remember? Mummy and Daddy's friend," she said, grateful that Flora couldn't speak. She was unsure her fitness for duty would have borne interrogation. "I'm looking after you and George."

The next part was not on the list of Michelle's instructions.

Mary set off slowly down the stairs, crablike, feeling for each step. "We'll have a little wander," she said to the hot hair that pressed her cheek. She planned to take the baby to a place of quiet and headed for the dining room, at the back of the house. "Now, now, it's sleep time, Flora," she said, patting the baby's back. Saying the child's name made her feel more convincing. She pushed down the door handle with her elbow. The air was so solidly warm it barely budged for her; she had to force her way through it, while it fetched itself up her nose and down her throat. There was more extrava-

gantly leafy wallpaper, which only exacerbated the impression of
jungly heat.

The room was in early twilight, the same gently darkening blue
as the world outside. Mary and Flora stood before the patio doors,
fathoming the murky shapes of Michelle and Eric's shrubs. Unlike
Mary's garden, everything here had been kept to an appropriate size.
"There you see," she said in a lullaby voice, "the birds have gone to
sleep. Mr. Squirrel has gone to sleep." She turned to show Flora the
view. "Neville's cat has gone to sleep." She caught sight of her own
reflection. She had made the right choice with that dress. Midnight
blue—so good with her chestnut hair. But how faint her face looked
in the glass, an apparition not fully formed, an intermediary between
herself and the outside world.

Further back in the garden, something moved to disturb the
reflection, its movement, even at that distance, immediately claiming
the foreground. As the fox came into view, acquiring substance, her
own face and Flora's seemed to recede. He was running at speed,
supplanting them in the window. It hadn't occurred to Mary that
he visited other back gardens too. But perhaps he didn't and had
come only because he knew she was there. Something dangled
between his jaws, pink and flipping. Her right foot took a step back,
then her left, instinctively trying to reinstate lost distance. He was
coming closer to the glass than she was now. She watched him step
through her reflection.

He hit the patio doors, two forepaws on the pane, the hard firm
thud of hairy footpads, the tap of claws. Impatient. Now there was
only the fox in the glass, and the pink thing, which was his tongue,
pointed at its tip like an arrow. She saw the black speckles on the
white of his muzzle where whiskers sprouted, the lustrous hair on
his chest. His front legs, propped against the door, in this posture
resembled arms. They were bushier at the top and short-haired from

the joints down, as if he had pushed up his shirtsleeves of fur and left himself bare below the elbow, like a doctor at the bedside. He looked capable, ready to attend. Up close, his eyes, which she had read as dark in her own garden, were in fact pale amber and rimmed with liquid black: the eye makeup of a New Romantic.

They were examining her now. Not shy or frightened or, as she had heard people say of dogs making eye contact with a human, judging his chances in a fight. The look was more of . . . keen appraisal. One ear bent down and up, then the other, flagging the movement of his eyes. Mary watched them shift from left to right, and back again, as if he were reading lines on a page, wondering what she was doing, in this home that was not her home, with this baby that was not her baby.

He hadn't seen her before in this leaf-walled place.

So.

This was where she was hiding.

Strange hideout.

He could look in. But not go in. His snout nudged the window. Open / not open. Hard as a frozen puddle but hot and dry and anyway. Not the season for ice. Nudged the window. Dark with the grass and leaves and everything in his place moving in / over the human den with the humans watching him. Watching them. Watching him. Watching. Human Female lively at last. Been going round with her head stuck in a limbpit, the time it took her to see him but. She saw him now. Check the flicker in her eye.

An eye that keeps looking without legs that jump is a yes!

He swiped an ear at a hum. Adjusted hind paws. Stretched his neck.

High up, a window folded out like a giant cat flap. Sweet food promises fell down like fruit from the tree. He caught them with his tongue, and the promise lifted his tail.

Mary adjusted her grip on Flora to liberate a hand. She waved it in a broad salutation, mimicking the arc he was making with his tail. "And good evening to you too," she said. That seemed to be the gist of it.

He was still staring at her, so she said, not expecting an answer, "I assume it's you who's been bringing me things? Dirty old boxers I can do without, thanks. And you can keep your paws off my sandals." His head continued to nod on the other side of the patio door. She felt certain now that he had been looking for her. Me, me, me, she cautioned herself. This is what happened when you were single: too much time to think about yourself. The world shrank to fit. A gnat danced between them—Mary was unsure which side of the glass—and broke their exchange.

His snout began to follow the movement of the insect, the black tip of his muzzle tracing wibbly loops in the air. Clap, his claws slapped the window.

And.

Waited.

To lift his paw.

Tongue slid ready.

While the gnat flew free inside the human den, and his claws skated after it, over the little face and the big face, down where the legs of the infant dangled, foot pads shining limp and pearly and pale, fine veins glimmering. His head bobbed. In the wall of the pen that was there / not there. The gnat landed on the Female's skin. Thirsting for blood. His tongue overlapped her as he gave the invisible window wall a lick.

The wet smear on the patio door seemed to Mary proof that he wanted something, that he was reaching out to her. His body, so comprehensively attentive, expressed the same desire, the same sense that he was here at the window with a particular intention. She scratched at an itch on her arm. There was nothing accidental about him, neither his behavior nor the way he looked. He was beautiful by design, as if his shape answered a special purpose. His leather pads pushed flat on the glass, and between them his fur flared into five tufty points of a star. His isosceles ears lined up with the bridge of his nose; his eyes and the black circle of his snout made three corners of a triangle.

"Flora, meet Mr. Fox. Mr. Fox, meet Flora," she whispered.

He stood still and looked past her, as if seeing only now the Ercol-style sideboard and matching dining table, a porcelain lamp in the shape of a bulldog—they would have got that in Islington—with a pleated shade on its head. He was examining the room unhurriedly, without embarrassment, and for the second time this week Mary felt a little slighted to see that his greater interest lay elsewhere. She put her right hand on the glass and tapped a few times with her fingernails—not hard like a rap, more like a sound for "Can I come in?"

He registered the knock and stood gallantly down. One forepaw slid to the ground in the join between the door and the adjacent pane, as if he were feeling for a handle. Mary had the impression he nodded. She knocked again, thinking he must have misunderstood and thought she was telling him to leave, but he was already darkening. She waited to see where he would go next, but he walked his shadow into the shadows at the end of the garden, and it was impossible to tell if he had gone over the back to the woods, right toward her place, or left toward Neville's.

Mary gazed down at Flora then. Somehow, having been seen with the baby made Mary feel more with the baby. She had lulled Flora to sleep, and he had seen her do it. The sleep and his seeing it, without any big show of having done so, had created in her a little bud of thought. With Mark, it had seemed absurd to plan a new life when she hadn't sorted out her own. Maybe if she'd got Dawn's job, made time for the master's degree she'd always talked about, she would have felt different. The magazines were full of stories of women choosing between their career and their maternal instincts. But what if you had neither? What if you were still waiting? "That wouldn't have been a good start for either of us," she said, resting her brow on Flora's scalp.

Her mind reeled back to New Year's Day when her and Mark's argument, about to enter its second year, had finally boiled over. It was their last proper fight, the one that had produced the irrefutable evidence that they had reached the end, and after which their demise was purely administrative. Up and down the stairs they had chased and shouted—they always argued on the stairs, one of them trying to escape the other. No, she didn't want to set a date for the wedding. No, she didn't want kids. He cornered her in the bedroom, by the wardrobe. He wanted to try for a baby. New year, new life, he said. The same old argument. She wasn't ready. *She always said that.* Well, he always asked. Maybe if he left her alone . . . *He'd tried that.* Not for long enough. The wardrobe pressing her back. His words goading her, his eyes cold as blades. She shivered to remember. She had seen things in both of them that day that she hadn't known existed.

Mary carried Flora up to bed and snapped her gently inside her sleeping bag. Then she pulled the fanlight closed. The blue of the sky was thickening, and when Mary returned to the lounge, she shut that window too and refastened both latches. She heard the cat come into the kitchen.

Michelle and Eric would be back soon, and Mary had the curious sensation that she was erasing all proof of her visit, making herself as elusive as the half-face in the window. She switched on the fan, plumped the sofa cushions. It was absurd to feel guilty, but she went about these jobs with the nagging sense that she was faking the scene. She ate a biscuit and slipped another into her pocket to save worrying about food later. The next glass of wine took her down to a third of the bottle—the amount she had thought, prior to unscrewing the cap, acceptable for three hours of responsible baby-sitting (there being no limit specified by the bottle or Michelle's instructions). She sat on the sofa and started doodling on the edge of the notes. She drew three small dots, the corners of a triangle: two at the top for the eyes, one at the bottom for the nose. Somewhere in that geometric puzzle of a face was an answer for her, if she could only find it. His features were diagrammatic, like part of an equation, $\because$, she knew those dots had a mathematical meaning, tucked somewhere inside an old schoolbook, but she had no idea what. It was only later, when she looked it up on her phone, that she found they were the symbol for "because." She drew two triangles on top of it all for his ears. It looked pretty good, so she drew another and another. Each fox was slightly different, but they all said the same thing. Because, because, because.

Outside, the street was raising a murmur, dribs and drabs heading down the road to the next stage of their Saturday night. Mary turned from the window and caught herself in the mirror above the sofa. Michelle and Eric were tall, and the frame cut her off just below the neck, as if her face were a stone that had sunk to the bottom of a vessel. She wondered what she and Mark had looked like from here, to Eric and Michelle—and how many of their rages her neighbors had heard through the writhing stems and antlers. It seemed reasonable to assume they had heard the ones that ended with Mark's head or fist banging the wall.

They had argued and argued, but there was no arguing away the fact that they had been engaged for more than four years, and engagement had led them no closer to marriage. She infuriated him, but his fury only made her delay further. Each time she thought "No" or "Yes but not with you," she failed to free the thought. Her mouth was a cage that kept Mark out, but only by locking her in.

His humors, good and bad, and the quick shifts between, were the walls of their relationship. They held them both in place.

She looked up at the ceiling, thinking again of their last fight, in the same room as the room above her head, in their house that was now her house. Slowly she turned Granny Joan's diamond on her right hand. She had waited until the last minute, after the valuation, to tell Mark about her inheritance. He had been hassling her to pack, but with a mortgage there was just enough to buy him out. Meanwhile, he got to live with his parents. Last month a postcard arrived. The oast houses of Kent.

She was still waiting for him to remove his things from her head.

MICHELLE CAME IN first, keenly scanning the wine bottle and biscuit plate in order to make her own deductions about what was different. "Everything OK?"

"All fine. Not a peep from either of them." Flora and George were asleep. What did the rest matter?

"And no sign of foxes?"

"Only that one," Mary laughed, pointing at the cushion.

"Michelle's obsessed," Eric called from the hall. "She's going to organize a mission to hunt them out. I told her about the mess outside yours last week, so I'm afraid you're on the committee."

"Did you have a good time?" Mary asked.

"Lovely, thank you."

"Even if Michelle did check her phone every ten minutes in case you were trying to call." Eric had come into the lounge now. "Seriously, Mary—thanks. We needed it." He rubbed Michelle's back. "Will you come over the weekend after next? Off duty, this time. We're going to have a barbecue, invite a few friends round."

Mary saw Michelle yawn then, and Eric took it as a cue too. "You know, the really great thing about living next door to the babysitter is that you don't have to drive her home."

She laughed. "I charge mileage though, and I'm going the long way."

FOR THE SECOND time that evening, Mary stood in the shallow porch. The sky was darkening properly now. Saturday evening; beautiful, and still so hot at 10 p.m. that you could be out in a gauzy but carefully chosen dress with nowhere to go and not look adrift. For the first time in weeks, she really wanted to be out. At the bottom of Eric and Michelle's path, she turned right instead of left toward her own home. She passed Neville's, the new-builds where she didn't know the neighbors, and reached Shepherds Bridge Walk.

Cars streamed by, and she veered off at the first side street, walking parallel to her own terrace. Ashland Road was much grander than Hazel Grove. The houses along here were larger, set further back from the pavement. Some were four stories tall and, judging by the bells beside the front doors, had been divided into flats. No one was walking down here; they had already gone out. Or perhaps they were walking down her road, the straighter path to the pub and the park.

She pushed her hands into her pockets and found the second biscuit. She ate it with one hand and swung her dress with the other; the alcohol had loosened her up, she thought. Either that, or she was happy! Somewhere behind her, a front door shut. Footsteps faded in the opposite direction. These houses were the ones she would see from her place if the trees weren't so dense. The little woodland lay behind them too, so that in effect she was making a large circle of her house and garden, pacing the circumference of her territory. Perhaps he visited here as well. She listened for him, but she could hear only the squeak of her left sandal; it had made that noise ever since she had found it in the garden.

The night was still and breezeless. All was quiet, except at the edges of her vision, where everything twitched and jangled.

A shape slipped under a parked car to her left. Her eyes gave chase, but not so much as a tail could be seen. By now he could be any-where. At the end of the street, she may as well turn on to Drovers Lane and complete the circle back home.

Perhaps because she had been looking for something in the mid-range of her vision, Mary screamed when she turned the corner and came face-to-face with an imposing foreground. He, on the other hand, smiled. He appeared to have been expecting her. On her home ground, she had walked right into Mark.

CHAPTER FOUR

He had shed his winter coat. That was her first thought. His hair was shorn—not shaved, but trimmed close to his head. He was dressed for the heat, so her survey of his outfit was brief: shirt, shorts, deck shoes, no socks. Laces fastidiously bowed. The fastidiousness was the only thing that belonged to the Mark she knew. Head to toe, Mary recognized not a single item of his clothing. Then she realized that the shape inside the clothes was different too. Her eyes followed the creases that pulled across his chest in a tug of war between one beefy shoulder and the other. He had always been lean, but now a hard ridge of muscle climbed his forearm. Like a rope, she thought with a shudder. He had bought a new wardrobe and built a new body too.

She raised her eyes to his face and saw that he was watching her with a smile, and even his smile came as a shock. Maybe it was the moonlight, but his teeth appeared whiter.

"What are you doing here?" she said.

He laughed. "Hello, Mary. It's nice to see you too."

"What are you doing?"

His lips glistened, straining into a smile. "Five months, and that's all you can say? Go on. Have another try."

"You're meant to be in Kent."

"Yeah." He laughed. "That's not a whole lot better." He gave a nervous flick of his head, as if he was still getting used to the fringe having gone.

"But you are meant to be in Kent."

"I was in Kent," he said.

"What do you mean, 'was'?"

He eyed her patiently, giving her time to catch up with him. But she wasn't trying to catch up with him. She was thinking it seemed an impossible coincidence that he should be here on this corner, just as she happened to walk around it. "Were you coming to see me?" she asked.

He pressed his lips together, trying to stop something from escaping. "I was on my way home."

"Home? What do you mean 'home'?"

Nothing about Mark—not his outfit, his posture, not the slant of his body on the pavement—gave any clue to his reappearance. He may as well have dropped from the sky and landed on this spot, on the very next road to her own.

"Hey, stop grimacing at me like that! You're making me nervous," he said.

"I'm making *you* nervous?" She suppressed a scoffing noise. "You're the one who's turned up on my doorstep."

"Not your doorstep, though, is it?" he said calmly.

"So you were on your way home, and you just happened to be passing my road . . ."

He let out a long sigh. "Actually, I deliberately avoided your road."

A street lamp flicked on over their heads, and now Mark's skin glowed with an amber sheen. His whole person presented itself as a sort of warning light. She wondered if that was how she appeared to him, if the whites of her eyes were orange too.

"We can do better than this," he said. "I'm going to start again. How are you, Mary?"

His arms hung loosely at his side, giving the impression of openness. His propensity to smile suggested ease. But the steel-blue eyes examining her were two circular shields, flinty flecks lodged here and there, and she knew that whatever she said would be brutely defended. He was watching for her next move.

"Where are you living?" she asked. "I think I've got a right to know." Two minutes in his company and already her voice sounded feeble. But Mark chose instead to address her underlying thought. Or perhaps it was just the thought he preferred.

"I missed London."

"You're in London? Where? Because you said you wanted a total break. You said it was the only way to get over—" She was going to say "us," but in her head the word sounded horribly solicitous. There was no way to use it without appearing to wish to apply it to them now, and even though "us" was something she had thought and not said, she felt herself redden.

He laughed. "That's true. But you can't legislate for accidents."

He put one hand in his pocket; she heard his keys flinch.

"And is this an accident?"

"Oh, I get it! You wanted to bump into *me*. You trailed me all the way to my sad little bachelor pad with borrowed furniture, for which I have paid an extortionate deposit and now must pay an extortionate rent each month, and you kept watch on the place, possibly from behind a parked car or a lamp post, until I stepped out. And then you devised a way to walk into me."

She looked at Mark doubtfully. The speech had an air of rehearsal. "Tell me where."

"Don't get worked up," he said. "You knew I wouldn't stay with my folks forever, right? Anyway, it's a big place, east London." His lips parted, and he gave her a tinted grin. She fixed on the black hole between his teeth. Somewhere in there, she supposed, was the old Mark. Maybe this big new Mark had swallowed him whole.

His eyes cruised slowly down and up her dress. He made no effort to disguise his interest, and his unguarded gaze seemed to contain its own defense: just looking, nothing to hide.

"Nice dress," he said. "Where are you off to?"

"I've been. And now I'm coming back."

"That's early."

So she told him, "I was babysitting. For Eric and Michelle." She had made the calculation quickly. Telling the truth had the drawback of suggesting a deficient social life, but the advantage of surprise. Babysitter was the last thing he would expect her to be. His final words to her—actually, not his final words, because he'd said them on New Year's Day, a few weeks before he moved out, but they had come to seem like his last words—loitered permanently on the edge of her consciousness. Basically, she was cold and selfish and too remote ever to perform the great act of self-sacrifice that was procreation. "What's wrong with you?" he'd cried, after years of defying her better judgment to assure her there was nothing wrong with her. She would never have kids, he'd shouted. Not with him, not with anyone. Thank God, because she'd fuck them up, silly bitch. Just like her mother had done. There goes fucked-up Mary and her fucked-up kids! She'd lost it then. Every kindness he had ever said, every reassurance he had given, was recast in an instant as the cold means by which he had tried to get what he wanted. All the worst things she thought about herself, he thought them too. Time and again he'd saved her from those thoughts, but only so he could keep her.

It was so satisfying now to break the news to him that she had been entrusted with someone else's children. It was about as perfect a riposte as you could get. She remembered Flora's body warm on her chest, Flora's eyes shut against her shoulder, the immense validation of being whimpered and then slept upon. She was still enjoying the sense of that, when he laughed.

"Ha! They asked you too!"

Splinters of thoughts lodged in her head, the dark outlines of question marks looming there like alien objects on an X-ray. Michelle and Eric were still in touch with him. Michelle and Eric knew he was here and hadn't told her. Michelle and Eric had asked him first, even though she lived right next door and he lived—well, where? They were her neighbors now, but they had gone behind her back with Mark. The shock of the betrayal was so great, some inside self seemed to limp off to lean against the wall of the house she and Mark were standing outside. "Why did you say no?" she finally asked.

"Had plans."

There was no safe follow-up to that, so she said, "You're not going to their barbecue, are you?" She was careful not to specify a date.

He shrugged and asked, "So if you were babysitting, what are you doing here? It's not exactly on your way home, is it?"

"Are you kidding?" she said. "I'm the one who lives round the corner. I've got a right to be here." But he was no longer paying attention to Mary. His eyes had swerved over her shoulder.

SALTY SNAIL ODOR tunneled into his muzzle. From the fresh male who was an old male who was a slithery male. Squaring up to the Female here in the outer edge of the inner tread of his patch. Snails, he thought when he saw him, so snails he smelt. Maybe because of the sloppit of shells that clustered in the wet / always wet behind this male's fence. When he scraped under the slats and came up in the woods, his claws clipped their shells. Flip, crick, squelch. He shucked a few to warn against complacency. It was a habit, though the texture was unpleasant, and the scrape served only for back itch.

The human male walked his trail when the sky was light and when the sky was dark. Quiet feet, in and out the woods, looping the human dens. But the human male didn't mark his territory. Didn't want anyone to know he was there. So ho, the territory wasn't his then, was it? No mark, nobody's. There. Now he was watching. That's right. My patch.

He brisked his whiskers. The air poked damp and saline. Come fresh to stalk around the human Female with sly feet and rippety eyes. Spruckling toadsome. Just the thought made his shoulder fur thicken. He took the smell of him to show the human Female. But she did not smell him. Bad human nose.

Interesting that earlier, when he went inside her den, there was no smell of this male.

MARK CLAPPED HIS hands and sprinted two steps into the street.

"What?"

"Fox. Gone now. Standing, like this, right in the middle of the road." He dropped his shoulders and lurched his head forward, gazing right at her. Then he stood up properly again. "I swear it was staring me out."

She peered behind her at the empty street. "What did he look like?" she asked.

Mark gave a laugh of real affection then that twisted back her head. "Er. Four legs and a tail?"

The beast had made her smile.

"Right," he said. "I'm running late." And then he added, as if answering a question she had thought but not voiced, "Not now. But another time. Maybe we can get a drink."

He reached forward and hugged her with one arm. His hand held her upper back, then snaked around to her arm, which he squeezed. The muscles, she thought, as her eyes filled with water, but she refused to express surprise or pain. She was stronger now too.

"You're wearing perfume," he said. "You never wear perfume." She let him think so.

On her fourth or sixth step Mary heard the squeak in her shoe catch her up, as if it had been wrong-footed by the suddenness of their farewell. She wanted to turn around, to steal a glance at Mark from behind. She felt defeated by their meeting and gripped by the urge to take something back. Some small, private piece of information. Just to know, for instance, how the new close crop behaved when it reached that part of his nape that she used to slip her fingers under his hair to feel.

But now she was moving, it was impossible to stop. She passed the house where the honeysuckle hung over the garden wall, then the house where the door was a sheet of studded metal. Mark would hear any disturbance to her footsteps as a sign that their encounter itself had been disturbing, and she didn't want to reward him with that knowledge. She cursed the squeak in the sandal that would give her away. Meanwhile, his new navy deck shoes made no sound, and the conviction that he was watching her juddered down all the articulations of her spine. She felt her dress cling to her thighs, fold into the gap between her strides.

She rounded the corner. At the double-fronted house, the first building on her road, she stopped safely out of sight and pressed her back against the wall for cover. What the—what was Mark doing there, on the next street to hers, a short walk from her home and just a few strides from the alley to the woods?

The bricks chafed her back, their abrasions pulling at her dress, studding it with little burrs of loosened threads. What did he want? There was no doubt that Mark wanted something. He had claimed to have been on his way home—location notably unspecified. Or on his way out. Now she was unsure. How close was he living? She tried to remember what he had said, but the words slid into each other, and she could hear his voice in none of them.

She tracked back around the corner and ran to the crossroads where they had met. Four directions opened up, but there was no sign of Mark.

She needed to get home. She touched her pocket, relieved to find her keys still there. It made no sense to feel relieved, except in terms of her impression that during the course of their encounter she had been somehow plundered. A cat's tail poked out from beneath a parked car, so dark it made a tail-shaped hole in the road, and she watched it quiver as she started to walk. She turned into her own road, pronouncing in her head the number of each house she passed, a countdown to the safety of 53. One before her own, she stopped. This hedge was so overgrown that it was impossible to see the house number. Since old Mrs. Farnworth had died, the gate was permanently shut, and even the house name was disappearing, its engraving steadily being backfilled with lichen and moss. One day soon, no one would know the place was called Tangle Wood. She snorted. She knew these roads were once farmland—the elderly couple they'd bought the house from used to graze goats on the land that was now the woods—but it still annoyed her that people in cities named their houses as if they lived in a pastoral. Maybe she would put a nice carved sign on her front gate, saying Bricks & Mortar.

She reached her path and glanced at Eric and Michelle's house, half expecting to see some outward sign of their betrayal. The lounge had gone dark, and the upstairs room—which had been dark—was light. She bristled at this update on the progress of their evening. But after what Mark had told her, she was going to bristle at everything Eric and Michelle did. Getting ready for separate mattresses in their boudoir of chaos.

She fished her keys from her pocket and finally turned to her own home. It gaped back at her, the front door flung wide, the house openmouthed with the soft, yellow light of its interior. Sweat ran to the dent at the base of Mary's spine, the place where panic pooled. The lounge, bedroom, and hall were all fully illuminated, as if someone else were home and she was being summoned inside, an expected guest arriving at the appointed hour.

CHAPTER FIVE

Inside her pocket, Mary's fingers squeezed her phone. She should call the police. But what would she say? That she couldn't remember if she had left her own house open? That certainly sounded like a cry for help—of the clinical kind. She could knock on Eric's door and ask him to go inside with her, but then she would have to explain that she'd popped home while babysitting, and she was unsure how Eric would feel about that. She raised her eyes to their window again, just in time to see the light go out. That was fine. Eric and Michelle were no friends of hers.

Mary looked up and down the road. The only other neighbor she knew well enough to ask was Neville, but stepping into the street, she saw that his house was dark too. She tried to replace herself at the scene, three hours ago. She had found her book and run down the stairs. At her gate, she had looked immediately right toward Eric and Michelle's. She looked left toward it now. She had been so preoccupied with the idea of keeping their door in sight, was it possible she had forgotten to shut her own? Her heart slammed sharply against the bars of her rib cage. God, the miserable self-insufficiency of living alone. This was exactly the sort of job Mark would enjoy, if Mark were here to do it. She used to tease him about his heroic tendencies, then one evening soon after they moved in, a gang of girls materialized in front of her two streets from home. She had already handed over her phone, when they—barely teenagers—demanded her purse. In panic she had looked down the street again, just as she was doing now, only to see Mark sprinting toward her. The girls fled. It was a coincidence that he happened to be heading home at the same time, but that's what it was like with the two of them. Back then, he made her feel safe. He was her lucky shadow. But that was a long time ago.

Be brave, Mary.

She took two steps inside and heard each step and each step's echo, four knocks on wood. The air smelt different: outside air, indoors. It had a visiting tang that could have traveled from any-where. A peppering of smoke, the spice of someone's barbecue. Her house had opened up and let the world blow in. "Hello?" she asked quietly. When she had called out earlier, in Eric and Michelle's hall, the question had felt rhetorical. But now she was less sure there would be no reply. She left the door open, for a faster exit.

In the hall, by the entrance to the lounge, she found her hand-bag, sprawled on its side with its contents spilt—crumpled receipts, the wrapper of her favorite health bar, a lidless lipstick forlornly crimped. The long strap traced a wobbly shape on the floorboards, like one of those outlines detectives used to chalk around corpses. She crouched to check for her wallet and was surprised to see it, the sight of it immediately undoing several hypotheses. Maybe she had got away with leaving the door open, because surely no one would have broken in and left her wallet?

Mary was unsure where to start. If someone was hiding on the other side of the lounge door, going to the top of the house would give them a chance to escape. "Yeah, I'm going upstairs," she said aloud to her imaginary assistant. "Meet you here in a sec." With a glimmer of inspiration, she darted to the kitchen and from the wooden block withdrew the cleaver.

She stamped her feet and coughed theatrically on the stairs, the blade joggling in her hands. After the bathroom—all clear behind the shower curtain—the first door she reached was the study. She flicked on the light and jumped as her own face leapt in the window. Christ! She looked like a madwoman with that knife. She switched off the light and let the darkness resettle, nestle back into its basket. How different the room seemed compared with the same one next door, where barely an hour before she had bent over the rail of Flora's cot. Little legs kicking. Her fist climbing cords of Mary's hair. The honeyed smell of her. Along the wall where Flora's cot would be, half-empty shelves of books collected dust. You couldn't have a study and a nursery in these houses, which said everything about what became of women when children arrived. Beyond that, the room was sparsely furnished. There were more books in boxes. One of the two remaining dining chairs—her share of the set— was tucked under the old desk, its surface a patchwork of bills and solicitor's letters. The room was inviolate. Not inviolate. The room, like all the rooms, was empty. It rebuffed any question of trespass with its explicit sense of desertion.

Mary checked the linen cupboard—clear—and crept to the spare bedroom. The blind was down, and again this space struck her above all as uninhabited. Maybe it was the act of searching that made her see it, but each time she pushed a door in dread, it was the emptiness that hit her. Mark had left behind the bedside table and lamp but taken the bed. Which made it just a side table. The walls, which he'd painted a few years ago, looked grubbily blank, apart from where the furniture had stood and left its crisp outlines, the pristine white ghosts of a bed and a wardrobe.

Mary reached her own room last. She strained for a sound from the floor below but heard only a closet thudding shut on the other side of the wall, the vibration of a low voice of indeterminate gender. She swapped the knife to the other hand and wiped the first hand on her dress. Space was pretty tight in her wardrobe, but she scooped the clothes aside to check, throwing backward glances to the door. She opened Mark's wardrobe and gasped at the musty lunge of trapped air. Her free hand brushed the few leftover clothes. She squeezed the arm of a shirt, and the pale blue cotton was cold. On her way to the door, she stooped to pick up a slim yellow leaf from the floor: a riddle, in this innermost room, where all the windows were shut. As she slipped the leaf into her pocket, she stumbled over a gruff sound below.

She tiptoed toward the landing, obeying a sudden urge for quietness. Sweat slickened the handle of the knife. She looked over the banister. The stairs, a slice of hall. The knife twitched slippery in her palm. There was a movement, a knocking.

"Are you here?" she heard.

She let out a long, deep sigh, a rush of all the captured breath from her patrol.

"Mary?"

"Who is it?" she called, thinking where the hell had he sprung from, and how dare he! Mark's upturned face entered the square of hall, caught in a cage of balustrade spindles.

". . . I got worried . . . ," he was saying.

She watched the bottom stair to see if his foot would appear on it, but the hand that held the knife stayed behind her back. She didn't want him to think she was afraid of life without him. "I'm coming down," she said, and as she descended the stairs, Mark edged toward the front door, as if she were pushing him. That was more like it. By the time she reached the bottom step, he was outside. "Hold up," he said, thrusting a foot onto the doormat. "Are you OK?"

"Why wouldn't I be?"

"Well, I thought I heard you scream. I hadn't gone far. I ran back, saw your door wide open . . . I'm an inconsiderate git. I should have walked you home."

"Did I scream?" She was asking herself.

"So you're OK?"

She laughed. "Look. Thanks. But really, I'm fine. Tired is all. So, thanks, but goodnight . . . OK?" She began to shut the door, then changed her mind. It would be better to watch him go.

After she had drawn the bolts, Mary walked back down the hall and noticed that Mark had neatly propped the lounge door with the hen doorstop. She entered the room, frowning. She walked to the front window and closed the shutters. She checked behind the sofa and leant over the top of the TV, but her search had become perfunctory. There was no one in the house. The whole place crawled with loneliness. Please let Mark not have seen that.

She checked in the cloakroom, and in the kitchen dropped the knife wearily into the block. There was nowhere for anyone to hide in here. The room was tiny. She unlocked the back door. A few stray stars glimmered, and the sky seemed peaceful. She filled her lungs with the night, the same free air that had roamed the house. It tasted good. That was the funny thing: it had been refreshing to come home and find the place different. She wished she had wine, she thought, opening the cupboard where she kept the glasses to prolong the wish. Her hand on the knob stiffened. Just beyond the kitchen wall, a steady drawl of flip-flops was scraping the silence. Crossing the patio. A slap of soles. Out the window nothing to see. Just her own face sharpened. The knife block, somewhere off to the right, behind her, she was thinking. Around the edge of the door came a determined jaw, stiff, wiry whiskers, the summit of an ear. She was watching these things appear, piecing them together to form his face, lost in his quartz eye, when the lino click-clacked with his front claws. Christ almighty, he was half in the house.

Block his path to the hall, she should. But she was on the wrong side of him for that. The kitchen so narrow. To pass him, she would have to touch him. The black circle of his snout strained toward the worktop, while her hands wrapped around the handle of the cupboard to keep her fingers safe, and her toes recoiled in her sandals. Would the fox bite or jump or otherwise exercise his intellect for sudden movement? She stamped her foot, and he watched her with a puzzled expression. But he did not move, and she took a couple of sideways steps to open up a view of his flank. His hind legs arrowed behind him in a fractional crouch, as if their mission were perpetually to point against the direction of his body. They made him look two-faced, capable of sudden reversals, but he was not reversing now.

"Not indoors!" she choked. A strong smell hit the back of her throat. It went straight there, bypassing her nose, and she knew it first by taste: a burnt sweet flavor, like a misjudged toffee. Infiltrating the sweetness was a strong dark note between malt and musk, with a smoky edge as if blown through an exhaust. He shifted his paws a couple of clicks. The scent circled the kitchen. It had her surrounded. He hoisted his tail high over his back, training on her the white torch of its tip. It occurred to her that he could be on his own patrol for intruders and, who knows, believed he had found one. Behind him loomed the wall of Eric and Michelle's side return. Imagine, just imagine, she thought. If Michelle could see me now.

One after another his hind feet gained the concrete step.

"Go!" she said. The word cracked in her throat. Fascination had stolen her power to move or speak, and in a small corner of her head, a voice was telling her to watch what he did when given the freedom to choose. That it was the only way to find out what he wanted. But it was one thing to see him in the garden, the house was—no way. Just no way. There was nothing to rap on. There was nothing between them. "Out!" she shouted.

He lifted his nose and continued to examine the air.

Just a faint streak of mouse, long dead.

"Go! Go! Go!"

For a moment he lingered on the threshold, half in her world, half out, as if he wanted to take the air and doing so inside was as invigorating for him as a walk in the park was for her. His body was busy in its stillness, twitching with diligence and industry, the workload of constant attention, checking and rechecking, a job to be performed every second and never completed. His snout tipped up. His nostrils widened and contracted; the black dome glistened, caviar speckles. The stainless-steel bin flashed a patch of white chest, like the rolling beam of a lighthouse. Then he swooped his muzzle to the floor and gave it a lick.

From behind Mary, in Tangle Wood, a door clicked. She guessed the fabled son, whom Mrs. Farnworth had loved to talk about but apparently never saw, had dropped by to check on the house. The fox heard it too. Before she could say a word, he sprang round, his tail brushing the side of the units. She watched the light of his tag dim into night.

It was a relief he had gone, but the relief was tempered by the knowledge that he had been there at all. It seemed to pace around her, like his smell. His intrusion was an affront to all that she had won when she had lost Mark. There she went again. She caught herself in the moment of weakness. Lost Mark! What she meant was, the fox threatened everything she had won when she had got rid of Mark: a place of her own, whose walls worked hard to keep the world out and her safe inside. But tonight she had lost that too, and no locking of doors would get it back. Now all the knots in the floorboards would scurry and jump like round-backed mice. He had barely stepped inside, but already the house felt alive with other lives.

She leant outside to satisfy herself that the fox had gone, and her eye snagged on something in the place where he had stood. A discarded glove sprawled on her step, its fingers stiffened by heat into supplication. She picked it up and thumbed its palm. Even in this state she could tell that the leather had once been expensively soft. Embroidered across the wrist in elegant cursive was the phrase *Town & Country*. First boxers, now this. She felt confused. He had brought her a gardening glove, but there was no sign of its pair. He hadn't carried the glove when she saw him next door, so where had he got it? And why just one? It took a moment for her to realize that this was a symbolic gift rather than a practical one. It was a token, the kind a knight pledges before going into battle. The glove was an oath of allegiance.

He was in her service. And she was in his.

WHEN MARY WOKE that night, it was a sudden, definitive awakening that carried her straight to full and open-eyed consciousness. She was alert so quickly she had time to witness her own lids opening, the creak as her eyelashes unstuck, her feet swiveling to the floor. "You haven't seen me in five months," he'd said. At the time, she had registered Mark's comment as a reminder of the duration of their separation. But now it seemed to disclose an extra, silent clause within—one in which he implied that while she hadn't seen him, he had seen her. Over and over she replayed the conversation, but each time verified only the previous playing. She had no way of knowing if what she remembered hearing was what she had heard or what he really had said.

Mary kept her perch on the edge of the bed. The duvet, thrown off in her sleep, frothed in a heap on top of the clothes on the floor. Sweat slicked up the side of her finger as she drew it between her breasts, and she kicked herself for wondering, yet again, if it was possible to incite an early menopause through lack of sexual activity.

She went to the spare room to open the window there too. The white blind ran up like a flag, and she thought she saw something in the woods behind the garden, a sliver of light, a bright ellipse, like a beam or a giant eye turned partially in her direction and then borne away. She grabbed the cord of the lamp and flicked the switch on. Off. On. Off. On. Off. She waited for a reply, and when it didn't come, she went back to bed and dreamt that the woods were full of search beams. Out of the light Mark came walking up her garden, into her kitchen. He kept walking at her until her back hit the units, a cupboard doorknob kneading her buttock. Then he took the hem of her dress in his hands, and, while it floated up, he edged his fingers inside the leg of her knickers like a blade opening a tin. With his new muscles, he lifted her up, the dark sky creeping into the house behind him. And then, just as she started to judder, Mark's face began to disintegrate. First his eyes went, then a strip of his cheek, his chin. She panicked. He was vanishing in segments. Her body stilled, waiting, but she knew what was coming, and she tried to stop it, but there was no stopping it. This picture of Mark was rearranging itself, piece by piece, into the face of the fox.

THE NEXT MORNING, Mary took the glove to the shed. It didn't belong in the house, but she was disinclined to bin it. Tucked at the dark end of the garden, by the woods, the shed was a place she rarely visited. Occasionally, if Michelle was out, Eric would mow Mary's grass at the same time he did theirs. But since Flora had been born, Michelle was always home. Mary opened the door, and the shed puffed out the same strain of musk that she had smelt last night. Had she carried it in on the glove, or was the smell already in the shed? Light stole in dustily on the far side. She moved her foot into a clear patch of floor between the teeth of a rusty saw and a lawn rake whose long handle was jammed diagonally from one slatted wall to the other. She put down the glove and found the torch on its peg, a relic of Mark's thorough organization. The beam raked over the frames of lame deck chairs, a pyramid of empty paint cans, plant pots holding pieces of broken plant pots. Crouching, she aimed the torch at the panel where light crept in. A few slats had broken away. She swept the beam slowly round each wall, lighting up the raggedy windbreak, the wheelbarrow, two green eyes. Mary jumped and stumbled backward over the rake handle. There was a thud and a clatter from the back of the shed, and the bristly scrape of slats on his back.

FROM HIGH UP on his perch at the top of her lime, the pigeon looked down on Mary. He had found a spot of sun and so had she, sitting at the little table on the patio, the one the shop had said was a bistro table. She had slept so badly, just lying there, thinking about Mark, she couldn't stop rubbing her eyes. New Mark. Mark MK II, she ought to call him. He bore so little resemblance to the one she knew. Her hand lifted and dropped the phone on the table. She had the urge to speak to someone, to talk through the things she couldn't understand. Where was Mark living? And had anything else changed, beyond the muscles? These were the questions she had lain awake puzzling over, until she consoled herself that, if nothing else, they at least explained her dream.

That thought brought to mind the fox.

So far, he had not actually taken anything from her. In fact, when she analyzed the past couple of weeks, Mary had a distinct but unquantifiable feeling of gain. But if she tried to put her finger on what this comprised, she faltered. Certainly life felt busier. One by one over the past few years her friends had had children, and although at first Mary had visited them, her visits had petered out. Mark had organized their free time, and eventually the friends without babies had fallen away too. She thought about Saba and Charlotte, the people she had let slip. Mark had been gone for months, but she still hadn't found the courage to contact anyone. She was too lonely for that. She dropped the phone. Yes, the gain was quite straight-forward. At the end of her garden she had found a friend.

She bit into a slice of toast, and the crumbs began to seep greasy blotches into her magazine, but it didn't matter. She wasn't reading. The pages lay open before her, a decoy in case anyone looked over the fence from next door, a territory she now considered hostile. She could hear them all out there, fussing over shade and blankets and who had what and who didn't. Just an ordinary Sunday morning. In and out of the house to fetch forgotten things. Bollocking George for never doing as he was told. She sat there listening to their grip-ing while she raked over Eric and Michelle's act of treachery, all the permutations of its meaning.

She imagined Mark babysitting next door while she, Mary, spent Saturday night at home. Not implausible. He would be relaxing on the other side of her lounge wall, knowing she was there and with-out her knowing that he knew. She saw him walking past the house, looking in the window and seeing her not seeing him. He would love that. He would hear the TV and know she had nothing better to do. If she went to bed early, which sometimes happened even on Saturdays, he would listen for her feet alone climbing the stairs. In retrospect, her whole evening felt as if an invasion had taken place. How many times must she now sit in her lounge, wondering if the noise she could hear on the other side of the wall was really Eric and Michelle or Mark the babysitter? She scratched at the gnat bite on her arm. For all she knew, Mark was in their garden right now. She could smell their coffee. And on top of all this, the total insult of them thinking that he would make the better babysitter.

What did he want?

Her, surely. Her, and the house.

MARY MOVED QUIETLY to get the blanket from indoors. Eric and George had started playing football, and she didn't want them to know she was there. She shook the rug out on the lawn in the sun and lay on her stomach. It had belonged to Granny Joan and had a permanently unaired animal smell, of wool that lives folded up against itself. She turned her face toward Eric and Michelle's fence. Technically, it was her fence—according to the deeds—but Eric and Michelle had got fed up with its permanent sagging off the post and had appeared at the front door one evening in spring to tell her a replacement was being fitted. No discussion. And she had had to thank them for their generosity in paying for it. Months on, the fence still had that horrible orange newness, and the ivy and other things that had climbed up its predecessor had been casualties of the upgrade. Probably Michelle had wanted a new fence just to get rid of the ivy. The ball cracked the wooden slats, and Mary jumped.

"Eric!"

Michelle made his name sound like a curse.

Mary felt drowsy. She really needed to concentrate. She picked over her and Mark's conversation, trying to gather all the pieces of evidence of how he felt, what he wanted. The fact he had moved back to London. The way he kept staring at her dress. His grip on her arm. Then his sudden appearance in her hall. Michelle's voice drifted over the fence: "Have you measured up for that gazebo?" Eric and Michelle had asked Mark first. That was so insulting. She was feeling very sleepy now. She imagined again his one hand on her back. More than nothing, short of something.

WHEN SHE OPENED her eyes, all Mary could see were the white wiry hairs of the picnic blanket sticking up like antennae. Through that thicket, among the finer hairs of her own skin, a ladybug was standing on her wrist. His legs were bright red, as if the color had bled from his shell. She pushed herself stiffly up on her forearms and, meaning to blow him away, inhaled sharply.

The taste was fainter than it had been in the kitchen or the shed, but it was clearly a strain of the same earthily sweet scent, and her recognition of it confirmed a new intelligence. She had learnt to tell his presence. Keeping her legs and arms still on the rug, Mary turned her head slowly over her shoulder.

He was lying on his stomach with his hind legs and tail stretched out long and straight on the grass behind him, as if he had arranged himself in order to maximize the possibility of an even tan. His forelegs, which were black, lay flat on the grass, in much the same position as her arms. His chest and head were raised above them, just as she had lifted her own upper body from the blanket. He was about the width of a king-size bed away and had directed his muzzle to her so she could see the black hairs of its outline. Neither of them moved. Their bodies seemed to want to hold the reflected shape of the other, as if all their physical instincts were bent toward expressing a synchronicity they had each, separately, chosen.

There was a scrambling sound as Neville's cat appeared on the fence, and they both turned toward it. The cat rotated swiftly and retreated back into Tangle Wood. The red-legged ladybug continued to pick a path over the cracked earth. When Mary faced the fox again, she noticed something stowed in the space between his paws.

One brown egg, inscrutable in its ordinariness. Absurd, to see an egg on the lawn. She could just make out the orange lion printed on its shell. So he ate certified eggs! That meant he had not foraged for this one from an urban henhouse. It must have come from the supermarket, no doubt via someone's kitchen or bin or shopping bag. From the other side of the fence, she heard the slithery metallic recoil of a tape measure.

The fox opened his jaws wide and, laying his head first on one side and then on the other, clamped his canines around the egg, like one of those devices for removing staples from a wall. All the while the egg stood upright on the grass, a paw flat either side. It was as

puzzling as a cryptic clue, which its shell, so slippery and han-
dleless, seemed both to express and disguise. He tried again. She
thought she heard it give, and for a second time he released the egg
from his jaws. But it was perfectly intact, sitting up perkily on the
grass. He let it be and gently licked it. She watched his pink tongue
lick and lick at the same spot on the egg, as if he were trying to
wash a resistant dirty patch or perhaps to befriend it.

His right ear moved before she heard anything. It swiveled almost
in a circle, like an old-fashioned tuning device looking for the right
station. He got to his feet in a jump, his ears flattened against his
head. His tail stood. She watched his fur enlarge. Dry twigs snapped.
Then a voice behind her.

"These bricks are bursting apart, Mary. You need to secure
your boundary here."

Michelle! The other side of the rear wall. And no "Hi" or "Sorry
to disturb you." Mary leapt up and brushed the wispy lime blos-
som from her shorts. She had the sensation that she had been caught
in a compromising position, and for a moment she stalled, looking
at Michelle and the something held under her arm. Dimly she registered fairy lights on the shrub above the fence. Barbecue preparations already! Didn't they have anything better to do?

"Hi!" she called, walking toward Michelle and calculating with
a quick sideways glance that the position of the shed would narrowly
prevent her neighbor from seeing her guest. He, meanwhile, had
understood the need for discretion. His bristles stretched out in pro-
tection of her, but his feet stayed put. "Are you having a restful
weekend?" Mary asked as she approached the crumbling wall.

Michelle looked at her as if she were mad. "Not really. I knocked
at the front door, but there was no answer. Are you on your own?
I thought I heard voices."

"No. Just me."

"I wanted to return this." She held out Mary's book, the pages thick with wear. Although their faces were cracked by creases, the two sisters on the cover exchanged a playful, secretive glance. "I found it this morning, between the sofa cushions." For a moment Michelle looked as if she would climb into the garden, but she must have decided that it wasn't practical because she waited for Mary to take the book, then held on too.

"I found it down the back of the sofa."

"You said. Thanks! I was wondering where it had got to."

"The thing is, I don't remember seeing it when you arrived. How did it get into my lounge?" Michelle's eyes were rimmed red. She looked unsure of herself.

The heat rushed to Mary's cheeks, but she managed to laugh. "You probably had other things on your mind." She had the uncomfortable sense that the three of them could be stuck in this uneven triangle for hours. From behind her, she heard a strange guttural clicking.

"Jesus!"

Michelle let go of the book and started yelling and clapping her hands, and Mary, in sole possession of her novel, watched the fox walk stiff-legged toward the part of the shed where she was standing and rub himself against its slatted walls. A damp smell of caramel on the turn wafted up.

"There's a bloody great fox in your garden!" Michelle yelled, but Mary maintained her composure as his brush flicked her leg. It was surprisingly muscular. Then he tapered into a rustle of ivy behind the shed.

"Didn't you know it was there? And your back door is open!"

"I fell asleep on the blanket. I didn't see him."

"God, Mary." Michelle's eyes were huge. "What's the matter with you, falling asleep in the garden? Aren't you worried? It came right up to you!"

"How are the children?"

She had thought she was changing the subject to the safe territory of domestic inquiry, but Michelle gasped. Leaving as she had arrived, without the courtesy of a greeting, she hastened back toward her own garden, where a tall, lockable gate gave her easy access to the woods and kept all intruders out.

Mary dropped the novel on the blanket with a sigh. From the other side of the fence, Michelle's voice, yelling for Eric, faded inside the house. What a close scrape. He had pretty much saved her. At the expense of his precious egg too. She reached for it and was surprised to find her hand fly up in the air. She had misjudged the egg's weight, expecting something heavier. But now that she was turning it in her hand, she could see that the shell was completely intact, apart from one hairline fracture through which all its contents had been drained.

CHAPTER SIX

The fox visited often. In just three weeks, Mary had entered his world. Or had he entered hers? When she walked to the station each morning, his hot blast of musk enveloped her—beside her front railings, as she passed the tree outside Neville's. The smell rose again at the new-builds at the end of her street, on Shepherds Bridge Walk, at the fringe of the park. It hit her intermittently, as if she were passing through chambers of scent. The whole neighborhood was his castle, all the roads and houses and gardens portions of some enormous floor plan to which she now held the key. How long had it been here, this invisible, pungent architecture? Had she simply failed to notice it—or was the first time she saw him the day he moved into the area?

Almost without looking, Mary spotted the signs of him, the tidy droppings by a lamp post, the food waste bin upended. Their two worlds were coinciding. As she left the park and turned toward Haggerston station on her way to work one Monday morning, a gang of crows dispersed over the rooftops with a sudden cawing. She imagined him stalking below, his shoulders dropped and rolling, belly dusting the ground. The crows were a clutch of black kites, and he held their strings.

After work that day, Mary came straight home and lay on the blanket in the garden. She was dozing when the fox's mellow spice began to solidify around her. The scent gave her the sense that she had awoken in his home, and when she turned her neck to see him nosing at the corner of her rug, it was not fear she felt but relief, because she had not imagined his presence but accurately divined it. They eyed each other cautiously. They both knew their relationship was entering a new phase.

On Tuesday Mary returned from work half an hour earlier than Monday, and again he strolled through the long grass to greet her. This time, he sat a little closer and dropped a rag between them, a funny thing with knots at each corner, and when she picked it up, she saw that stitched into one was a smiling face. She watched his claws extend and retract in the thinning lawn, toying with the invisible string that divided his space from hers.

And so the week went on. Without either of them needing to say, they settled into a routine. Mary would come outside, and he would appear. From the woods, he heard her footsteps or caught her cologne. He seemed to know her movements, to have a supernatural sense of her whereabouts, no matter how she tested him with small variations to her timing, or how quietly she drew back the lock and tiptoed outside. The fox knew more about her comings and goings than her mother, her neighbors, and Dawn put together, even though Dawn sat opposite her for eight hours a day and today had even commented on how cheerful Mary seemed. Actually, Dawn sat opposite her for eight hours in theory. It said a great deal about how little people truly noticed Mary that she could slip out of the office unseen, yet she found it impossible to come home without being met.

On Wednesday, after Red—not yet his name, just something

she was trying—had sprung his exit over the back wall, she left the blanket outside. The sky had forgotten how to rain. And besides, he was no longer a threat. He was encroaching on her life the way any new relationship encroaches, and she shifted over to make room for him. The blanket was an open invitation, their sofa in front of the telly, the place where they met and crashed at the end of the day. At least, it was the end of her day—perhaps only the start of his. Later she learnt that he slept on the rug while she was at work, because it bristled with his smoky tang.

On Thursday, when Dawn disappeared into what was to be a long meeting, Mary took her chance. She arrived in the garden a whole hour earlier than Wednesday. The edges of the blanket curled upward in the sun, and this time when he walked down the lawn to meet her, he did not stop, but slipped his snout beneath a frayed corner. Mary pressed her stomach into the blanket, to fend against his tugging. "Easy!" she cajoled, as the plaid rucked and crumpled into new shapes over his head. Polite guy that he was, he withdrew his muzzle and hovered at the fringe with little snagging noises. Mary had been watching over her shoulder, and now as he approached the peak of his ear spiked the rim of her vision. Her limbs stiffened. How close would he come? But instantly his legs folded beneath him where he stood, and they lay there looking up at the trees, watching the shadow of a bee crawl across a low-hanging hazel leaf, trawling veins with its antennae. The hard part was done. They had got themselves here at last, side by side on the blanket. Now they could relax, lie in the sun, and talk.

HE WAS TOO busy to relax. His tail thumped the dead animal beneath his underparts. From the size of the fleece: a big beast. The fleece was all that was left. She must have eaten the rest long time gone which made. Hungry. His ears blinked at the tangle of sounds.

Sounds were food. He avoided making sounds. Not wanting to be food himself.

Human Female was singing pigeon. Pigeon in the tree. Wrens squeaking. Infant Beetles chewing. Later, he would whistle them out of the log. A wood louse drummed on a crispy leaf. Most there was noise. Just he wanted rest. Puff, puff. He breezed some scent from the notch in his tail. A formality. The human Female was his. The fleece was his. The grass was his. The tunnels and dens and diggings were his. They all knew his. He was here in his. Not hiding. Busy being seen. Not resting. Watching. He was the Fox of the land. Tip tap tip tap went the wood louse across the. Leaf tipped. Louse flipped. All those little legs, w a g g l i n g fascinatingly. Stretching, straining, leaning, this way, that way, this way . . .

His snout was swaying, watching something. It was not a thought she could share with any human she knew, but Mary believed, from the way his muzzle bobbed in excitement, the happy thump of his tail on the blanket, that he enjoyed the sound of her voice. He was so easy to talk to. He seemed to understand her.

The thing was, she *had* loved Mark. "He was—in the beginning—a nice guy," she said. He was affectionate and open, and the openness was a foreign thing for her. He needed her, he loved her, he told her that he loved her. He wanted to spend time with her. It was the opposite of being a child. She had absolutely no sense of being an aberration. She was his normal. He chose her every day, and his choice, in turn, gave her purpose. She adapted to his ways, grew herself to fit around his shape. "You can see why it's hard to work out what I am without him," she said to Red. He lifted his snout, and regarded her intently. His pupils cut a dark slit through his amber iris—the narrowest ovoid, as beckoning as the gap between closed curtains or the score line on a pill.

"I did love him," she said. "Maybe still love him." She had

better clarify that. "Not actively," she said. "Like the love spent a long time soaking in and left a permanent stain."

It was hard to explain, but her submissiveness had become for her an effective way to keep the peace by second-guessing Mark's needs. She applied herself to them, and the self-consciousness of her application, the way she complied and pandered, made her feel that somewhere inside she was reserving for herself a kind of discrete emotional autonomy. "I've been so used to keeping this little part of me locked away that now he's gone, and I can do what I like, I can't get used to the freedom," she said. She was contemplating, among other things, the fact that she still hadn't called Saba, struggled to enter a supermarket or get to work on time. Red's head swayed as if he didn't quite follow. She tried again. "Imagine you're in a trap. It's hypothetical," she added, seeing his uncertain expression. "You are taken to be released into the wild. The trap opens, you see the fields or woods, smell the grassy air. What do you do? I bet you wait inside for a while. Maybe the trap feels safer. I bet you don't rush out. Am I right?"

There was no answer.

"Do you know where he is?" she said suddenly. "Have you seen him?"

If he knew Mark, if Mark lived within his territory, maybe he went through Mark's bin. A bin was very revealing. But Red just coned his snout into the long grass.

"What are you crunching on?" she asked, smiling at him, companionable and independent, a cipher to crack her indecipherable life.

"Thank God for the house," she said. This house was all she had. This nice den.

He looked around for another. Snappy things with a chew inside. Not much effort to—Especially if they were in easy—

Her voice soothed him, she could see by the way he tucked his snout under the bushy hairs of his tail, and his eyes shrank to a wet seam. But his ears never slept. She watched them, flickering and twitching as she chatted, their minute movements like an electronic readout of her tenor–bass balance. Up, down, down, up. Or twisting round when she heard the clatter of dinner things next door, then when Eric and George called again and again for their cat, "Tiggy Tig-Tig!" He was so caring that when Flora grizzled, his ears lifted and quivered. They were large ears, and their size told a truth about him—he was an excellent listener. It occurred to Mary that, contrary to Mark's evaluation of her, she might be an excellent talker. All she had needed was someone to give her the space to be one.

"Do you know," she said, "when I was small I used to write letters to myself. The house was so empty and quiet. Dad at work, Mum around but not around, prepping for lessons. After school, no one to talk to. *Dear Mary, How was the day, and what do you think you're going to do about Stuart Biston, then?* Actually, I did go out with him in the end, but only for a week." She had never talked to anyone like this before. She glanced at her fox, and his ear bent in encouragement. She chuckled. This was a bit like thinking aloud a letter. *Dear Fox . . .*

"I wonder what happened to them," she said. "I was desperate to post them. So I would receive them. I, erm, borrowed stamps from Mum's purse." She raised her eyebrows at him, and he nestled his snout forgivingly between his paws. "I stuck the stamps on, but I couldn't do it. Post them. Release them into the unknown. It seemed such a . . ." She looked up again and was aggrieved to see that he appeared to have fallen asleep. She coughed sharply, and the near ear turned frontally to face her. Inside, the dark hair made a narrow black line, as if his ears had pupils too, and through them he saw and heard her in unison.

"I was going to say 'risk.' It seemed such a risk to post the letters.

And by the way, it's fine if you want to sleep but please don't think this is weird. People talk to animals all the time. All the time."

He resettled himself then, folded his haunches into a crouch beneath his rump. Even lying prone, his legs never looked fully relaxed, but already committed to their next move, whatever the next move might be. They pulsed with intention, the quickness of his instinct. And when it was time for him to go—

he decided this—

he stood in one fluid motion. Black legs steeped in stealth, he rippled his way to the far corner of the garden and vanished. It was as if he had a secret transportation station tucked away in the dark sliver between her shed and Tangle Wood. He was an escape artist, she thought admiringly. Maybe he could free her too.

WHEN MARY STEPPED outside on Friday morning, she had the distinct impression that Eric had been waiting for her. He was putting out the rubbish, and she took his yellow rubber gloves as another sign of his and Michelle's prissiness. Then she realized that he was on her side of the railings. A scent of veiled rancidity rose from her front garden: the sort of aroma that warns of its high calorific content. Honey nut loops, sweet food with added sweetness. White things were strewn across the ivy.

"What's all that?" she asked.

"This," Eric said, with a theatrical sweep, "is what breast milk looks like when it comes out the other end. I'd say there's two days of Flora's nappies here. Or there was till I made a start. I was hoping I could clear up before you came out. He left them in your garden."

"Who?"

"Fox."

The word wrong-footed her. It sounded abrupt, like hearing a friend referred to by his surname. But she was unsure about Red and had not yet produced any better ideas. (She had wondered briefly about Fantastic, but he was too modest for that.)

"How do you know it's a fox?" she said to Eric.

"They like the smell of breast-fed babies' nappies," Eric said, shrugging. "They're famous for it. Apparently, it's all my fault. Admittedly, as Michelle mentioned, I put the rubbish out last night. Admittedly, as Michelle also mentioned, I overfilled the bin, contravening her particular instruction to make sure the lid was shut. And now this lot's all over the garden." He waved his gloved hands. With his shirtsleeves and tie, he looked like a waiter forced to help with the washing up. "They're getting worse, Mary. When I got home last night, one was walking down the sidewalk with a Big Mac in its mouth. Still in the box. As if it had come from some animal kingdom drive-through. You'd think it would get off the sidewalk when it saw me, but *I* had to get out *its* way and walk in the road! We need a few more like that one in spring."

"Which one?" she said.

He pulled a face. "It was a bit grim actually. In the road. A health hazard. Michelle called the council. The pest people came to shovel it up. Good job too or we'd have had an even bigger problem. The guy told Michelle it was pregnant!"

"They obviously don't like me," she said. "I never see them."

Neville stepped onto his path from the front door the other side of Eric's. "Nappies," Mary said, to answer his inquisitive look. "Eric thinks a fox did it."

"Not thinks. Knows."

"Vermin," Neville said.

"Hey, while you're both here," Eric said, "have you seen Tigger? He didn't come in last night."

"If he's anything like Baxter he's probably overindulged in the woods," Neville said.

Mary shook her head. "Sorry, Eric. Look, you know you said *he* left the nappies? The fox, I mean. The one you think did this. I was wondering how you knew it was a he?"

"What? What the hell does it matter? It's a crap way to start the day. I've got to go and change now. I'm soaking already." He pulled his shirt free of his chest. "What are you doing up bright and early for work, Mary?"

"Got an appointment."

IT WAS LATE in the afternoon when Mary dared to come home. Late, considering she had spent the day doing nothing. After she left the doctor's, she had taken his letter straight to the post office, then looped the roads around her house for hours, looking for Mark. She knew it was ridiculous to try to catch him in the same place, but she had nothing else to go on. And the whole time the squeak in her shoe tagged every step, as if someone had planted a listening device in her heel. When a shoe got a squeak, did the squeak ever go?

In the hall she kicked off the sandals beside her mobile, which lay darkly on the floor next to the landline. She had not thought to unplug the other phone, because it almost never rang. But now a red 7 limply flashed on the answerphone. She pressed Play.

"Hi, it's a message for Mary. Hi, Mary. It's Dawn! From work. Umm. Just wondering if everything's OK? Are you coming in? Umm. Where aaaare yooou? Are you there? Are you there? Nope? Umm. Hope you're OK . . . Let me know. OK? Yeah. Byeeee." Beep.

"Hi. It's me again. Dawn. Er. It's twelve o'clock. No sign of you. Your mobile's off. Give me a call." Clunk. Beep.

"Mary. It's Michelle. From next door." A heavy sigh. "The postman's just woken me up with a parcel for you. It would be good if you could avoid ordering things when you're not going to be there to receive them. It's given me a really bad headache. Whatever you do, don't knock on my door. I'm going to have a sleep. Don't knock on my door. Don't knock on my door." Beep.

"Hello, love. Just calling because it's Friday. I know you're at work, but I'm going out later, so at least you'll know I rang. Speak soon. Hope you're well. Love, Mum." Beep. Mary pressed Delete. Her messages always sounded like brief letters, written under sufferance.

"This is the UK's Eco Fund. This allows you to have your loft and cavity walls insulated for free . . ." Beep.

Clunk. Beep.

"Mary. Give us a call. I'm sure there's a good reason for this, but you need to get in touch. This is an HR issue, for God's sake." Beep.

On Monday, Dawn would get the doctor's letter and everything would be OK.

Mary deleted all messages. She wanted no one else's voice in her house.

IN THE KITCHEN she filled the kettle. The blast of water brimmed in her ears and drowned all the voices there. When she turned, the fox was watching her. All four feet were inside, and the room had shrunk. Her mouth opened and shut, but her words were dry. She felt her muscles contract and loosen of their own accord, to swallow the jolt of surprise.

Get a grip, she told herself. They had known each other for weeks. Almost a month. Of course he'd want to see where she lived. It was the natural next step. Sometimes, taking control meant surprising yourself, disobeying the familiar instincts, thwarting the same old you's perennial attraction to the same old you's typical decisions. It was like living in confinement, inside this head. She felt a fierce retaliation against the way her world had narrowed. Well, tonight she would not surrender to her lonely Monday, Tuesday, every night lock-in. Tonight, she was throwing open the doors.

She stepped aside with a flourish and said, "Come in."

He nodded.

It was so easy. One simple decision, and life was a different place. She felt as good as if she had let some second self out of the cage.

He lifted his muzzle and dropped it again. His nose dabbed the ground, trying to filter signals through the interference. An electric hum zigzagged—floor—claws—shins. Bounced about his knee joints. Messing with the messages. His paws shifted, padding for information. Ground a thin pierceable skin. He hesitated while he. His own scent was the only fox scent. That was good. He pulled up his tail and released some more. Better. Coming through strongly now. The earth hummed with the strange calls of what? His claws curled into the floor. The floor clung to his claw. To get rid of the stickiness, he lifted a leg until the floor let go.

Mary felt a twinge of shame. If she ever got the money, the lino would be the first thing to go. Then, seeing him delay, she gestured into the house again. "Come on. After you."

He was in her world now. He was everywhere in this room. She could see his reflection in the sheen of the bin, the silvery steel of the oven, the glint of the toaster and kettle. Then one by one, all those mirrors emptied themselves of him and darkened. He was on the move. He seemed to know where to go. A small step led up to the hall, and his paws knocked warmly on the floorboards. He stopped to examine his toes. Each noise made a larger noise than it should.

An echo was nesting under this wood.

He moved slowly down the hall, his muzzle probing the boards, his feet proceeding only at its say-so. It dropped with every lift of a paw, as if his nose were the thing that clenched and pulled the strings that moved the feet. It bobbed over her handbag.

Something inside smelt good.

She scooped the bag out of his way. At the entrance to the lounge, he balked, and Mary pulled up too. The room was as dark as if autumn had come. Over the past few months she had scarcely both-ered to open the shutters. What was the point, only to close them again later? But now, looking over Red's shoulder, she saw the place through fresh eyes. The lounge was horribly uninviting. Besides the sofa, stained and tatty, there was only Granny Joan's old chair and a decorative rug. To the right, in the so-called dining room, the table with no chairs. It was all too obvious why he—her first houseguest since Mark had left—chose to stand in the hall. At last he nudged the patchwork hen doorstop.

He clamped his jaws around it. Gingham tail feathers poked perkily out of the side of his mouth, and he clicked forward. Mary followed, sensing the door bounce softly behind them. For a moment, Red stalled in the middle of the room, his head facing the opposite direction to his feet.

Bury the chicken / not chicken.

He stuck his haunches in the air and scratched with his forepaws at the rug. He appeared to want to conjure a hole right there in the mock-Moroccan diamonds. After a while, he looked up. His snout pointed side to side, and whichever way it faced, his tail swung the opposite. Left, ri— "Watch out!" Her grandmother's ornamental brass hearth tools clattered to the tiles. Red leapt back from the commotion, the hen still locked between his teeth, and, as he jumped, his tail toppled the china lamp that stood at the far corner of the hearth. Its base opened cleanly in two, like an Easter egg. His head swayed while the pieces rocked on the floor.

"Steady!" Mary cried. "I know it's shabby, but don't wreck the place!" She glanced at the door, which had come to rest at a point not fully shut. His being in here had happened so fast she had given no thought to how much freedom she was prepared to allow him. Was it best to contain him in one room, or would the sense of enclosure panic him as it was panicking her? She did not want to be in thrall again to the unpredictable instincts of another living being, and he seemed wilder in here than he did outside, a liability in a way he never appeared in the garden, where he knew when to come, when to leave, how to lie peacefully. Indoors he took up so much space, and his wishes were unguessable, as if they might advance in any direction, and he was continually reconsidering the options.

His brush swished her knees where she hovered on the edge of the sofa, and again he headed to the hearth, his claws making tinny taps on the tiles as he dropped the hen into the grate. He bent an ear to the window. A car door shut outside, and he spun to face it. The quiet lounge revolved with his speed. Then stilled with his furtive crouch. Family voices drifted indoors. Eric back from nursery with George, maybe. Red strained at the sounds even when the sounds had stopped. At last he returned to the hen, giving it a firm thrust under the logs with the tip of his muzzle. Down and down his snout drove. His hind parts were raised, and he whisked his tail so violently that the paper light shade began to whirl in its airstream. Mary tucked her feet beneath her legs. Now they were both indoors, his tameness seemed selective.

At last he was satisfied that the hen was buried, and she watched him look about, wondering, as he seemed to wonder, what he would do next. She had not specified that upstairs was out of bounds, and she glanced anxiously at the door. She was about to get up and close it when the neighboring sofa cushion dipped beneath his weight.

He lifted and replaced his paws. The resting place was trying to swallow his feet. He kept pulling them out out out out and somehow out out they were dry.

He didn't like the sofa. She could see that. Despite her invitation, he had declined to sit and was staring at his feet with a look of pure suspicion. Maybe he thought it would eat him. Death by Dralon. She started to laugh, but a switch inside flipped, and a few tears came instead. She wiped them. She was not going to cry. Why was she crying? Everything was fine. She refused to worry about Mark. Work would be sorted. A fortnight of fully paid leave. More if she needed. Her mum could get off her case. Then more tears came because her mum was never on her case. She inhaled fiercely, and one last drop rolled onto her cheek.

"Relax and the sofa will stop moving," she sniffed, patting the cushion.

She showed him her dark bit of ear, which meant yes, and he gave her a lick.

Her mouth opened to speak, but a laugh escaped because he had turned his snout away and was pointing it toward the window, as if he knew he had overstepped the line and was pretending that the lick had nothing to do with him. Mary wiped her cheek with her wrist, studying the side of his poker face. He had licked her! It was a huge transgression, but when he turned back his head, his warm amber eyes addressed her so respectfully, she knew he had meant no harm. It occurred to her that she might have given him a sign. After all, she had no experience of this situation. As a child, her parents steadfastly refused all requests for a pet. The only animals she had been allowed to keep were imaginary.

She looked at Red. At last he deemed it safe to sit and was lowering himself into the cushion, but his ears yearned upward, and she wished she understood why he had turned away. With time, she would learn to read him better. On a hunch she licked the back of her hand: it was typical of her lack of confidence in social situations that at first she thought human skin must taste bitter or contain some repellent only he sensed. But then she heard the feet on her path, and her eyes widened in horror. She laid a finger on her lips, trusting that he would behave. They waited, and then it came, the knock on the door. She shook her head because whoever it was could come back later.

A second knock. "Mary?"

He was off the sofa, stalking across the room, hips rolling.

"No!" she whispered, overtaking him at the door, scraping his bristles with her thigh, his flank muscles rippling against her leg.

As she opened the door, his muzzle probed her hip, trying to see past her into the hallway, where the letter box was folding inward.

Eric's voice sounded closer this time. "It's me," he said, more quietly. "Only Eric."

"Don't move a muscle," Mary hissed to Red. "Not. A. Muscle." She backed down the hall, staring him into place, until she reached the front door, which she opened a fraction.

"Ah, Michelle said you were in." Eric squinted through the gap. "This came for you today. I'm not disturbing you, am I?"

She widened the opening to take the parcel.

"Looks intriguing," Eric said, staying on the step, as if he meant to watch her open it. "Hold on," he said, as she began to close the door. "Have you got a sec?"

"Er. I'm a bit busy," she said, moving her body to block his view into the house.

"Oh, I see! I'm interrupting, am I? Good for you!" He strained to see past her. "Look, I just wanted to say, about tomorrow. It's going to be great! The gazebo's up—pretty tricky to get it straight, but I did it. I've got a fridge full of cava—"

"Oh, the barbecue!" she said. "Actually, I don't think—"

"Right. Yes, I see. Well. This may not be relevant, then. But, there was one other thing. There's a small chance Mark will come. Very, very small. Almost infinitesimal."

"What! You invited him too?"

"Not exactly . . . It wasn't like that . . . We asked you. We wanted you to come . . . We want you to come. But I ran into Mark outside the station. He mentioned it, and I couldn't not invite him. Please come. You can bring—your new friend."

She narrowed the door opening further and checked over her shoulder. "I have to go. He's got to leave soon," she said.

"But will you come? I promised Michelle numbers," Eric persisted.

"Well, tell her I need to think about what you've just told me."

Mary took the parcel to the kitchen. The label had been stuck on messily with too much tape, and her address was written in thick, faded felt pen. They had misspelt her surname as Greene, as if the correct spelling were insufficient. She racked her brains. She knew no one in the United States. Tape was wrapped so tightly around the corners that it took her ages to work beneath it. She looked up as she picked away with fingernails that used to be longer, and saw him watching.

"That was Eric," she said confidentially. "Mark has got himself invited to the barbecue tomorrow! What d'you make of that?"

He registered this information with a small flick of brush. His attention was divided between her and the front door. He fixed on it as if an enemy lurked behind there.

"Oh, he won't come back," she said. "Way too busy. More fairy lights to put up. Intestinal tracts to be extracted from giant prawns." His tongue slid out between his jaws. "Eric, do this. Eric, do that." There was no budging the tape. She yanked open a drawer, and he leapt back as it glided out on its rollers. She laughed and grabbed the scissors.

"I hope this is something interesting . . . ," she began and stopped. Surely not that, not so soon.

The package was just a little larger than the letter box, and its corners had been scuffed by Eric's, Michelle's, and probably the postman's efforts to push it through. Mary snipped the seal and pulled off a long ribbon of brown paper. Eric had said that the chance of Mark coming tomorrow was extremely small, which showed how much he knew. The ribbon kept coming. So Mark had mentioned the barbecue to Eric, had he? "How very interesting," she said. "First he bumps into me; then he bumps into Eric. That's a lot of bumping into people." She reached the end of the sheath of paper and started to unwind the bubble wrap. The miniature portholes of the final layer magnified the label, and she read it easily. She knew her fox was watching, and she felt herself redden.

"Nothing interesting!" she said brightly.

The box itself was surprisingly small, considering how much it had cost. She slipped out the vial and hid it in her hand. All that packaging for this tiny, cool thing. The glass was tinted brown, and when she tipped it up, she could make out powder slipping darkly from one end to the other. It had got here fast, and yet it seemed to her that she had ordered it in a different age. It was hard to think of a less accurate representation of her feelings toward Red than the poison she held behind her back.

He watched expectantly, but she wasn't going to explain what it was. "No need for that now, is there?" she said. "Look, it was a mistake, that was all. I was scared. I listened to Eric. And the Mark in my head. He's gone now."

Red appeared, as he always did, to agree.

She scooped up the packaging, but her hand wavered over the bin. Maybe the bin was a bad idea. What if the glass broke, and the powder leaked into the bag, and what if he knocked over the trash can and licked it up . . . In fact, it would be dangerous to dispose of it anywhere in the neighborhood. Her house and garden were the center of his territory, but she had no idea how far it ranged nor where she would have to dump this to be sure he was safe. She trembled as she checked that the cap was secure. Then she buried the vial in the cupboard under the sink. The previous owners had fitted a child lock on the door for their grandchildren, which Mark had pointedly refused to remove, and it amused Mary to think that she was repurposing his harassment, that his family planning would now keep the poison out of harm's way.

"Eric's visit has certainly put a different complexion on the barbecue," she said. "Did you hear him say I could bring you too?"

The fox cocked an ear, and she smiled.

He came when he heard. The click that
meant drink! The open that meant food!
Through the snug in the fence, into this
human run. The grass so long. Anything
could hide among. Butterflies spun out
and jerked his snout. Squalling bees. He
sprayed and squeezed till his odor
flowered in the long and humming.
He slunk his stomach to the floor, and
the grass dusted his shoulders. The air
fuzzed with pollen and mites. He liked to
creep through here. Then. Grass stopped.
Tread on stone. Near the human den.
The male carrying a puddle.
Sausage sausage egg egg. Water slopping
his snout. Such a thirst. He drank,
looked around. Waited. Watching the
male. Sometimes the male brought again.
Something to bury for later.
Would the male bring? Bring! He
said this by staring at the male and
tweaking one ear. But the male sat at the
edge of his den, looking back.

He didn't do begging. He had seen the
mastiff do that. He sat. He began to
wash. Watching the male. The male
watching. It often went like this.
Strange sort of fight, no touch. Next the
male would fetch something, hold it out.
There! He waited, then. He heard his
feet. Pads, on the stone. Each step,
his choice. Human male held more food.
Taking food back, back, back into his
den. Less experienced foxes would walk
right in. But even though he had done
this before. He waited. Took steps slow.
Paused. Took steps. Paused. Took the
food. Left.

CHAPTER SEVEN

When Mary stepped outside on Saturday morning, the sky was full of small planes. Vapor trails scored the blue, then fuzzed and faded. Her own garden, her neighbors' gardens, the woods—they were all one swath of green to the humans up there. They would know nothing of the yapped commands coming from the other side of the fence, the frantic bustle and cries and scraping of furniture and testing of electrics as Eric and Michelle raced to complete their preparations, all of which made it so hard for Mary to decide which would be worse: to listen to the barbecue or to go to it.

A couple of hours later, she fortified herself with a final glance at her fox's favorite places and, on a whim, darted to the lawn, her apple-green sundress fluttering, to shake out the picnic blanket. She was unsure whether he would prefer to wait there or in the shade of the patio, but now he would know to make himself at home. The party would not detain her for long, and when she returned he would be waiting, she thought, smoothing out the rug's creases.

Her neighbors' hall was as gloomy as a church when she stepped in, with that unvisited dimness which the insides of buildings muster on bright afternoons. Tom with the sandy-gold hair—who had answered the door—laid his hand on Mary's shoulder. "Vroom, vroom," he said, steering her down the narrow hall. Her feet felt their way toward the back door, a blaze of light that smudged and yellowed at the edges like a camera flash. In the kitchen, Tom made a braking sound. Bottles crowded the worktops, throwing sunny green splodges onto the ceiling. "Here," he said, handing her a glass. "You're going to need this. There's not so much of the good stuff." He waited while she drank, then poured more, his shirt falling forward to show the hairs on his navel, which were darker gold. "Ready?" he asked.

Mary nodded. She felt disingenuous allowing Tom to believe she needed a guide—she knew the layout of the place as well as its owners—but she was relieved to follow him. Since Eric had dropped by last night, she had gone to bed, got up, got ready, all in a kind of reverberating hope. She hoped Mark would come. She hoped he would not. She hoped he was here now; then he would see her with this Tom. She stepped through the blazing doorway.

Mary felt herself to be stalking the brink of some tremendous informational gain. Instead of wondering where Mark was, what he was doing, here was a chance to watch the answers. At first, their troubling encounter on the street corner had left her wondering if Mark had really changed. But slowly over the past fortnight that question had spawned a second, more unsettling one. Had *she* changed enough? After months of stateless gloom, she was slowly beginning to take charge of herself, to find her shape. Since Red— not Red, Sunset, maybe?—had come into her life, she had felt her strength increase. What he had given her, and she was slowly learning to exercise, was a fresh and powerful perspective.

Today she was going to discover what Mark was up to, and she was going to do so from the happy vantage point of a new relationship. In the early evening, she would go home to Sunset. The more she thought about his name, the less sure she was of it. Never mind.

It was a comfort to picture the time later when the two of them would relax together in the lounge and make sense of the day.

"What are you smiling at?" Tom asked.

"This place!" she said quickly. "Looks amazing!" Crocheted bunting hung from shrub to shrub, and a sweet scent of jasmine wafted over in drifts: from the tea lights, extravagantly lit in midafternoon, or the white flowering shrub that had been trained along wires on Eric and Michelle's side of the hideous orange fence. But now Mary saw that Eric and Michelle's side of the bright orange fence was not bright orange. It had been stained tasteful jet, so the small shiny leaves of jasmine gleamed upon it like gems on a jeweler's black velvet cloth. People clustered in threes and fours on the lawn, barely a dozen in all. There was no Mark.

Mary followed Tom across the patio with the growing sensation that she had traveled much further than next door. Eric and Michelle's garden was a different country. The flower beds were edged with little cliff faces of mud, cut with a sharp blade into a clipped lawn. Even the dirt knew how to behave. The fence erased all sense of her own property, which in some ways was a relief. She didn't want to be the shabby neighbor any more than she wanted to be the uptight one. "I can't imagine my place ever looking like this," she said with genuine bewilderment to Tom.

Despite her neighbors' claims to be fighting an infestation of foxes, it seemed implausible to Mary that any wild thing had lived or would want to live here. Thinking that thought was enough to evoke a picture of him, and he flicked his tail across the sunlit amber field behind her eyelids. Careful, she cautioned herself, opening her eyes for a quick check. This was hardly the place. Sometimes she thought of him, and then, as if her thoughts were a summons, he appeared.

"Mmm. Or ever being sufficiently arsed to make it look like this," Tom said.

"Is there going to be a wedding?" Mary said, cheerfully pointing to the gazebo at the end of the garden, a sort of miniature marquee.

"Just a renewal of vows," he said. "They want to replace the 'Till death us do part' bit, which isn't really working, with something a bit more modern. 'Till we tear each other apart' maybe. How does that sound?"

She spluttered her laugh into a mouthful of insurgent bubbles. "That doesn't scan," she quipped. The talking-to-humans thing was going better than she had imagined. She smiled again because that thought sounded back to front but was nonetheless true. Her voice was finding its way out, unimpeded by the little pause that habitually overruled it when she lived with Mark, in which she doubted whether what she had to say really was better said than thought. She felt brighter than she had done in weeks. Her new relationship was releasing her confidence. Someone—and not to be bigheaded about it, but someone with a large pool of humans at his disposal—had chosen her.

"Ah. Here comes Eric," Tom said loudly. Her new friend shifted gears easily: impressive, to have located geniality so smoothly after disloyalty.

"Mary, you came! And I see you've met Tom," Eric said. "Sorry about him."

She laughed. "You should be. I can't believe you've got him on the door."

Eric was looking around. "Where's your new man then?"

"He couldn't make it, I'm afraid," she said, feeling a prickling in her cheek.

"Meanie! I was hoping we'd get to meet him."

Mary laughed. "I'm sure you'll see him soon enough. Hello, Flora, and how are you today?"

The baby's heavily upholstered bottom hung over the edge of

Eric's arm, which disappeared like a ventriloquist's under the frilly yellow valance of Flora's dress. She appeared smaller than a life-size doll. Mary reached out and stroked the baby's knuckles and in triumph watched her finger vanish inside Flora's quick fist. "What's up, Flora?" she said, trying to wag her finger. Flora held on, and Mary had the feeling, from the baby's secretive look, that the squeeze was a little message slipped into her hand. She was probably asking to get the hell out of here. Mary's mother had once told her that an infant's grip is so strong, you could hang a baby by its hands on the washing line and it would stay there for hours. She looked around. Presumably a washing line would spoil the vista.

"Here, Tom, take Flora, will you? I'm going to show Mary the new barbecue."

"Christ, she doesn't want to see your new barbecue. Do you, Mary?"

"Actually, I've come all this way especially. Flora, I'll see you later," she said, wiggling her finger free. "You've promised me a cuddle."

ERIC RATTLED HIS fork up and down the bars of the grill, silver and black in the sun, and gleaming menacingly like a giant orthodontic brace. "Guess how big the cooking surface is?" he said, squinting at her.

"You tell me."

"Oh, come on, humor me!"

"Four feet?"

"Eight hundred and thirty-four square inches! Official capacity is twenty-four burgers and/or chicken breasts, but I reckon I can get more on than that. How many burgers do you think the average adult eats at a barbecue?"

Mary glanced up at the open doors of the dining room, where she and Flora had stood last weekend. She looked toward the back fence, where her fox had started his run, and imagined him galloping through the gazebo, pulling down the manicured nonsense of the garden, bunting and fairy lights tangling in his wake. She mentally closed the doors on this image of him.

"One? Two?" Eric was saying.

"Er. Three?"

"Really? They're quite big."

That would never happen, by the way, with the gazebo. He was incredibly civilized. Every tiny movement was governed by immense self-control. She looked again at the patio doors. If Mark arrived— if, if, she kept reminding herself—she would almost certainly see him before he saw her. But the house gaped blankly. She was able to glimpse inside only as far as the strange bulldog lamp on the sideboard. Just a dark shape, a shadow guard dog.

Eric lowered his voice. "Hey, while it's just us? I'm so glad you came." He gave her hand a sweaty squeeze. "I'm sorry about Mark. I hope that's not why your new man didn't come . . . ?"

"It's fine," she said.

"I was walking back from the station—"

"Eric. It's fine."

"I'd had such a long day at work. The truth is, as soon as I'm on the train, I'm already dreading putting my key in the lock. Every night someone's crying—"

"Oh really? I'm sorry to hear—"

"That was all going through my head. Who will it be tonight? I didn't even see him till I heard him say my name. He probably won't come. And if he does, you probably won't even know he's here. I don't even know if he's here."

He wasn't there.

Mary glanced again at the two doorways, saw Neville step into the garden.

"All right, mate," Eric said. "I was just showing Mary the new barbecue station."

Neville pressed his beer bottle against his cheek and caught her eye. "Impressive bit of kit, that. Tell me, Eric—did you find Tigger?"

"Nope. George is gutted. Tiggy's his best mate."

"He'll turn up. They do that, cats. Disappear for a few days, then wander back as if nothing's happened. The garden looks great, by the way. I like your little pavilion. What goes on in there, then?"

"Ha! You'd have to ask Michelle. The gazebo's her baby. Talking of which—where is Michelle?" he said, looking around.

Behind Mary the garden was filling with people. Tom was chatting to a pregnant woman, who was holding Flora. There was George, pushing a toy truck around the lawn. But no Michelle. Along the left side of the garden, Neville's fence made a narrow strip of shade, and Mary's eye followed the line between green grass and black down to the rear wall, where it bisected a new figure.

He was standing in front of Eric and Michelle's gate to the woods, almost exactly straddling the line so that his left side was in bright sunlight, his right disappearing in deep shade. From the way one foot stepped forward, it occurred to Mary that she was witnessing Mark's arrival. Had he come through the house, and she'd missed him? Or was it possible that instead of knocking at the front door like every other guest, he had slipped in through the back gate? No, Michelle would definitely keep that bolted.

Mary's stomach was a furnace. Heat rose to her throat. She sucked down champagne to quell it and heard Eric faintly from within the swill of extinguishing foam.

"I don't s'pose you've seen Michelle, have you, Mary?"

Panic gave the wine an aftertaste that was sharply mineral, a lick of a rusty blade.

"Mary? Are you OK there?"

"Er. No. Sorry. I ha-haven't seen her," she choked. She looked again at the back wall, meaning to overlay the outline of Mark in her head onto the real thing. But the shape in front of the gate had gone.

"Can't be far," Neville said.

Mary had to find a way out of this corner. She ran her eyes around the periphery of the garden, and a bird called helpfully from the top of Neville's copper beech, its strange song like the continual clinking of marbles in a bag. There was Mark, in the thick of the party now, next to a woman in a floral skirt. Impossible to tell what they were saying. Only, from the tilt of their heads, that they were saying something. Red hair hung in waves down the woman's back: one of those people you need see only from behind to know they are pretty.

"Hey, Rachel!" Eric called to the pregnant woman. "Have you seen Michelle?"

"Nope. Me and Tom have found a giant fox hole though."

The mention of her fox tugged at a muscle in Mary's cheek, and she tried to restrain the twitch. Her underarms moistened with the thrill of guarding an intimacy that no one else knew, and her heart gave a silent applause to his bravery, his refusal to be intimidated by Michelle.

"Oh, Christ! Another one?" Eric raked his hair, and the sweatiness of his roots made it stand on end, in a look of continual shock.

To Mary's surprise, the pregnant woman, Rachel, was pointing with her free hand to Mary's own fence.

"Ah, I know about that one," Eric said with relief. He took Flora from Rachel. "That's Michelle's. Or it was Michelle's. When she went back to plant her rose, something had dug where she was digging. She won't touch it now. Says it's the foxes' hole!" Eric rolled his eyes. "I've filled it in twice, but it keeps getting unfilled. I'm going to have to stuff some bricks down there."

Mary smiled at Rachel. "Will you show me?"

* * *

"Here. It's pretty weird. It's, like, a hole within a hole," Rachel said. "Is that even possible? I think I've just invented a new philosophical problem." The main excavation was about a foot deep, but out of its side a second opening had been burrowed, which sloped toward Mary's fence.

"What are you doing?"

"Just having a look," Mary replied. The grass was warm under her knees, and her body threw the hole into shade.

"Don't put your hand in!" Rachel cried, but her voice already sounded distant to Mary, who was reaching down to where the air in the hole cooled. She patted the base, sides, up to the point where he had begun to scrape out his tunnel. Then she leant in, caterpillaring her fingers slowly along the track. It was quite narrow: he was still digging it out. Eric and Michelle's garden must be a sort of anteroom to her own. "Probably best leave it, yeah?" she heard Rachel say, but she shuffled her knees forward on the lawn as her elbow entered the coolness. She was feeling her way into his fortress, crossing the underground boundary with her own garden. This was the last thing she had expected to find. She had come to Eric and Michelle's primed to be a good guest at a rather boring barbecue, but now she realized there was a second, hidden occasion, tucked inside the advertised one. They were all her fox's guests. And she was the only one who knew it. She was practically a cohost!

"Are you OK? How far does it go?" Rachel called. She looked worlds away, her face a small dark circle, sunshine frizzing the blond tips of her afro.

"All OK," Mary said. She shifted her arm cautiously forward, as if her hand might be inching toward sharp teeth. Beautiful, earthy air prickled her nostrils. Then her knuckles knocked on a mud blockade. The tunnel stopped short. It was only a pathway between these two gardens, or it would be when it was finished, but just by kneeling here, her forearm wrapped in earth, she felt she was finding him. It was a hole made out of another hole, nothing dug out of nothing, but inside this cramped, damp, crumbly sleeve she felt her two worlds converge. A powerful sensation of ownership or belonging—it was hard to separate the two—puffed out her ribs. He was here at her neighbors' party. He was here, in Mary's heart, in the mud beneath her fingernails, and with the tight earth gripping her hand almost to congratulate her on the discovery, she thrilled with a sense of comfort and opportunity. The sensation was tremendously fortifying. Energy bolted up her arm. Her right ear dipped into the hole, as if her head were searching for a shoulder to lean on. All she could think was dear fox, fox, fox. Her mind dug up a memory.

Rome, four and a half years ago. Her thirtieth. Mark's idea. Mark? What was her head doing, finding him in the hole? He'd booked the flights, the hotel, packed her case, chosen all her clothes. Waited till the airport to tell her the plan. She pulled her ear from the opening, sat back on her heels, and brushed at the mud on her arm, trying to stop the memory. "Just one last thing I want you to see," he'd said on the Sunday afternoon. She shook her head, trying to shake Mark out of it, but she was following him down cobbled lanes and across a main road to a church, Santa Maria in Something, his hand pulling her forward to a large stone face, a sort of drain cover with a grimace. One of its giant eyes had cracked into a tear-shaped fissure. "The Mouth of Truth," he had said. He'd stayed on his feet. That was good. She hated clichés. Especially with the queue watching. When he asked her, he took her fingers in his and slipped them into the stone mouth. "You'd better answer truthfully," he said. "Or it bites your hand off." Looking back, this struck her as threatening, but at the time it had felt exciting. They had been together two years. They were happy. There was no lie to tell. With her palm on the cold stone, she had said yes. She could still see his fingers laced over hers in a protective claw.

"No!" she exclaimed, snatching her hand into her lap.

"What is it?" Rachel asked in panic. "Did something bite you?"

Mary stood slowly and pushed a stray hair behind her ear with her wrist. "I just got spooked, that's all." She straightened her dress. Was that why Mark was here? Because he had worked out that he was competing for her headspace with another living being? He had a knack of understanding the things she kept unsaid. And here he was, breaking into her thoughts again.

"Of course you're spooked!" Rachel said, brushing at the mud on Mary's shoulder. "It could have been in there." Smoky fumes wafted upwind from the barbecue; the breeze rattled the leaves of the lime overhead. On the patio someone shrieked as a young guy broke out of the circle, walking on his hands, while his friend clapped together two beer bottles. "Er, so, Mary, isn't it?" Rachel said to her. "Erm, Mary, how d'you know Michelle, then?"

"I live next door," Mary said, gesturing at the fence, where the fox's digging had broken the bottom of the panel. "That's my garden."

"Ah, right! Now I get it!" Rachel looked relieved. "Course you're worried about the foxes! You should talk to Michelle. Get someone round to deal with them."

"I was looking for her," Mary said, "but she seems to have vanished." She raised her voice to make herself heard above the noise of a large group that had drifted across the lawn behind her. Something cotton brushed Mary's back between the straps of her sundress. "So how do you know them—Eric and Michelle?" she asked Rachel. She felt the garden grow smaller, its sides creep inward. Particles of the conversation behind her flew up. Distinct words or phrases that evaporated as soon as she heard them. She strained for Mark's voice.

"My boyfriend, Farooq—have you met him? Skinny, beard, checked shirt?" Rachel looked around. "Over there with Eric, on the guided tour of the barbecue. Those two used to be flatmates. Michelle and I met through the boys." The smoky smell was thickening, lugging its heavy, beefy juices up the garden. Raucous laughter. The person behind Mary was standing so close to her, she could feel the heat of his body on her spine, as solidly warm as if she were leaning against a radiator. She let one foot venture back to investigate.

"Michelle started going out with Eric about the same time I started seeing Farooq," Rachel said, resting her glass of water on the little shelf of her stomach. "After a month we'd both moved in. Double dates, the works."

Mary was considering this picture of the youthful Michelle when someone behind her sniggered quietly, and his quietness, so distinct from the group's boisterous laughter earlier, gave her the answer. A few hairs softly grazed her right calf, a grope of millimetric precision. She tensed her right calf to double-check on his whereabouts, and the tips of Mark's hairs fondled her once more. She was meant to find this hair's-breadth mauling enticing, was she? There was something gross about the way he wanted the gesture to pass for accidental when it so obviously wasn't. Their bodies joined by one hairy thread. He must have tracked her to this side of the lawn, on his own prowling loop of the garden. Well, he was going to find that this calf was a closed door.

There was only a small space in which to maneuver, but Mary edged toward Rachel and turned. Now she had Mark exactly where she wanted him. His back faced her, so she could see him and he could not see her. She was free to look as much as she liked, and the one-sidedness of their proximity—hers unseen but understood, for he knew she was there—seemed to confer its own kind of power. She was going to enjoy this.

Inside the espadrilles—yet another new pair of shoes—his ankles were bare. Mary's eyes fastened on their knobbly handles and climbed those wayward, naked calves. She had seen him standing like this at countless parties over the years, she thought, as she scooped over his buttocks. They had known each other inside and out with an intimacy embedded in the bones of daily life. She was thinking that she had no idea how much of him she still knew when her gaze bumped over his beefy shoulders and stalled sharply at his nape.

Mark had clipped his hair so short that the skin beneath gleamed through, and here Mary saw four red blotches orbiting a larger stain. He had never told her he had a birthmark! Had he cut his hair in order to reveal it? Or perhaps he didn't know he had one, kept under wraps all his life at the back of his head, and now unwittingly disclosed as a by-product of his post-breakup makeover. She took it as another proof of new Mark, Mark reborn, as if in shedding her he had uncovered previously unknown parts of himself. The stains looked uncannily like a handprint.

She turned to Rachel and coughed. "Slightly awkwardly, that's my ex."

Rachel's eyes widened, but before she could reply, Mary was reaching forward and prodding Mark firmly on the shoulder.

He swung around with the edges of a smile that instantly contracted because Tom began to call out. "Mary! You're overdue a top-up." He was swinging a bottle of champagne as he strode toward them. "And how about you, Rach?" Mark nodded to Mary, then turned back to his circle. "Come on, Rach! Special occasion," Tom said. "It clears your system faster than wine, you know. Nope? OK, more for you then, Mary." He held the bottle vertically to shake the last drops into her flute.

"You two coming for food?" Rachel asked.

Mary scanned the patio and the lawn, but in the time it had

taken Tom to fill her glass, Mark had vanished. "Er . . . I think I'll just check out the gazebo," she said.

A pigeon flew up from her lime, clattering a leafy branch like maracas.

"Do it," he cooed.

INSIDE, THE TENT was so cool and dark, Mary felt she had entered some kind of shady human burrow. Rows of upside-down glasses glimmered on a white cotton tablecloth. Unopened bottles chilled in a box, although the ice had long ago melted, and water rose around them. A soggy label floated free. There was no Mark. The gazebo was deserted. She turned to go.

"Help yourself."

Mary jumped. In the gloom she hadn't seen Michelle, sitting very still, barely ten feet away.

"Michelle! Are you OK?"

Michelle said nothing.

As Mary's eyes adjusted to the dimness, she could see that her neighbor's gleamed with tears, and her lashes had stamped kohl smudges onto her under-eye bags. "What's the matter?' she asked.

"You're the first person to come into the gazebo," Michelle said.

"Am I? That's not why you're crying though?" Mary crouched beside Michelle and ventured a rub of her arm. Michelle smelt of wine and looked as if she might bite. "The gazebo's beautiful. I love the fairy lights," Mary said, searching for the right thing to say because the right thing would get her out of here faster. "And all this will be so handy for future parties. Come on out!" She looked at the doorway, half expecting to see Mark part the drapes and exercise his strong instinct for rescues.

"There are no parties in the future."

Mary cursed herself for crouching, which made the exit seem further away.

"Anyway, I can't come out or everyone will see I've been crying," Michelle said. "Not that I want to come out."

"Let's dip this napkin in the bucket," Mary offered, pulling one from the tablecloth. "Give you a wipe, get you presentable."

"Can you put that back, please? Give it here. That's not how they're folded." Michelle reshaped the napkin, then regarded it forlornly. "Eric hasn't even noticed I've gone."

"Gone" seemed an exaggeration. Michelle was holed up in a tent at the end of her garden. It was the kind of running away that kids did. Comically, her blouse was printed all over with birds in flight, and Mary suppressed a smile at the idea that she had flown her nest. To a gazebo. The whole thing was ridiculous. "You're wrong," she said. "He's been looking for you. Why don't I fetch him? Discreetly. Or is there someone else I could get? Rachel maybe?' Her knees clicked as she stood. "Anybody you like."

"I see Mark's come," Michelle said.

"He has."

"With a new haircut."

"Yes. And that reminds me . . . Do you lock your gate to the woods?"

"Woods!" Michelle snorted. "It's a bloody wasteland, Mary."

Mary gave a heavy sigh. Barely a crack of light broke between the drapes. To all intents and purposes, she had disappeared into a sort of urban Bermuda Triangle, a strange parallel party comprising just her and Michelle, locked within soft walls. Someone stumbled against the gazebo then, rippling the canvas, and the whole thing briefly shook. A shout, then a laugh, and the voices receded.

"That'll be Dave, my idiot brother," Michelle said. "You know, when I had George, I left a shadow self behind me." Her eyes turned back to the floor. "I think of her every day, this other me I used to know. I see her standing at a window, looking out. Always at a window. Isn't that trite?" Michelle glanced up, and Mary shrugged. She was attracted to windows herself.

"All her life ahead of her, and God knows where she is now." Michelle was actually staring at the opaque plastic window in the canvas. "I left myself somewhere a long way back. I don't think I know who I am anymore. Even hearing myself say this, I think the saying isn't mine."

The chatter outside had receded, and in the silence Michelle's words seemed to fall on the floor before them, pieces of some shared breakage, unclear whose hand was on it last. Mary stared at the pattern of lime leaves swaying on the groundsheet. She was caught in a gazebo with a woman whom she knew by nothing more than a randomly generated proximity—the sort of terraced intimacy that makes you privy to someone flushing a toilet but reveals nothing of how they feel. And here she was, telling her things she should probably be telling her husband or her doctor. The truth was, she did know what Michelle meant. But she wasn't going to tell Michelle that. She said nothing.

"I love it in here," Michelle said, suddenly brightening. "When Eric takes this gazebo down, I'm going to get a shepherd's hut."

"I think it would be better to just come out," Mary said. "Eat, clean yourself up."

"Mark looks good with the new hair. You should get back together. Then you could leave Eric alone."

"What? Oh my God, you've got to be joking!" Eric! She hadn't sunk that low. "Eric!" she exclaimed, her voice taking over in fury. "No way. No way. No offense but it would actually be a compliment to you if I was interested in Eric. Which I'm not. For many reasons." Eric was a nice enough guy. Well-meaning. Harmless. She was annoyed to realize she was smiling. Picturing Eric's moon face, receding hair, the general air of sweatiness. What she felt for Eric tended to be governed by what she felt for Michelle, meaning that she veered between scorn and pity. "I mean Eric's a nice guy . . ." She did like him. But he was one of those people who had to be liked with a sort of physical disregard. Otherwise he became too gross. "Ugh!" she cried, her anger rising again as she belatedly registered Michelle's assumption that she was single. "And for your information, I'm seeing someone." She had already reached the drapes when Michelle called after her.

"Don't tell Eric I'm here. I want to see how long he takes to notice."

Mary pulled back a curtain and gave the supporting pole a sharp kick.

OUTSIDE, THE PARTY had moved toward the house, as if someone had tipped up the garden, and all the guests had slid to the patio. Sun glinted off the windows and blurred the humans clustered at the picnic table with a hazy rim. Soon her fox would be on the other side of this dark fence. Time was running out. She had to catch Mark, find out what he was after, then go home. Saturday night—and for once she wouldn't be alone.

Mary stalked across the lawn, following the scent of burgers. She dodged a bloke in a fedora who was running, but his friend, the one who had been walking on his hands earlier, thumped right into her, spilling the rest of her drink. "Watch it!" she barked, but they were too busy rolling on the grass to care. Rachel and Farooq bowed their heads over Flora as Mary passed. Ordinarily, such a display of disinterest would have felt belittling, but as she drew near to the patio, the air bled with the smell of meat, and she imagined Sunset—not Sunset, why was it so hard to find the right name?—smelling it too, and the thought bolstered her. It crossed her mind to fold a burger into a napkin when she left. That would be OK if she fed him. Which she didn't. "Mary! Here we go, this one's got your name on it!"

Eric called. "Pure grass-fed beef." A drop of sweat rolled off the end of his nose and sizzled on the grill. "Where are you going to take it?"

"Thanks. Have you seen Mark?"

Eric looked around, frowning in the direction of the picnic bench. "He was there five minutes ago, sitting with Neville . . . Look, take this, will you? You're my last customer. Unless Michelle shows up. I think she might have left me."

Mary made for the picnic table, but halfway there she turned and called out to Eric, "Try the gazebo."

IN SILENCE, NEVILLE filled Mary's flute. Tom, on the opposite bench, appeared to have abandoned his glass-watch. He was leaning into a blond woman, his arm sloping under the table. "Another fox hole!" someone shouted from the end of the garden. Another gateway to his brilliant, subterranean citadel, she thought. It tickled her that he was so big on home improvement, constantly adding new rooms to his floor plan. Mary looked over to see what Eric made of this information, but the barbecue had been abandoned. "Have you seen Mark?" she asked.

Neville was running his finger flat along her arm; the pain was like someone pressing on a bruise. "This looks nasty," he said, ignoring her question.

"Oh. That. I know." The gnat bite had stopped itching and started throbbing, as if an invader's heart beat under her skin. She bit into the burger, but she didn't feel like eating. Blood seeped into her mouth. All she could smell was beef. The insides of her nostrils were made of beef. Perhaps in some corner of the woods her fox was drawing his muzzle over his scent map, plotting her coordinates. Burger meets Boss. She was wearing Mark's cologne again.

"I think I need a glass of water." Mary gripped the table as she stood.

"I'll come with you," Neville said, pulling her out of the way of the guy in the hat. "Careful!" he shouted, and then to her: "Someone needs to tell those kids to stop drinking."

On their way to the kitchen, they stepped over a few alliums that lay felled across the path. Their heads had cracked, spilling mauve petals onto the concrete, and mud was scattered over the pavers.

"More fox," Neville groaned.

"You don't know that," she shot back. "It could be anything."

He lifted the reedy stems of the alliums with the toe of his moccasin, flashing his chestnut instep. "This looks like something wants to dig under the house. It's right by the air brick," he said. "This place is riddled with holes. Foxes are anarchists, you know."

"Really? They've never given me that impression."

Neville looked amused. "Are you fond of foxes, Mary?"

She shrugged. "I've got no strong feelings either way."

"Hmm. Cagey," he said, laughing. "Very bad for the electrics. My friend had them under his house. Some nights impossible to hear the telly. Squawking and thumping and clouds of dust puffing up between the floorboards. The foxes owned the freehold. Once they're in, you can't get them out. They can demolish a whole house from beneath you. We'll tell Eric about this one. After we've got your water."

Last night, her fox . . . She kept calling him that, but sometimes she wondered if he was her fox or if she was his human. Anyway, he had left through the back door abruptly, as if he had been called away. One moment he was in the kitchen, the next his ears flicked, and he was gone. He certainly didn't want to take over the house. Far from it. She wished he would stay longer, but he always had somewhere else to go, and she was trying to learn to accept the fact that he didn't do goodbyes.

"What happened to your friend's house? Did they leave?" she asked Neville.

Crows shook up out of the sycamores toward the western end of the woods, calamitous cawing, wings like black arrows jagging at the brambles below them. The same noise they made when they spotted him.

He was waking up.

He stretched forward his paws and curled his claws into the dust. He read the wind. He yawned a tall yawn. Cursed the crows for telling where he was. His stretch shook his shoulders and his back and wavered out his body at the tip of his tail. His hind paws walked to meet his forepaws; then he arched his back. The lid of a human food den slammed shut. His mouth wetted. The mastiff yelped, and the air convulsed with the tremors of meat on the wind.

". . . destroyed. Caught, then destroyed," Neville was saying. "The house had to be rewired. You grab your water. I'll tell Eric about this one. Listen to that bloody mastiff! Those people don't deserve a dog."

MARY GOT HER water and got rid of Neville. For the first time since she had arrived, she stood in the garden alone. Mark was not at the table. He was not on the blanket, not among the groups dotted on the lawn. If he had left without saying hello or goodbye, if their encounter had amounted to nothing more than the brush of his leg hair on her calf, then what had she to show for turning up? Just a grease stain on her dress and a hangover before prime time. Every stage of the barbecue had been dictated by her bifold desire to evade Mark and to confront him. Now he was gone, she felt as if the whole sticky hot afternoon had been dripping and dripping until it had melted down to nothing.

"Aha! You look like you want a baby!" The redhead in the floral skirt was smiling at her, less pretty from the front. "Only kidding!" she said. "I need the loo." She held out Flora. "Will you take her? I'll swap her for a drink when I'm back."

Mary settled the baby on the perch of her left arm. Her other hand went to Flora's back, her ear inclined to the child's head. Their bodies adopted the position easily, as if each had stored a memory of it. Mary breathed in, a warm, milky smell. "Do I look like I want a baby?" she asked, and Flora exhaled heavily in reply. It was such an adult sigh, a misplaced breath from her own body.

She walked into the shade of Neville's fence—the strip had crept a third of the way across the lawn—humming and swaying her hips. She was singing into Flora's fine, dark hair, lips moving in the dampness of her scalp. Farooq and Rachel were on the blanket. The redhead was spinning under the arm of the guy in the hat and, just a few feet away, his friend in a waistcoat was taking a piss in Michelle's shrubbery. A glass smashed, and then another. Someone cheered. Mary wondered which one was Michelle's brother. The redhead was kissing the guy in the fedora, his hands complacently cupping her buttocks. Tom had rejoined the blond woman, and a child was climbing onto his lap. Her fellow guests were transforming before her eyes into building blocks of family life, clicking into place as the day drew on. Had these couples been together when they arrived, and she had failed to see them as such?

"Just you and me," she said into the soft spot on Flora's crown. It pulsed against her lip. "And it's lovely to see you again too," she said. Then she whispered, "I'm seeing our friend Mr. Fox later." A sudden cawing broke out of the trees a few houses down, and the sky became a raucous din of wing flap and yakking. Something had rattled the parliament of crows.

Mary kept humming. Flora wasn't exactly company, but she did provide an occupation, something to hide rejection behind. A baby: a passport to socially acceptable solitude. Under the cherry tree with Flora, cuddling her, it did not hurt to have been deserted. She was standing in the place of loneliness, where loneliness should have been, but with something else instead. Intense heat glowed down her left side, hot as skin on skin, as if Flora's body had dissolved the memory of clothes and was burnt onto her own.

Mary stared dreamily toward the end of the garden, where the gazebo drapes were shut. A breath touched her neck, near the ear where Flora nestled.

"You're a natural."

Mark blew the words at her, and she felt them tweak the wispy hairs that had come free of her ponytail. "She looks so peaceful asleep," he said. "I had a go earlier but couldn't get her off."

Mary turned. "I was looking for you."

"Were you?" Mark sounded pleased. He laid a hand on Flora's head and with the other lifted a magnum. "Do you want a drink? I found Eric's secret supply."

The sun was still so high it was impossible to tell whether it was 4 p.m. or 7 p.m. Mary glanced at Mark's wrist, but his watch was turned inward to his body, as though his time were a private matter. "I think I've had enough," she said.

Mark breathed in deeply. "There is no way to put this without weirding you out, but you smell really familiar," he said. "Sort of sandalwoody."

The hairs on Mary's neck stood and leant toward him, hundreds of fine probes inclined toward detection. Mark's body had no discernible smell. No sweat, soap, alcohol. Even his follicles were a covert operation. He had shaved so thoroughly, it was impossible to see where a beard would grow, though he had worn one last winter. He was twirling the rings of his house keys around a finger. A blackbird cranked out an alarm, like one long squeak sliced into lots of smaller squeaks. Mary pictured her fox on his way to her. It was nearly time to go home to him.

"I was looking for you," she said, "because I wanted to know why you were here, where you've come from . . ."

Mark laughed. "I think it's safe to say I had a longer journey than you."

"I get that," she said irritably. "It's not a game, Mark. I want to know."

"I came via the off-license, and it was probably a mile." He sighed. "Look, Mary, if you want to know where my flat is, I can take you there now, or after this. I'd like you to see it. And I really want to talk to you. And not at our neighbors' party."

"*My* neighbors' party," she said. "That's my house next door. And it's my street. Unless you've secretly moved in."

"Of course I haven't."

"Well, I'm busy this evening. So why don't you get on with it and tell me where you're living?"

"What, you want the information without any conversation? That's kind of harsh," he said, reaching again for the fringe that was no longer there. "Please. Just text me when you're free, anytime, and I'll come and pick you up. What about tomorrow?"

"I don't know what I'm doing tomorrow."

"Oh, cheers. I bet you do. You're out tonight, you said. And by the way, I know you're seeing someone. Michelle told me."

Mary chewed the inside of her lip.

"You could have told me," Mark said into her silence. "Do I know him?"

She sighed. "Look, maybe Monday. But don't call for me. You'd better tell me where to come," she said. "And try not to be evasive."

"Me, evasive! You won't say who you're seeing. And you could come and look at my flat, but no, you're 'busy this evening,'" he said in a voice she understood to be an impression of her own. "Are you sure you're not the evasive one? Now you've made it really difficult for me to ask you anything. I was trying to ask . . . Are you wearing my aftershave? I could have sworn I packed it, but I never found it in any of the boxes."

She hated that word. It was cologne. The two things were different. "Certainly not," she said. "Ah. So Eric has found Michelle!"

Mark gave a low whistle. "Doesn't look good." He bent to pick up his keys, and Mary was surprised to glimpse the little orange ribbon she had once tied around his house set. Sentimentality was not something she expected from him. "She wanted the perfect barbecue," Eric said. "Wanted to show people she could still do it. I mean, look at this place."

"Still do what?" Mary said. It was like the old days: side by side, heads leaning in so no one would overhear, finding in someone else's misery a wisp of intimacy.

"Hold a party, I guess. Have a life. Eric's worried. I got the impression she's in a bad way."

"I saw her earlier. She told me not to have children." Mary kissed Flora's head. "Sorry, darling. I didn't mean that." A wasp began looping figure-of-eights around Mary and Mark, joining them, dividing them.

Mark gave her a look. "I'm not going there. Anyway, you seem to be doing well. Didn't I say you would?"

She ignored him and, looking down at Flora, caught sight of the three-headed shadow that poked over the shade of Neville's fence. So this was how they would have looked. Grouped together like this, they could have been posing for a family photo. Their shadows were already a family. Woman holding baby, apparently doing a brilliant job. Baby blissfully sleeping, nowhere else she'd rather be. Man watching protectively. "You're a gorgeous girl," Mary said to Flora. For the first time, she felt what it would have felt like, the fruitful reorganization of life.

"Is she OK?" Mark asked.

Mary flapped at the wasp with the back of her hand. Of course, it wouldn't have been like that with Mark. There was too much in the two of them that she had grown to fear. "I think so," she said, "but what do I know? Maybe by letting her sleep I'm being the opposite of a good parent. At some point, she must be meant to eat."

He smiled.

"What's so funny?" she asked.

A squirrel clattered down the fence from the woods.

"Because you sound like you know what you're doing, I guess. And because I'm not sure you're going to be able to help with the food." His eyes dropped to the breast that was free, that was not Flora's pillow, rising and falling with her breath. Mary straightened her back, just as the wasp settled on her arm and began to walk, his head bent determinedly low. She was watching him climb the steep, tanned hill toward her shoulder when Mark flicked his fingers fast over her arm. She heard the sharp click of his nails on the wasp's articulated body; saw the poor fellow hurled into the air, and then dip, his body a dark dot charting a seemingly inescapable plummet until the point where—and she knew how hard it must have been to do this—he gathered his strength, switched direction, and soared up, beautifully, heroically, converting the force of Mark's swipe into his own power of flight.

"Sorry," he said, straightening.

He smelt biscuity now.

Biscuity like her fox.

But he was nothing like her fox. She sniffed again while Mark's hand guided Flora's fine hair around her little ear. As his knuckle passed close to her face, Mary caught a clear, potent waft of musk, malt, damp earth, as if some smell had got up and started walking around them, in and out of their legs. She was unsure if she was seeing Mark or if she had suddenly unlocked his aroma, the flavors spliced with close-up glimpses of him, oddly angled fragments of his face and body: the heel of his hand coming down on Flora's skull, the yellow bone-shine of his knuckles. It took her a moment to order all this information, to realize that she was watching Mark and breathing in someone else.

The last guest had arrived.

He was standing on her shed.

On his shed, in his garden. His muzzle prodded the sky for scent spirals of beef while his claws filed the shed roof, and he licked his lips. Loops of air were stringy with chicken / chicken smoking upwind.

Look—Who's—Here. Mary mouthed the shapes of the words into Flora's ear with each outward breath, too scared to sound them. He was statuesque up there. The shed commended him like a plinth. The sun, filtering through the outer branches of the lime, tipped his coat gold, gilt fibers on end, as if some unseen hand had stroked him backward. His snout was raised: flicking through his Rolodex of known scents. Was Mark in there, logged from some previous encounter on overlapping territories?

Of all the humans, Eric and Michelle were standing closest to him, but they were still arguing outside the gazebo. Their proximity to her fox reminded Mary that Eric had insisted she invite her new friend, and it was tempting to picture herself walking right up to them and making introductions. She suppressed a giggle. But she didn't feel like laughing. She felt ashamed. The barbecue was gross: debris everywhere, drunken humans sprawled on blankets soppy with spilt beer. Uneaten hunks of burger pooling blood on the plates that littered the garden. The annoying young folk had slumped over the picnic table, apparently asleep, the worst behaved of them melted down to just a fedora on a plate. Her fox, in contrast, bolt upright on the asphalt roof, cultivated a posture of lofty detachment. But maybe he was not so much the final guest as the elusive host, evading the partygoers swirling around his land with the hospitality of Gatsby while he kept a low profile in some hidden quarter of his estate.

"Get out of here!" Michelle screamed, a ringing, throaty cry, like someone banging hard on a glass with a spoon. Mary watched heads turn, saw them all thinking: screaming at Eric?

"Hey! You! Yes, you, vermin up there! Get away from my garden!"

The fox sat down. "Move it!" she shouted.

Far from deterring him, the screaming appeared to interest him. He dipped his muzzle toward Michelle. He seemed to think that by paying full attention to her hysteria, he might understand it, and a desire to placate or help her motivated him. His ears strived upward, keen to please. He lifted a front paw—whether to ease some stiffness in his joints or out of embarrassment at Michelle's display, Mary could not tell. It was not a salutation.

"This is our home! It doesn't belong to you!" Michelle heaved through her shrieks.

Mary watched her fox stand. He declined to advance or withdraw, but only raised his tail so that the tip pierced a drop of sunlight and glowed, a flare to catch her eye.

Mary turned her palm on Flora's back in reply. He opened and shut his jaws, emitted one loud bark. The sound was a sharp "Wo," like a question that could have been where, why, or when. Why are you here? maybe, or When will you be home? Mary realized it was the first time she had heard his voice. It was surprisingly deep. Eric had given up clapping and shooing, and wrapped his arms around Michelle instead; she shrank to fit inside his hold. Whether owing to the power of the spectacle or to the strange impasse of this particular hour of the day, the afternoon facing up to evening, no one else moved. Only George ran to his parents. Then the fedora lifted itself off the table.

Mary locked her eyes on the shed. She felt her own edges sharpen as her fox directed his muzzle to her, and his muscular shoulders heaved a query. "Here with this lot?"

"Jesus. The size of that monster!" Mark said beside her.

Simply by being in the same garden she felt implicated in Mark's leering and Michelle's grossly uncivilized behavior. But then her fox's eyes engaged Mary, black holes from here, as hers must be to him, and he waved his brush—it was as wide as his thigh—in splendid salute. She guessed it had occurred to him too that they were standing together, Mary and him and Flora, just as they had been two weeks earlier, at the patio door.

Mary turned a little, to show him the baby. Flora had opened her eyes but made no fuss, and her calmness seemed to Mary proof of a certain kind of progress. She would not repeat the mistakes of her own childhood. She had begun to teach the little one something no one else would, quite unlike the suspicion of nature that had pervaded her upbringing, the injunction never to go near animals in the park, always to wear shoes in the garden. His wildness was a gift. She wanted never to forget the immense favor he did them, the kindness of reminding them that no matter how lonely the city became, you could open a window or a door or even just an eye and find a mass of life that listened back.

He shifted his paws and looked down at the loose asphalt of the roof with proprietorial anxiety.

Flora began to fidget. "There, there, it's all right, darling," Mary said aloud. She meant to soothe the baby's whimper but immediately felt the cold draught as Mark left her side. "Wait!" she called. "Mark! Stop! She's not scared; she was just stretching!" Oh Christ, what had she done? In quick straight strides Mark crossed the line of shade— over the blanket, people leaning out of his way, the reproving clatter of a bottle toppling on a plate—and stalked to the end of the garden.

Mark looked at the fox, and the fox lifted his snout.

Him again?

This snail smell spreading where it should not be. Causing him to spray extra. He stooped to refresh his scent on the roof, everything in the wrong place, the world. Scrambled. Scents fighting on the wind. The whole run covered with humans. Big job to sort out. He was looking at the new swaying human den behind the male. They had put that on the grass where he liked to root for worms. The worms were his. So the grass on top of the worms was his. So the den on top of the grass was his.

A nerve in the male's eyelid twitched and flickered the way the mastiff pulsed before she jumped on her chain.

Mary began to panic, and maybe Flora sensed her agitation, because she pulled away, sucking at the apple-green cotton, soaking it in dribble. Even in this heat, perhaps because of this heat, Mary's skin felt ominously cold. She began to walk the forty feet toward Mark, tightening her hold to stem the baby's wriggling. If it was a question of making the peace, she could do it. She knew how to calm Mark. And she knew her fox meant no harm. How she wished he had waited for her at home instead of coming to meet her here. But even as she thought it, the scene in the corner of the garden struck her as the logical conclusion of the past few weeks, as if all those crossed paths, indistinct sightings, shadows overlaid on shadows, pledges, and misgivings, had led the three of them to this moment. One seemed poised for attack, the other alert in every golden fiber to defend her.

He was her friend. He alone knew that she was not so strange.

She caught that last thought for inspection, then let it go: it did not seem strange to think that of him. More than anyone else, he understood her, saw her best self, and found no fault.

Mary was still trying to square the bizarreness and the truth of this when Mark reached back. His forearm swiveled on the elbow joint. His upper body cantilevered backward, and Flora joggled up and down in Mary's arms, plates and glasses swerved, and the black fence bounced as Mary broke into a run, her cry dividing with each step. "No!"

With one brutish lurch, Mark threw the bottle.

Mary did not see it land. She did not know where it hit and broke. She saw the movements not as a sequence of events, but as a single overlap of images: one's funny little hop as the force of the throw threw him off balance, juddering into the gazebo; the other's bewildered jump. She heard a thick clunk of glass, then its disintegration into several discrete new noises. The scrape of claws on the roof. The lime rustling violently as the pigeon took flight. The warped wobble of the asphalt. A hiss and fizz of booze. There was a long hush, an eerie time delay, while all those fragments were in flight, in which Mary pictured the trajectory of Mark's previous missile. His mug whistling past her ear and smashing against the bedroom wall. Coffee streaming down the white paint, brown tracks dividing and multiplying. She had stopped running, and now in her ears there was only the muffled rustle of broken shards nestling into leafy overgrowth.

Stiffly, without turning, the fox's forepaws took the place of his hind paws. He performed the maneuver with immense dignity. His reversal was not a retreat—more like the courteous accommodation of his thuggish guests. After they left, he would return.

The asphalt buckled again beneath his pads. Really must fix that roof.

Mary flashed her pale palm to say she would be home soon.

"Sorry about that. It was pretty much empty anyway." Mark shrugged to all the gawping faces.

He was walking toward her, and Mary knew from his look, she just knew, that he had heard her shout and, unlike everyone else here, had understood that her panicked cry of "No" was aimed not at the so-called intruder on her shed but at him.

Behind Mark, with a flip, fold, thud, the gazebo collapsed.

CHAPTER EIGHT

It was the idiot in the fedora who started it, who observed Mark's violence, and in its quiet aftermath began to stir beneath his rim. A few humans turned to watch him climb onto the picnic bench, where, encouraged by the attention, he clamped both fists to his mouth and made a bugle sound. "Tallyho!" he shouted, jumping lightly from the bench to the tabletop, his trousers rolled for action. "Ladies and gentlemen, welcome to the first ever Hackney Hunt!" Mary looked around, expecting a responsible adult to intervene, but Michelle was sobbing on the grass next to the gazebo while Eric tugged lamely at corners of canvas, a cloth thrown over a catastrophe.

The guy in the hat cupped his hands to his mouth again. "Kill the fox!" he yelled. "Kill—the—fox! Kill—the—fox!" His shouts roused his friends, who began to beat their hands on the table while the slats flexed beneath the fedora's stamping feet. Louder and louder, faster and faster—an incitement to something, the next thing, whatever the next thing might be. "Hey, Dave, that's the wrong kind of hat!" someone shouted, and he touched his brim self-consciously. So this was Michelle's brother, Mary thought. The friend who had chased him earlier, the acrobat who had nearly floored her, ran to Eric and Michelle's side return and came back with the lid of the old kettle barbecue. He handed it up to Dave, who pounded it with his bottle. For the first time in an afternoon of impeccable behavior, Flora let out a piercing cry.

The picnic-bench crew whooped a welcome to their new recruit, and at the end of the garden, Michelle started to run. Certain that she had heard Flora and was coming to take her, Mary tensed her muscles to prepare for the loss. But Michelle sped past without a glance, and the dark house gulped her down.

"Who wants to be whipper-in?" the fedora yelled. The woman in the floral skirt stood up, jangling all the bangles she'd picked up while traveling.

"For God's sake, calm down!" Mary heard herself shout, but now a second guy climbed onto the table, the halves of his waistcoat flapping like saloon doors. A pack of crows flew up from the direction of the street. Was her fox safely out the front while the humans were all back here?

"You need dogs for a hunt!" the redhead shrieked, darting into the house. With one hand on his hat, the fedora sprang off the table. He half staggered, half danced to the corner of the garden where Eric was lamely huffing over poles and tarpaulin; rebuilding the gazebo evidently trumped both the job of reinstating order and of going after Michelle. Mark sauntered to Mary's side, just as the fedora jumped and snapped off an overhanging branch of her lime. She opened her mouth, but Mark got there first.

"What the fuck is he doing to our tree?"

"*My* tree!" Mary said. "And it was my garden the fox was in! It's no one's goddamn business if he's on my side of the fence."

"That fox has ruined the barbecue," Mark said.

"*You* have ruined the barbecue!" She glowered at Mark, his fingers jerking at his sides in quiet, involuntary spasms, as if his brawling adrenaline, having found no other exit, was running itself down in those dead ends. "Couldn't you just control yourself?"

He blinked at her in surprise. "God, there's no reaching you, is there? It was ripping chunks off your shed roof!" His eyes were examining her, bitterly blue. "Do you know what I heard when I threw the bottle? Your voice. Telling me no. I only did it for you. I was trying to help. Is that so hard to understand?"

"Hey! Mind those burgers!" Eric shouted, slinging gazebo poles to the grass and running to the barbecue, where the fedora was poking branches into the coals. "All right, Dave! Leave that, will you? Let's calm down, shall we? Think of your sister!" But Dave shook him off, whooping as the branch took light. He passed it to his friend and shoved in another. Down the garden they danced, lithely dodging Eric, waving their smoking sticks, while the guy in the waistcoat looked about for a better plan. The redhead emerged from the dining room with the ceramic bulldog lamp tucked under her arm. "I've found a dog!" she said. She had wound the electric cable around her hand like a lead, but Eric apprehended her and took the lamp with a firm, "Thank you, Sky."

On the blanket, Farooq helped Rachel to her feet.

"Don't go!" Eric said. "Michelle's made a trifle. Guys! Cool it! Bring that stuff back here!" he shouted as other guests began to gather their things. "There's children around!"

"We can't just stand here!" Mary said to Mark. "What will they do if they find him?" If she had one of those baby slings, she could march into the woods and confront them, but she was unsure her fox would approve of carrying young into that sort of danger. She studied Mark, wondering if there was any way he might be deployed. A faint sheen of sweat shimmered on the near side of his neck. Suspect seepage that betrayed a fault in the coils of his inner air-con. He looked at her and said, "So what I'm wondering is, what's it to you if they find it?"

"You can't hunt an animal like that," she said. "It's barbaric."

"So? You hate animals. You were always asking me to get rid of foxes." He checked over his shoulder for Eric. "And cats."

"That was different!" she said, reddening. She had forgotten entirely that there had been foxes in the garden before her fox. They had borne so little resemblance to him. How instructive, she thought, that now when she tried to picture them, she could call up only their generic mid-distance stare. The simple fact was, she had never got close to them, never wanted to. Why was that? "Maybe because I never had pets when I was a child," she said to Mark, "I grew up fearing them. So animals always looked wrong in the garden. Like they didn't belong." She thought about those last words. "Actually, the problem was, they looked like they thought they *did* belong."

"You want a pet, get a pet," Mark said, watching the guy in the waistcoat slip through the gate to the woods. He gave a deep sigh of exasperation. "They're not thinking it through. Do you know what my granddad always said was the hardest part of killing a fox on the farm?"

Mary didn't know and she didn't want to know. She curled her fingers around the baby's calf, a human stress ball, the perfect size for an adult hand, but Mark was already telling her. The hardest part of killing a fox was finding it. Mary squeezed so tightly she could picture her fingerprints on Flora's bone. "Look," she said at last. "That fox is doing no harm." She tried to think what the average, reasonable person might say. "It's nice in a city to encourage wildlife."

The trees started to chatter. The branches shook the leaves hard, the first Mary had heard of them in all these weeks of still heat wave. There was the tear of splitting wood, a shriek, a crash, a cheer. A magpie's rattle cut across the racket, and Mary traced the sound to her chimney, a sort of sentry post, where the bird's long tail stuck out straight against the sky like the barrel of a gun.

From side to side it turned, discharging clattering rounds. "I need your help," she said, looking up at the bird, and he flew off into the woods, strafing the idiots below.

Mark shook his head. "Fuckin' Neanderthal hipsters." He looked back at Mary. "What sort of help?"

She made to go—his life was in danger, they had a pact, she needed to get to the woods—but Mark pulled her back. "Think of the baby," he said. His hand stayed put, and at his touch her arm began to tingle. Mary willed her blood to leave it, so all Mark would be holding was the dead arm and none of her feelings, but instead, just thinking about it made the whole of herself hasten to the muscle that his hand clasped, her head, her thoughts, squeezed inside his grip. She met his cool eyes and saw their silent addition. "And think of your sanity." It was the moment when she knew she had him. The way he held her arm. She had him right there, if she could handle him. He was going to rescue her, from marauding foxes, from herself, from anything she needed rescuing from—if she let him. Well, she didn't need rescuing, but maybe he could rescue her fox. Mark would never agree to that. But he would want to save them, Mark and Mary, his idea of them, and he would protect the green lushness of the backlands, his leafy memory of their shared life. She had only to blow on the idea to make it rustle.

"Our woods!" she cried. "We must save our woods!"

Shrieks rang out from the other side of the garden wall. Judging by the manic clacking of hazel canes, she supposed the hunters had found his hole and were trying to shake him out.

"I'll go," Mark said.

HE WAS NOT in his den. He was creeping through the brambles with his back dipped long and low, weighing up risk with a vrim of whisker. Quick paws, felt feet; this way. Fern, fern, mud, mud. The path halved beneath his pads. Humans escaped pens. Rushing out. Like cubs seeing their first sky. The air a hive of new smells. Well, let them. Just up here was his den / other den. Two hazels bent together. Best resting place for quiet. He stopped. Even this den busy with human howls. He would go to his other / other den. Down the track to the park. Through the nettles. Nearly at the end of—

She had lost him. She was urging him forward, but then she lost all sense of him. That was her worst fear. She desperately hoped he would escape, but only so he could return to her. What she dreaded was not so much his dying, his death in itself, but a world in which she would never see him again.

"This is meant to be a party, for God's sake! Come here, Georgie!" Eric said, scooping up his son. "Michelle's gone to a lot of trouble." A guy in a patterned shirt hugged Eric and thanked him for a great day; he and Maeve had to make a move.

Eric looked relieved to spot Mary.

"Sorry about this," he said. "Dave is a selfish git. He knows Michelle's in a bad way. Or he would if he could bring himself to look past the brim of that fucking hat. He's ruined her party, and for what? That fox or one of its gang will be back tomorrow."

"Do you think so?" Mary tried not to sound hopeful.

"I know so. They're on to a good thing here. Footballs, pot plants, even Flora's beloved raggy they've taken." He stood George back on the grass and tousled his hair.

"Actually, Eric, I think it's time I handed you Flora," Mary said. "I should really head home."

Eric's face fell. "Don't go. Please? Just five more minutes so I can find Michelle."

THE BABY WAS beached on Mary's breast, with her mouth squashed open like a dry spout. She was exhausted and hungry, and Mary was pretty sure her nappy needed changing. There was still no sign of

Eric. She entered the kitchen and glanced down the hall in time to catch Farooq and Rachel slipping out, the world closing to a thin slice of light between the front door and the jamb. Lucky them to have escaped—the house, and the whole afternoon, behind them. A couple of bottles had rolled onto the floor, and she kicked them gently to the skirting. The kitchen glistened with a sickly fermented smell, sweet and dejected, of a spillage dried sticky. Mary had the sensation she was breathing in another person's outward breath in the last conversation of a long night. Between her temples a hangover had begun to move in. Where were Eric and Michelle?

In the hall, Mary whispered Eric's name. She appraised the stairs, but at the half-landing, darkness roped them off. When she had babysat she had been free to go where she pleased in the house, but she was aware that the parameters of acceptable trespass had narrowed. The doors to the dining room and lounge were also shut, so she bent an ear to the nearest keyhole. Were Eric and Michelle in there, or had the stags on the wall got the run of the place? From up on its perch, the ceramic owl looked down and saw—

No. The keyhole was blocked.

How claustrophobic this hall was. Mary was boxed in by wooden panels with knobs she must not turn, as if she had found herself at the center of one of those little wooden puzzles that Mark had bought. She put her nose into the soft folds of Flora's ear and nuzzled her. She twisted her head to look at Flora's face, and with a thrill saw the baby raise an eyebrow in sleep. Mary repeated her nuzzle, a little more vigorously, and the eyebrow lifted again. "Mmm. You're delicious," Mary said.

It was her voice, but not her voice. The words thrummed in her chin and with a tacky sound unstuck her lips. It was the first time she had spoken to Flora without embarrassment or pretense, in just the voice that had come to her, not singsong nor parentally derivative. "You really are good enough to eat," she said. Oops. She wiped the dribble off the child's neck, rubbed her lower lip up Flora's lobe. The cartilage in the curve of her ear was such a tender balance between supple and resistant that, as she did so, the ear rolled up like a tuile. She gave it a nip.

"Baby's ear." There is a shell called baby's ear. She shut her eyes to listen better. It's her mother's voice, come to her tangy with salt. Found on some shingle beach of her childhood. Such a solitary childhood. She holds out her hands, and her mother tips the shell into her palm, pale and smoothly breakable as thin porcelain. Her thumb idles across the porch, polishing the red frill, the pearly ridges of the entrance floor. The swirl darkens into some unseen inside shell cave where a drop of sleeping sea curls. She shakes the shell. She shakes the shell . . .

She remembered that she had shaken the shell, but the droplet clung on. She had heard its faint rattle, sniffed its briny prickle. But no matter how hard she shook, there had been no loosening it. No seeing it, whichever way she held the shell or turned her head. With a shell like that, you could never round the final bend into complete discovery. God, she'd been lonely. She'd always been lonely. Even as an adult. She'd spent whole days sitting by the canal, watching the gas holder rise, just to be near another thing that breathed. She shut her eyes again and pressed her own ear to Flora's ear. She longed to hear something, something coming back at her, mother to daughter, the wash of foam on a shore, the rebound of a wave, an answer from another place.

It swept against her ear and rolled back to Flora's. It poured from one to the other, and there it was, the soft hiss she had listened for, wished for, and which she recognized now as the crash of life itself, the steady, reassuring surge and hush of the baby's breath. The sound lifted her up, and she floated in on its tide.

Flora's dark hair was matted on her scalp, but she smelt soporific, of warm, sweet milk, and a floral fragrance, pretty as lily of

the valley, which her skin seemed to emit and was probably there-
fore the aroma of intestines bathed solely in milk. What an amazing
thing this ear was. Mary gave it another nip. Her lips hovered. She
wiped them up and down the baby's cheek, swallowing the excess
saliva, but more saliva kept coming. She had a relentless thirst for
the child, which made her wonder: Would her own mother, with
her dry pecks and brittle hugs, ever have salivated for her? Footsteps
entered the dining room from the garden, and Mary stiffened,
unhunching her shoulders only when the steps faded back the way
they had come. It was a very simple thing her mouth watered for.
She wanted a kiss. Was it OK to kiss someone else's baby if someone else wasn't there to see? Stuck here in the quiet hall, Mary felt
sneaky, though God knows she had no need, having cared for Flora
better than anyone else all afternoon, better than Michelle, better
than pregnant Rachel, better (by his own admission) than Mark.
Mary looked up, ran her eyes around the cornice. A few cobwebs.
No eye watching.

So was it best to kiss the baby somewhere obvious or somewhere
hidden? Behind a wall or a door, she heard a woman laugh, and spun
her head one way, then the other. She glanced up and down the cor-
ridor. Empty hall. Empty kitchen. Silent stairs. She nestled herself
against the dining-room door, the darkest spot in the hall, hun-
kering inside the frame like a vandal at the bus shelter. Hurry up,
woman, before someone comes. She was so nervous that when the
hand that held Flora's back began to pulse, it took her a few moments
to realize it was her own heart she could feel, hammering through
the child's body and pegging the infant to her palm. She pressed
her lips to Flora's lips.

Flora's eyes opened.

"Hello, darling," Mary said. She had not spoken for a while, and
her voice came out as a growl. All she had done was kiss the baby,
so why did the kiss feel stolen? She had kissed Flora as any motherly

person would kiss any child person. Kissed her out of love and kissed her out of craving, and the craving sated gave her courage. She swung open the lounge door with such force that it hit the sofa with a thud. "Thanks for a lovely party," she called to the ceramic owl. "We're leaving now."

She walked to the front door, her sandals clomping on the wooden floor. There would be nothing surreptitious about their departure. Every left step squeaked. She was a walking alarm—but that was good. Noise was collateral. Go ahead, floorboards, and creak your worst. She cleared her throat. "No?" she asked. "No one here?" Anyone would think Eric and Michelle didn't want their baby. "We'll get some air, darling," she said to Flora in the same husky rasp. It hit her only then, this brainwave, that the three of them could spend the evening together, and even though Mary had not shared this thought aloud, Flora smiled. Some strange cord of understanding bound them. The baby's top lip stretched out in a long, languid M like a seagull in flight. Her fox might be there now, waiting, Mary thought, and a picture of a peaceful family evening hovered before her. She would let him in, and Flora would lie on the sofa between them. She would return to him the funny rag doll, and he could give it to Flora. That would start them all off on a positive footing. As a dare to anyone listening, Mary rattled the letter box. Then she pulled back the latch and thumped the door shut behind her. She had no key. There was no turning back. A trail of saliva gleamed on the baby's cheek. They were free.

The street was in shade, and it occurred to Mary that instead of finding the exit, they had merely gone deeper into the backstage area. "What have Mummy and Daddy done here then?" she trilled to the baby. "Looks a bit excessive, no?" The lid of Eric and Michelle's household bin was garlanded with iron chains. "We'll go home, my darling," Mary said. "See if Mr. Fox is waiting." She lowered her voice. "That's not his real name, by the way. I only call him that when I'm with you." The truth was, she had thought of countless names and dismissed each one. Red, Sunset, Darcy . . . She could go on. But he really wasn't hers to name. In her head she called him "my fox," because that was what he was. "What do you think?" she said to Flora. "Will it do?" They were walking down the path. At first "Fox" had sounded lacking, but she was beginning to prize the accuracy of the shortcoming. The word, never enough, included her hankering for more. In any case, there was no rush. She would keep trying to think of something better.

At the bottom of the path, they turned left and ambled beside the hedge toward Mary's own house. She plucked a nice, cool privet leaf and tickled Flora's cheek. When a shout came from behind, she continued walking. They were so close to her path. Two steps from home. She could make it if she kept going. "Mary!" The word was a dart in her back, and she faltered. Footsteps approached, grew heavier, and when she turned, Eric was hurrying toward them. Staring at her from further down the road, clustered beside a parked car, were Michelle, Farooq, and Rachel. It was Eric who spoke, out of breath from his run.

"Mary, I'm so sorry! You've had her for ages! I was meant to relieve you, wasn't I? I got waylaid saying goodbye to Rachel and Farooq."

Michelle strode toward them, and Mary heard the car doors bang shut behind her.

"Where were you going?" Michelle asked. Someone had tidied her up, removed the black from under her eyes.

"Looking for you. Couldn't find you anywhere, could we, Flo?"

"We got caught chatting," Eric said apologetically. "I think it's done you good to see friends, hasn't it?" he said, smoothing his wife's hair.

Michelle stretched out her arms, but Flora had scrunched Mary's dress into her fists and screwed her fists to Mary's left shoulder. Since

Mary herself had no experience of passing back a baby, she did what Flora did and held on tight. Together they watched Michelle unpick the lock click by click of each tiny digit until the hands opened. The baby was gone.

"Thanks, Mary. You've been heroic," Eric said.

"No problem!" She pumped her arm to work the stiffness out. Adrenaline took over, and the arm kept pumping. She beamed at Michelle.

"I'm going to take her in for a feed." Michelle was already unbuttoning her blouse as she turned toward the house. Flora's little face watched Mary from over her mother's shoulder. She missed her. And then the face switched back to neutral again.

When they reached the front door, it opened without their needing to knock. Mary caught Michelle's brisk farewell to the person behind the door, and Mark stepped out.

"They're going completely mad back there."

"I can't deal with that," Eric said. "They'll have to work it out of their systems. Knowing Dave, they're fully coked up."

"Fair enough. I thought I'd have a go at fixing the gazebo," Mark said.

"No, mate. Leave it. I've seen enough of that bloody thing." Eric moved to go indoors, but Mark had something on his mind. He said, "There are four ways to get rid of a fox. One, you can trap it. But then you have to release it, and it will probably just come back. Two, you can put down poison. Illegal, but still possible. Though you'd have to keep the cats indoors . . ."

Eric shot Mary a look.

"Three, spray your garden with deterrent . . ."

"We've already tried that," Eric said. "Michelle even made me piss down all the holes."

". . . Four, shoot it. No problem there, provided you have the correct license."

Eric took in this information silently.

"I could probably help you with that one," Mark said.

Mary glared at him. "I thought you were meant to be keeping things calm." This was not part of what she had asked him to do. "I think you'd better leave this to those who live here, don't you?" She saw Mark raise an eyebrow at Eric. "This is really a discussion for people whose properties adjoin the woods," she said.

Eric stared at the floor, embarrassed. "Did you buy poison?" he said, finally lifting his eyes to Mary.

She felt her cheeks burn. "I tried. They took the money, but it never arrived."

After they said goodbye, Mary patted her sides, her pockets. She had the sense she was leaving with less than she should be. She began to walk the short distance to her own front gate, with Mark following. At the foot of her path, he looked up at the house next door, and his question seemed to come at her out of the corner of his eye. "Ever see anyone?"

The two houses were separated by a low wall. As usual, the curtains were drawn. She snorted. "No. But I'm pretty sure someone's living there at the moment. He's got a dog. What a stupid pet for a recluse. He can never be taken for a walk." Then she said, "You don't really have a gun, do you?"

He smiled. "Don't worry. Just stay inside tonight, what with the foxes and those loons over the back. Will you be OK?"

She nodded, and he reached to wipe a streak of Flora's dribble from her shoulder. He left his finger a moment on her bare skin. "I want you back," he said. She pocketed his words. Some only-child glitch in her reciprocation instinct forbade a reply.

On the other side of the door, Mary lingered at the peephole. Mark's head bulged on a stick body. It grew larger and larger. He was coming up her path. His head curved around the peephole, so close, his body seemed to melt into the door. She held her breath.

And then, just as if he had knocked and found no one home, he walked away. In the fish-eye, the street stretched out behind him. The houses on the other side of the road rose grand and distant, though they were really neither. Mary watched him wheel around the rim of that little circle world, until he passed Tangle Wood and slipped out of the ring.

CHAPTER NINE

"Only me," she whispered.

Speckles of dust rose. The air rippled with his peaty scent. Mary shut the shed door and waited for her eyes to adjust to the dark.

"I'm going to put on the light," she murmured, feeling for the torch. She crouched and swept the beam gently around the wooden walls, hoping to ignite the gleam of his eyes. She stayed there for a few minutes, the torch resting in her lap, lighting her thigh through her green cotton dress. The noise in the woods had dropped to a low burble, but there was still no sign of him. She wanted to tell him that it was safe to return, that this place was his place still, but how could she get a message to him, cooped up in here or in the house? Without budging, she strained in her crouch until at last a trickle ran hotly down her bottom and made a small pool on the floor. She didn't expect anyone else to understand this, but it felt comforting to squat there, her knees against her chest, enjoying the privacy of a message only he would find, and the warmth of it. A trickle was all she could manage. It would have to do. He would understand.

She stayed stooped for a while, and when she finally went indoors, her wet clothes had turned cold. But even the wet kept the thought of finding him close. She went on pulling the cotton away from her body, while she checked the places where she usually saw him. At the wrinkled pane in the lounge she watched the reflection of a passing cyclist disappear into its seam. The sky was aging before her into the beautiful deep blue that precedes true darkness. In the glass, three pairs of eyes, which were really the bulbs of her cheap chandelier, glinted back at her, and she began to cry. The six eyes fuzzed and multiplied. She had lost him, and the loss seemed to bear the ruins of all her other losses, emptiness dug out of emptiness. Flora gone, old Mark gone, then gone again in this new Mark who would not bloody go. Her mother always further away than she should be.

Mary smoothed the bodice of her dress, eyeing in the darkening window the place where Flora's fist had scrunched the fabric into starbursts. She could pin the silence of the house to a very specific place on her body. It was her front left side that felt empty. "Empty" was such a cliché. She knew that, but knowing it was just another dispossession, as if this kind of wanting stripped all intelligence to an urgent, trite desire. She had never thought of herself as a mother in waiting, nor even as what her own mother had once described as "mother material," implying that a good eye and a talent for craft would suffice. Her own parents had to take responsibility for this. And where were they? Dad in Spain, with his new family, which was ironic since he'd never much wanted his old one. Mum in Dorset, where Mary herself had never lived, their whole relationship boiled down to a perfunctory weekly call, recently reduced (owing to the presence of a new boyfriend) to a perfunctory weekly answering-machine message, deliberately left at a time when Mary would not be there.

What did it say about any mother, to have given birth to a daughter who did not want—had not wanted—to be a mother herself? Perhaps because her mother had always given the impression that after Mary she had wanted no more (possibly wanted less), as if once Mary had been born, a hole had closed behind her.

It was impossible to be empty, never having been full. But she had held Flora, and holding Flora, some sort of fourth dimension had opened up inside.

She had not wanted to let go.

UP THE STAIRS she went.

What an idiot she was to have gone to the barbecue. She had broken their fledgling routine, and in the early days, breaking a routine could break a relationship. Now neither of them knew where they stood. What am I doing? she thought as she entered the spare room, the best lookout in the house. All this time we've been together, I have talked and talked to him about me, but I know nothing about him. I never ask him how he is. I never ask him why he came because I worry that if I ask he will leave. That has always been my problem. She opened the window, let the smoky edge of the night, of the bonfire, and of him, she hoped, enter the room. The scent and the darkness wafted inside her. "Don't go," she said. There. She had let the words out. "Please don't go." She hung her arms over the sill, leant into the air as far as she could, opened her mouth, and sucked it all in. Pain and longing climbed in her lungs, and the noise they made was one she could never have made without him. A rising cry of song that stretched and wobbled as it escaped her mouth, her howl whole and precarious as a giant blown bubble, sealed with the end of her breath and sent into the night to see how far it could fly.

She waited, and then she heard his reply.

THREE YEARS OLD was pretty long in the tooth for a fox. Almost unheard of. To be clear, he was a fox in his prime, but a fox in his prime in these parts was as golden as a free-range chicken. They all died so young. He stretched his jaws a moment, ran his tongue over his lower canine. Prize tooth. If it ever came out, which it wouldn't, it would show three rings. One for every year. True story. Fox teeth. Grew like tree trunks.

He won this country two summers gone, after his first mate passed, and he smelt a vixen here that he liked. Musky and fruity. That was her scent. For all the blackberries she ate. Slipped through the trees, shaking with the rattle of the first falling leaves. He came in the dark, crossing the stinklines of many foxes, and he fought for her. He waved his tail for victory! The other male was older and smaller. He knew it when he landed on him. But he fought like a cat. They rolled and gekked and spat. Teeth hacked teeth. Made his lip curl. Just thinking of it. The little one's snout thrusting open his jaws. Whiskers in his eyes. Fur bristling gum. They spun and clawed in the brambles, thorns pulling at his tail, well, let them pull, blackberries bursting. The scent of her. He got to his feet. Reared up and lunged at the little guy. Clawed his shoulders with his paws, swagged him back. He was only one. But big for one. Biggest at home. Biggest now. He didn't need his teeth. Strength won it. He was the dog. The small fox wiped the ground with his stomach. Yapped. Yes sir, no sir, Beetling backward. He went to him. Stooped. Rubbed himself on the small fox. Made the whole place smell him. Then he stood on his hind legs, folded his forelegs across his great white chest, and danced in circles around his new mate. She thumped her tail on the dusty ground and perked him with her ears. He knew how to behave around Females. He scented her too. Neither of them noticed the little guy leave.

The place was all set up for living. Plenty of everything. Salty frogs and dusky rats streaked the air. Scrapes dug under fences. Gardens ripening with human food. Only thing he had to redo was the scent. The first year they had four cubs, all boys, in the earth under the hazel. When the sun sank and cooled and darkness stretched, one left, one left, one left, till they were all gone. Off to fight for their own homes. This year—This year—The pain. No fox, human, Beetle should know. He filled the days, filled the nights, hunting, foraging, lying, resting, sleeping, sunning, curling, uncurling, sitting, watching, digging, filling in, and patrolling; then he double-checked it.

There was only one fox.

She was right about that.

THE OUTSIDE AIR in the room gave Mary comfort. He had begun to come alive for her again. She shut the window to keep the sense of him inside. It must be late, close to ten maybe, because outside the shrubs were blackening, outlines blurring, shifting into their nebulous nighttime mass. In a window on the far side of the woods a light flicked on yellow, and she blinked at it quickly. Just some random person going about their ordinary Saturday night. Probably it went on every night, and she was not in this room to see it. A shadowy form appeared in the new window; then a blind rolled down quickly, leaving only a thin line of yellow. Mary squinted at it, and the light shot outward, its fine rays like whiskers. Everywhere she looked, there were reminders of him. And then the window snapped black. Mary was sure the houses on Ashland Road had always been invisible in summer. The beginning of a fear twitched between her ribs. She pulled down her blind.

There were still plenty of haunts to search.

THE NIGHT WAS so still that Mary, on her hands and knees, heard quite distinctly the metallic wobble of a pet bowl behind the Tangle Wood fence. That weirdo made his poor dog go outside to eat! She dropped her back and crawled through the long grass. Stones chewed her shins. Even when something sharp pierced her palm, her stomach muscles flattened her gasp. When she reached the wall, her hands felt their way up the bricks, and she stopped, as at the door of someone else's bedroom. Through a gap between the trees, Mary caught a flash of floral silk, saw a fedora hung on a branch. She heard a muffled giggle, fed under breath from one mouth to another. The redhead moaned. Well, let her moan. Mary dropped to the ground in the woods and licked her hurt hand; then she began to edge toward Eric and Michelle's. To her right, a fire flickered in a small clearing. Far from raging, it crackled calmly.

The gate was open. She didn't even need to push it.

Eric and Michelle's garden was quiet, the rear windows in darkness, just a pale glow seeped into the dining room from the front of the house.

Mary crept up the lawn, past the fox hole in the border, sniffing for his scent. When she reached the patio doors, she pressed her palms against the glass, as he had done this time a fortnight ago, and then her nose. There was nothing to see: just the dinginess of unlived space. The hideous bulldog lamp was back on the sideboard. Out of curiosity, she tried the door handle. Eric had locked up. She slipped back down the garden. She was a shadow passing through the woods, learning to make no noise, to leave no imprint. She slipped under the big hornbeam and was heading toward the far side, to see where the new light had come from, when another shadow reached out and grabbed her wrist. She screamed.

"Ssh! It's me."

"Christ! What are you doing out here?"

"What am I doing?" Mark whispered, incredulous. "You asked me to come out here. What are *you* doing? I said to stay inside."

"I didn't mean you should camp out all night. Just manage the mayhem for a bit. But you've done that." Mary was unsure how much Mark had seen of her movements, so she said, "Brilliantly. I came out because I smelt smoke." He was still gripping her wrist. Once, when they had gone for a walk and started arguing, he had held her like that the whole way.

"There's no smoke. It's all under control," he said. "I've dampened the fire. Just like you asked. Our woods are safe!"

"Did you see the fox?" she asked, trying to take back her hand.

He frowned. "No. And neither did they. I thought you were out tonight?"

"Change of plan."

"Get yourself indoors," he said, suddenly letting go. "I'm keeping an eye on things out here."

Her heart sank. She had asked for Mark's help because what choice had there been? But now she worried she had unleashed a pet vigilante in her own backyard. She thought about all the ways he had helped her over the years. When she had been overlooked for the promotion, he had rushed to meet her, even though he had been on a construction site on the other side of London. For months afterward, he kept her afloat: patiently, repeatedly, enumerated her strengths. Then at some point, she couldn't say when exactly, Mark's comfort had begun to seem constrictive. She felt belittled by her reliance on his valuation of her. He praised her skills, character, sharpness, humor, her work rate and her ideas, and in all of that she heard her own dependency, as if she'd got stuck in his safety net.

A small, clear sound cut through the night from a distance, then again. Two barks.

"Get inside," Mark said.

"How are you going to get back to the street?"

"Don't worry about me," he said. "Eric's left the gate open."

"You're going soon then?" she said, and he nodded. "I think it's fine to go now," she said. "Job done. Thank you."

"I'll see you Monday," he reminded her.

Two more barks came, the same intonation, the same interval.

From far away he heard her. From far away he spoke to her. Wo wo. Go home.

As Mary walked back home, she glanced up to see that Eric and Michelle's house was as she had left it, but to her other side, in Tangle Wood, one top window dimly glowed. Its curtains were closed so tightly that it was impossible to see where they met: they had the look of objects that had stilled themselves only because they knew they were being watched.

CHAPTER TEN

How many cries can an adult human make? Mary's mother believed that babies had only three. One for hunger, one for exhaustion, and one for pain. Even when Mary entered her teenage years, a time when she hoped life would admit more possibilities, any sign of sadness was diagnosed as tiredness. There was no suffering that an early night could not cure. Adulthood had taught Mary to scoff at the limits of her mother's understanding, but she still sometimes applied the old family prescription to random sorrow. She was harking back to all this because a continuous sobbing had drawn her to the lounge wall, making her wonder whether anyone had ever studied the cries of adults the way they had studied those of babies. If there were such a thing as a lexicon of tears, she would like to own it. And she would have a second copy delivered to her mother. Mary leant into the tremors. Oh, oh, here they came again, each sob a broken gasp, regularly spaced and oddly uniform, like a stuck machine. The hardest kind to stop. Where the sob itself is a hand laid over a wound, and there's nothing to do but keep going because you don't want to hear the thing you know you'd hear if you . . . She shut her eyes. It was actually quite comforting to stand there and listen. It must be George, because the sobs were too grown to be Flora, too quiet to be Michelle. Now she thought of it, she had never heard Eric cry. "Georgie, Georgie, Georgie . . ." Ah, there was Eric now, so it definitely wasn't him. His low chant kept time with the cries, and the cries, enjoying the company, kept going. Oh Jesus, now what? Mary lifted her ear from the wall in disgust. She'd recognize that wailing anywhere. Michelle! What had set *her* off again?

The screeching was too much for Mary. She was already in the hall, through the kitchen, out of the door. She halted in the middle of the lawn, which was where the ringing in her ears stopped.

How quiet it was. Some guy's saw drowsing through wood in a garden down the street. An airplane silently splitting scraps of cloud overhead. She exhaled noisily. Because where the bloody hell was he? The sun lit a white butterfly, and its wings strobed briefly in the laurel, then held their peace. In the Sunday stillness, her lawn and borders and everything out here pronounced his absence. She looked in at her shed and screwed up her nose. No news. Rather than leave empty-handed, she grabbed the glove-oath he'd brought her weeks ago. She would take it indoors because the sensible course was to follow police advice for loved ones of the missing and make sure she was home when he returned.

Mary walked slowly toward the house, trying to decide whether she hoped the noise from next door had stopped or whether it might be soothing to listen to someone else doing her crying for her, and she felt rather than saw the thing under her foot. Hard and stiff, like a tenderized muscle. She picked it up. The leather—it was a shoe—had been chewed to an indigestible putty, and the laces eviscerated from the eyelets. Her fox's glorious rank truffle hit her nose.

A shoe, a glove . . . In the kitchen, Mary set the two deliveries on the sill beside the funny rag doll. It was becoming a squeeze up there on her little shelf of treasures. She lifted the magic egg, which looked whole but was really empty. Even when you knew the truth, its lightness still surprised. She moved it next to the glove, the pledge that had started them off. She could count back all the weeks of summer by these . . . Something was missing. Before the glove, of course, were the boxers, which she had dumped in the bin out front. She tapped the shoe and began to straighten an idea. When you looked at the objects together, imagined the boxers on the sill too, what he was really bringing her were the pieces of a new life.

They had known each other only briefly, but standing before her collection, Mary understood that he had looked at her, quite possibly before she had ever seen him, and taken her in whole. He had seen what she wanted. Though she scarcely knew herself what to call it. A relationship seemed too obvious. But when she shut her eyes, here with one hand on the sill, and the light and the thought of him flooding through the window, tinging the dark refuge behind her eyelids russet, that is what it amounted to. Solidarity, partnership, comfort, company. Care that felt like love.

What an idiot she had been to dump the boxers, which in this light took on the appearance of crucial evidence. The boxers and the shoe belonged to a man, which begged the question, which man? Was it the same man or two different men? Had her fox found someone he thought she should meet? Christ, she hoped these things didn't belong to Eric. Or maybe they were intended more generally. He was telling her that she needed male company. That was rich! She had male company. Or she would have, when he finally turned up. She glanced at the back door: she had left it open, as a sign to her fox that she was home and to herself that she had hope.

Her first thought in reply to the loud rap on the front door was that it must be him. But there in the fish-eye was Michelle, looking right at Mary. Her eyes were rimmed pink again, but the tiger-print top she wore cast the pinkness in a fierce light. Mary drew back the latch.

"I need to talk to you," Michelle said, slipping off her shoes.

IN THE KITCHEN, Mary watched her neighbor lean out of the back door, inspecting the dingy side return, while she boiled the kettle. She had no idea what Michelle wanted, but she knew what Michelle was thinking. She was well aware of the state of the patio with its cracked concrete, pots of nettles, and old watering can, long since conceded through disuse to a frog.

"That's odd," Michelle said. "There's an egg on your patio."

It was a relief to Mary that her head was in the cupboard, looking for unchipped mugs. The fact was, and it was important to be clear about this, she never left food for him. That was not at all their relationship. She and Mark had once seen a documentary about people who put out peanut butter sandwiches and apple pies. The foxes loved those people. But not in the way he loved her. He came every day, and she left nothing for him except herself. The egg wasn't food. It was a word from their shared vocabulary. All morning it had sat there, and she was starting to lose faith in its message.

"How bizarre," she said. "What kind of an egg?"

Michelle's stare was boring holes in her back, but what else was there to say about an out-of-place egg? It kept its secrets.

"Don't you worry about leaving this open?" Michelle said, pulling the door shut.

"Worry?"

Michelle looked impatient.

"Oh, the fox? I never get any trouble from . . . them." Mary remembered the plural just in time. The truth was, she never saw foxes. She saw only him.

She carried the mugs through to the lounge and watched Michelle settle herself into her own corner of the sofa. Her neighbor looked enormous. She was tall enough to lean against the backrest with both feet on the floor, and still her knees cleared the cushions. Mary felt freshly conscious of her decorative shortcomings, of this room's insufficiency compared to Michelle's lounge, with its ornamental knickknacks, its thematic organization. Granny Joan's old chair gave a surprised creak as she sat. Visiting was something that people did who lived further apart or liked each other better.

"Is that pigeon?" Michelle said, staring at the bluish paint on the wall.

"I don't know what it's called." It was duck egg. She had no wish to make small talk. She wanted Michelle to tell her what the hell she was doing here.

Michelle lidded her eyes and said, "My family." Mary waited for what was to come next while Michelle wheezed and patted her chest. "My family has been the victim of a horrific attack."

"What? Are you OK?"

Michelle gave a great sob. "Eric went into the garden this morning, and found . . . Eric found . . . Oh God . . ." She buried her face in her hands, and Mary strained to make out her words.

"Did you say a leg?" she asked.

"Tiggy's leg!" Michelle sobbed again. "I was going to bring it. To show you what killers the foxes are. But Eric wouldn't let me. He's buried it!" she cried. "It breaks my heart to think of poor Tiggy's last moments, of the fear he would have felt. Georgie's bawled all morning. How do you explain a chewed-up cat to a three-year-old?"

"Ugh!" Mary said. "How horrible. Poor George. Poor you. But are you sure it's Tiggy?"

Michelle shut her eyes again. "There was a patch of fur near the ankle."

"Well, a patch of fur isn't much to go on," Mary said, trying to sound bright. "And if it is Tiggy's leg, he could still be alive. You sometimes see cats with three legs."

"Don't be ridiculous. The animal that did this to Tiggy would not have stopped at one leg. Look. I'm not here to discuss the proof. The proof is buried in our garden. I've come to tell you we are sorting this out. Are you with us, Mary? That's the question. Are you with us?"

"Of course I am!" she said. "How do you mean?"

"We're going to get rid of the foxes. We are going to do this, Mary. I'd like to count on your support."

"Do we really have a fox problem? I only ever see the odd one."

Michelle laughed bitterly. "Don't be an idiot, Mary. That's what they want you to believe. You think you're seeing one, but really there's dozens. Like mice. One scuttles across your kitchen floor, you think you've got a little mouse coming to visit. It's quite sweet. In a funny way, flattering that it's chosen you? But it's not really a little mouse, Mary; it's a whole fucking family of mice. Under your nose all the great-aunts and cousins have moved in, and you're living in a mousetropolis!" She slumped back on the sofa. "You just can't tell them apart."

That was not true. Mary could shut her eyes anytime she liked and see her fox. The white rib marking the black of his front-left shin, his distinguished bearing, the small tuft of hairs beneath his chin, the exact weight of his tail, the notch in its fur. It was not an exaggeration to say, "his character." His face was his face alone.

"I'd have thought any animal would be mad to come back here after yesterday," she said, scarcely managing to keep the sadness from her voice.

"Mary, there's a half-eaten leg in our garden! It will take more than a few drunks to scare them off," Michelle insisted. "Anyway, I heard them howling last night. They don't see walls and fences, except as things to climb over or dig under. Perhaps you haven't noticed that the bottom of the new fence is already broken from where they've clawed under it, dragging God knows what carcasses between our garden and yours? They're even trying to dig under our house. Neville spotted it. They have no respect for our space or property. If I bang on the window, they carry on lying there. They have no fear. I can't put nappies in the bin. I can't leave the kids in the garden. I can't even open windows. I am penned in, in my own house."

"I'm so sorry for your loss," Mary said. "Poor Tiggy," she added. "And poor you, and poor children." She thought that covered it, but Michelle bowed her forehead and latticed her fingers tightly over her hairline. Like chicken wire to the brain.

Michelle looked up suddenly, and her eyes went straight to Mary's. "It's highly likely that someone round here is feeding them. That's what Neville says. Otherwise—what is it they want?"

It was a question Mary had asked herself many times. Sometimes she pictured him as she had first seen him, lying out there peacefully, warm on the warm grass, the point in the compass while the sun drew its arc around him. He had asked for nothing, taken nothing, except a small amount of space which the Land Registry said belonged to her. When she had rapped on the glass—she felt ashamed to think of it now—he had left immediately, without fuss. It was so hard to articulate, but really she believed that what he wanted was what she wanted. She had let him enter her head, with his printless steps and watchful respect, and she had come to feel his allegiance so totally that their desires overlapped.

"So what's the plan?" she asked.

"Eric's been making calls, but these fox experts are busy seven days a week. Our nightmare is playing out across the whole city. One guy told Eric ten thousand foxes live in London."

"Look, I've got the week off. I'll help. You've got enough on your plate with the children. Let me take the strain with this."

"Are you on holiday then?"

"Just home for a couple of weeks." To change the subject Mary said, "So where are the kids today?"

"Eric's taken George swimming to cheer him up. Flora's asleep."

"Indoors?"

"Yes, indoors. I can hardly leave her in the garden. She's sleeping, Mary. Sound asleep."

"What, on her own?"

Michelle laughed. "Of course she's on her own. Well, apart from Godfrey the bear. I'm not that irresponsible. She's in the cot. She can't go anywhere. The worst she can do is cry." She gave a heavy sigh, leant back into the sofa, and stretched out her toes. "Total bliss to walk out of the house alone."

"But what if she wakes?"

Michelle sipped at her tea and savored the question. "She might learn to appreciate me when I'm there."

"You know, if you ever need a break, you can leave her with me for a bit," Mary said, standing. "Give me your keys. I'm going to fetch her."

"FLORA! FLORA! IT'S OK, darling," she called from the hall. She took the stairs two at a time and arrived puffing over the cot, her heart thrashing in her chest, hands swooping over the side rail . . . then froze midair. Michelle was right. Flora was sound asleep, and her perfect peacefulness, instead of calming Mary, quickened her nerves. She was considering whether she still had a mandate to rescue the baby, when Flora's eyelids sensed her shadow and twitched in affirmation. One purple vein was raised on her left lid, as if a loose thread had been overlooked when she was made. Mary ran her finger along it. The baby was sleeping with both palms turned upward either side of her head, in an attitude of total surrender.

"Hello, my darling," Mary said. "How's my gorgeous girl? You are my gorgeous girl." When the words reached them, the fingers of the left hand fluttered singly, each pulling in a different direction, as if the hand had five heads that could not agree.

Mary thought of Michelle, alone in her house. Oh, Christ, what if her fox came back while Michelle was there? She bent over the broken rail of the cot and scooped up Flora. The baby opened her eyes and shut them again in perfunctory approval. She was with this nice mummier-than-mummy one again. At the bottom of the stairs, they paused. Today the doors to all the rooms were open. The place had been aired and scrubbed. Pine faintly scoured Mary's nostrils. The house and her neighbors held no mystery for her, she realized, now that she was completely alone with Flora. How liberating this unimpeded intimacy felt: it seemed to Mary that the tight wooden puzzle that yesterday had encased her had cracked open and lay in pieces.

She poked her head into the lounge on her way out. "Morning, Mr. Owl."

MICHELLE WAS IN the hall when they got home. "What's this doing here?" she said, waving the glove from the sill. "It's mine! It was in your kitchen. And by the way, it's ruined. And this," she said, picking up the doll. "I spent hours looking for this—Flora's raggy. Also ruined."

"Really? I found them in the garden."

"Found them?" Michelle narrowed her eyes. "Have you noticed how the foxes don't bring any of your things to us? Why's that, do you think?" She held the glove by the tip of a finger. "I mean, this is rubbish now. It stinks and the leather's torn. What were you doing with it? Why are these things in your kitchen?"

Mary shrugged. "I suppose I thought their owner would turn

up. You were right, by the way. She was fine," she said, smiling down at Flora.

Michelle rolled her eyes. "Obviously. People get so freaked out by sleeping babies. It's always fine. As long as you remember your keys and the oven's off."

This sounded unlike any parenting advice Mary had heard, and she began to justify her rush to Flora. "At least we'll know when she's awake. We won't be worrying." Michelle looked unworried. She did not reach for the baby but turned again to the kitchen. The bin lid flapped shut. "I've dumped them," she called. Mary heard her from the lounge. "And I'm making another tea. Do you want one?"

Mary did not. She wanted Michelle to go home and leave her in peace to enjoy this very nice cuddle with Flora and to retrieve her belongings from the rubbish.

"You need some new mugs!" Michelle sang out cheerfully.

"My good girl," Mary whispered. She ran a critical eye around the room. Flora was the first baby to visit, and Mary tried to envisage how this scrap she was holding would live in it. A little game sprang to mind. If she had a baby, where would the baby be *right now*? Asleep in the corner, in one of those baskets she had seen next door, while she, Mary, read or watched TV. Or the two of them could lie together on the rug and waggle their legs in the air to pass the time. She could fall asleep on the sofa with the baby sleeping warmly on her tummy. She tickled the underside of Flora's foot, searching for a souvenir. "Have you got a smile for me, Flora?" she asked, but the baby met her gaze with a serious look. "Smile for Mary," Mary smiled, watching Flora watch the edges of her mouth with a quizzical expression.

"She's not old enough. She can't do it yet," Michelle shouted from the kitchen.

Not for you, Mary thought. Who would? She was absentmindedly winding a few strands of Flora's soft dark hair around her finger, thinking, if a baby lived here, this is what I would do. It was so soothing, the silkiness, twirling, its slippery escape, twirling again. Flora still refused to smile so Mary gave a sharp tug. There was no cry, just a look of absolute surprise on the baby's face.

"Sorry, darling."

Mary rubbed the wispy hairs from her fingers and slipped them into her pocket.

Shortly after Michelle returned to the lounge, they heard Eric's car. The engine slowed and shut off. Then the sound of him jollying George out onto the pavement.

"He'll wonder where you are," Mary said.

Michelle sipped her tea slowly. "Let him wonder. Let him go inside and find me not there for once. Isn't it weird that we've lived next door all these years and never dropped in for tea or coffee?"

Mary rocked Flora, trying to seem too busy to answer, and Michelle said, "I suppose it's generational. Our mothers would have been in and out of each other's houses all the time. Probably had their own keys. We should do this more often."

Mary smiled indulgently. "I'm thinking," she said, "that we shouldn't do anything too rash about the foxes. Also, I would like to pay toward the cost and be, you know, organizer."

"Great! We always end up paying for everything," Michelle said. She gave a sharp double take, apparently noticing Flora for the first time, and her head continued to move from side to side while she stared at the baby, as if there were a thought inside that needed to be rocked to sleep or refused. "You're really good with her, you know," she said sadly. "You're really good with her."

They listened to Eric and George going inside, the door closing behind them. They must have removed their shoes because their footsteps petered out, and no further sounds traveled through the blue wall. In the silence, the two women sensed Eric's searching for them, a moment which Michelle evidently wished to prolong. But there was nothing more to say, and though Michelle kept sipping at it, her excursion was cooling in her cup.

Mary waited till the last minute to hand over Flora. From the front step, she watched them take the half-dozen strides to their own path. Then she called across, "Come and see me soon, Flora." That was another nice thing about babies. Once you knew the right tone, you could address only them.

IN THE GARDEN, Mary dragged the blanket to the shade and lay down, hoping to lose the empty space beside her in the comfort of his scent. Michelle's plans were troubling. And on top of that she had to manage the thickening sense that her relationship with her fox was precarious. It felt suddenly conditional—she had no idea on what. Now she was going to spend the rest of the day wondering if he would visit in the late afternoon, as he had daily for the past few weeks, or if his disappearance yesterday was the start of a new era, one that began just as abruptly as the last, in which he ceased to be part of her life. The day was crawling past in terror toward the hour, somewhere around 4 or 5 p.m., when she would have her answer. She tried to prepare herself for the worst, to persuade herself that today was tomorrow, that she was already surviving without him, that this was what it felt like to live without your cure.

She chucked aside her book; it always ended right, but sometimes, not today, the rightness felt more satisfying than others. To keep busy and to get a head start on Eric and Michelle, she searched on her phone for a fox rescue service. It seemed unlikely that Hackney would have such a thing. Sure enough there were dozens of wildlife charities but nothing specifically for foxes. She kept scrolling the results, and on the third page her thumb nudged the words *Fox Ambulance.* But the picture took ages to load, and in the end she had to swipe it away. In any case, a rescue might involve trapping him or taking him . . . She just couldn't think her way out of this mess. The rest of the afternoon hung in the air. Time slowed, just as it had done after Mark left. The trees waved gently from right to left, right to left, like a gif. All was quiet in the gardens either side. All was quiet. All was quiet. Until at last she was awoken by her own name.

"Did I wake you?" Eric was looking over the fence.

"No, I was just dozing."

"I woke you then?"

"What's up?"

"I thought you might have Michelle over there, but obviously not."

"Michelle? She came round this morning. She went home, didn't she? I mean, of course she went home. I saw her. She was on your doorstep."

He was leaning on the fence, and he flopped his head onto his arms and let out a loud groan. His crown had caught the sun.

"When did you last see her?" she asked.

He shook his head and said softly, "I don't know. I don't know. I don't know. I just don't know what the way out of this is."

Thank God for the fence, thank God for not being tall enough to need to reach over and hug Eric. He looked up and smiled. "Sorry, mate. You've probably seen enough of us this weekend."

"Has she got Flora?"

"Yes. And that's a good thing, you know, because it means she can feed her. Look, forget I mentioned it. I only asked because she said she was going to see you. But don't worry. I have become quite good at finding her." He gave a rueful smile and clapped both hands on the fence. "Oh yes, I'm getting to know all her places."

"Do you want a hand?"

"No, thanks. I'll start out there," he said, and Mary was surprised to see him nod toward the woods. "Georgie will help, won't you,

George?" he said, looking down between his arms. "He thinks it's hide-and-seek. You'd be surprised how many times we've found her there."

At dusk Mary resumed the previous day's post at the window, at the back door, all the usual checkpoints. The lights in the kitchen blew, the clock on the oven reset to 00:00, and she let it stay like that. Zero was the time she felt. His hour came and went. His next hour came and went. Again and again she gave him one last chance to appear, but he never took the chance. Damn the seam in the window for encouraging her with false hope. She returned to it over and over, putting her faith in its capacity to buckle experience, to let you see one thing while believing in the possibility of another. He was there; he was not there. In the end she gave up looking. Twilight came through the wrinkle, the garden fanning out into a kaleidoscope of darkness. Her phone beeped only once: Eric, telling her all was well in their world. Yeah, right. She turned in early.

Some things were best left for the night to fix.

CHAPTER ELEVEN

Way up in the sky, an owl hooted. Mary stopped. She had read that there were owls nesting in the warehouse by the canal, but this was the first time she had heard one. He had chosen the perfect mid-point of the night: too late for the rumble of traffic, too early for birdsong. She stood in the darkness with her arms lifted clear of the nettles, waiting to hear him again. The crisp, sharp air turned small sounds into big sounds. She rubbed her ear on her shoulder, trying to shake off the high-pitched whine of two winged things arguing in her hair. Something dripped nearby, though it hadn't rained for weeks. Tonight the woods gave her the creeps. And she was just another creep, creeping through them. She had no choice. If he was alive, she had to find him.

Her feet stabbed at the throng of stinging nettles, warping their hairy spines. It cheered her, the papery rustle their leaves made as they fell, dry tongues rasping last words on the woodland floor. Another one down! Another few inches closer to his den beneath the hazel. Too bad for those nettles. She had her own troubles. Her cheek blazed with their burns. And all the while, this hollowed-out feeling was growing within, as if someone were scooping out her heart until only thin, cold scrolls clung to the sides. He was gone. Gone. It donged over and over in her head, this thought, a gong that kept striking her loss—Gone!—that had rung out of the unquiet silence of the house and turfed her from bed, because what was the point in sleeping, just to wake to another day without him?

She had hoped he would come to meet her. But every step took her closer to the possibility that he was lost for good. Suppose Michelle's idiot brother or one of his friends had found him? She considered that unlikely, but there were other worries. He had seen her at the barbecue. What if he believed she was part of the hunt? He would surely sever all contact. She was so agitated by these thoughts that she continued to edge forward with her hands aloft even though she had plowed right through the nettle bed, and the weeds had shrunk to a kickable kerfuffle around her ankles. She dropped her arms. The sense of order and governance in this bit of the woods gave her the impression that she was approaching his den. She walked more briskly, and when she glanced up, his hazel flared darkly on the path before her. In relief she made a grab for the nearest rod but lost her footing when it flew down under her weight, then pinged back up, clacking away with the other sticks at its clever trick. The woods thrilled with the clattering of canes. She had rung his bell.

Mary took a step back from the place she supposed the hole to be—in effect, his front door—and waited. It was a new experience to be in the position of solicitous partner, and after a while she tired and sat. The air was warm. The sky was cloudless. The ground was soft with mulch. But even as she soothed herself with these comforts, she felt miserably out of place. Just being in his world should have brought consolation, but instead darkness rubbed its face in her face, solidified space so that all she could feel was obscurity. She was crumpling where she sat, her comfortable curl beginning to unravel as if she were being dismantled against the instructions. She pictured Flora—tucked inside her wadded envelope, tucked inside her cot—and envied her belonging.

Mary herself was barely a pinprick on the world. No one would notice if she were gone instead of sitting here with her face tipped to the sky. Not the stars or the airplanes twinkling overhead, not the hundreds of people inside those dots. That's where civilization was: up there, glowing with the borrowed light of street lamps and tower blocks. Down on the ground was desolate. It seemed to her that the purple haze of London's night sky had been lowered like a lid of light over the clearing to seal all the darkness in place and her inside. She was a tiny specimen in a giant jam jar, thoughtfully provided with a twig floor and cuttings of familiar habitat, awaiting examination through the convex lamp lens above. See how insect Mary burrows into the mulch for comfort. Someone bring her an insect friend.

She strained at the shadows, and everywhere she looked the night mask teased her. His ears pricked in the clumps of tall grass. His triangulated stare fixed her from the undergrowth. Each time his features sharpened into view, she let herself think that this time it must be him. But then his face receded again. There were dozens of them, these false foxes. They had her surrounded. Fantastical creatures with bramble legs and flickering fern tails and fidgety mice or haunchy toads for their wary footsteps. But he, her true fox, was nowhere to be seen.

In panic, she imagined him arriving, not recognizing her (or, worse, recognizing her) and leaving again. Maybe he would see her from afar and wonder what she was, a mysterious object disturbing the landscape. She was beginning to doubt she had the courage to last till morning, when she caught a faint, smoky tang from the direction of Eric and Michelle's.

THERE WAS A shape way downwind in the clearing that looked like none of the bushes he knew there. Stop.

Hitch a paw midair.

A new thing. Not a bush. Bushes grow slowly. A stump. Stumps come sudden. Like—This. It was pleasant, the fresh sawdust powdering his hind claw while. Focus. Eyes on the thing. He inhaled. Juicy, leaky blackbird feathered his snout.

His paw hung.

New is danger is wait.

The thing could be anything. Stuff flew into this land. Humans. Food and not food for sorting and scenting. A big fox. Just waiting outside the earth. To fight for it. His worst nightmare. This thing was still with the quivering stillness of the living.

He couldn't get a clear scent. When he lifted his nose, the wind, not really wind, was blowing the wrong way. All he could smell was. Blackbird, beautiful blackbird. He opened his jaws. The bird thudded to the dust. Dead, but. Take no chance. His paw clamped it. Claws parted feathers, silfling barbs. His mouth filled wet while he watched this thing too big for a cat, too unhappy alone to be a cat. He triffed his paw where the blackbird's heart tickled his footpad and pierced it. He put a new paw on the bird, licked the first paw. Replaced the first paw, licked the second paw . . .

He was doing this when the thing quavered, and he recognized the song of the human Female.

MARY HAD SPOKEN quietly. But the trees were listening, and all the half-awake things in the woods were listening, and in her ears her voice boomed. She scrambled to a stand, tugging down the ankles of her jogging bottoms against another assault on the nettles. Her ears buzzed with a distant drone. She strained in the direction of the scent, trying to glean some reliable outline from the darkness. "Are you there?" she called again. She felt herself to be in the eye of an intense, unlocatable gaze. Not a shadow flinched. She stared at the place where she thought she smelt him.

"It's me," she said again.

She pictured his ears pricked into two pointed portals, opening up their dark, Gothic chapels, snuffing out all the night sounds like wicks till the only flickering was her breath. She inhaled with a fluty whistle, which winged its way toward him. Soft and sad.

His ear wavered. But. New information. Another noise. Upwind. Leave the bird / check the fresh noise. Scrape out a quick hole, flick her with earth, give her a squirt. An ear peaked at. Cloud of noise. Rumbling upwind causing. Its own wind to disrupt the. Round and round sounds and smells sliced into scuttle and leaf blurt dust the world stirred into a swirl in this. Dark growl that swallowed—

A police helicopter.

How odd, Mary thought. It usually came on Saturday nights. The sound shook up Shepherds Bridge Walk and began to thicken overhead, churning the sky on the other side of this dense screen of leaves. It hovered above her as pure noise, its blades scissoring ominously at the stars, its barrel bulk hammering at the soles of Mary's feet. She put her hands to her ears. She could almost feel her teeth rattle. Three years since she saw the dentist. You would imagine they were looking for her, the way they hung there, staring.

Now Mary felt the opposite of safe. The helicopter shone a light on previously unsupposed dangers. It was scary out here. Pitch-black. Not a soul in sight, apart from, perhaps, the one they were searching for. She had no idea how many houses and flats backed onto the woods, who lived in them, or how many gates opened onto this land. She knew just three of her neighbors by name. Why had she thought it safe to come into the woods at night? And why, in her terror, was she grateful to the sycamores for hiding her with their hands from the whirring overhead? She felt all the fear of the pursued and all the guilt of the pursuing.

The noise was a long, jagged thunderclap. It whipped the air into a vortex that drilled cool blasts down to the fox's snout.

Hairs blew out from his ankles. He put his paw on the black-bird dirt mound to guard the bird. The dark was busy with voices. He strained through the sky alarm for another sound, the one that jabbed his ear close. Grating, scraping. Impossible to make out. Rumble fading. Rumble rolling away. And. There.

Clunk.

Human preparing to exit den.

The barbs of a feather bristled between his teeth, and he fuzzled them with his tongue. He regretted leaving the bird. But he had to. His feet trotted while he bent one ear back \ to the human Female on the move through the ferns / one ear forward to the new noise.

The air began to wobble as the helicopter circled again, chopping and dicing. The pilot and copilot looked down on east London, laid out with its venous strings of orange lights. Below them the woods were a small rectangle of pure blackness. And then they steered the helicopter west.

Mary took her hands off her ears. That bloody thing had drowned the sound of him. She waited until the rumble had completely faded, and then, in the new quietness, she heard a bolt shot. She imagined Michelle unfastening the multiple locks of her back door.

Mary set off again, striving toward the brambles as her fox dipped his paws in and out of undergrowth. Why didn't he wait? She groped her way along the boundary wall, hit the ironwork of a gate, its handle warm as a hand, grappled along a chain-link fence, round a hornbeam—and at last she saw him, barely fifteen feet ahead.

He looked different in the dark. His fur was tinged gray, as if she were seeing him through night-vision goggles. She walked toward him, and with each step she took, he acquired color. She was warming him through gray-brown to auburn. Mary hauled herself toward the next trunk, breaking the stem of a bindweed heart with a moist snap.

Like a frog bone.

He was coming to life before her eyes, less than ten feet ahead of her on the path. His feet stilled; his muzzle addressed her. She approached cautiously, waiting for the moment when she would cross the line, trip the invisible switch, and vanish him. Was it him? It had to be him. There was only him. Six feet and closing. Five feet, four feet. Her last step. Eye to eye. She sighed.

Her sigh, warmer than the warm air, blew on his muzzle and made it twitch. Hot and cold currents swirled his whiskers.

Mary liked the way his face wrinkled. It looked like snout for "hello."

"You're OK," she whispered, dried ferns crunching beneath her knees as she crouched. She had hoped he would copy her—that they would sit together awhile—but he stayed on his feet, forelegs locked decisively at the hinges. "Where have you been? I was worried about you! I tried to stop them . . ." She watched one ear pitch away from her, and her heart sank. She knew him well enough to understand when his attention was elsewhere. "Won't you sit?" she said. A twitch pulsed in his cheek. There was no point trying to persuade him. He was the great uncrackable code, and even trawling his eyes as close as this, she had no idea what he meant, except in relation to herself, and she knew that he was leaving. His eyes answered hers with interest rather than deference. He would share only so much. That's what he was saying. He was honest enough to tell her, and in his amber eyes she found kindness, something more alike than unalike. It was the same color she saw inside her own lids in sunshine.

Her hand snaked out toward him on the woodland floor. They both looked at it a moment, some foreign thing that had traveled between their worlds. Then he dropped his snout and licked it.

In hindsight, that was his farewell gesture. In an instant he faced the opposite direction. He seemed to have interchangeable front and back legs. His nose skimmed the ground, shoulders rounded in his posture of habitual industry, as if he had dropped something along here earlier and was intent on finding it.

Mary tagged him as far as she could, but he was too quick. Beneath her feet a dry crackle broke, and a wispy fragrance of ash rose, which made her think she must be where Mark had guarded the fire yesterday, and her fox was drawing her toward Eric and Michelle's. She tried to keep up, but at some perfect point where distance equaled darkness, he began to silver and fade for her, as if his fur were intercut with night's invisible stripes, and it was no longer possible to know for sure if she was seeing him or seeing the night behind him. He vanished in stages, reappeared, vanished. It was impossible not to wonder: he was alive, but was he still hers? Because the one meant nothing without the other. She watched him where she could. It was like watching through the wrinkled pane in the lounge, through glass warp and time warp, a moving picture that overlapped and jumped, that repeated and cut, and through which all things were possible.

CHAPTER TWELVE

There was a baby on the back step. A white bundle, downward sloping, spilling two arms and a head, the head looking at the edge of the step precariously. Not really looking. The eyes were shut. One hand lay beside an ear, fingers stiffened into a fist that might have held something or lost something. Such a beautiful hand: its sliver of palm was streaked with shimmers of purple and blue, veins rubbed with moonlight.

The surprise came not from seeing the baby, but from seeing what was around her. A baby on the back step. It was the step that was wrong. She was meant—Mary turned to check she was alone before she finished the thought. She was meant to take the child into the house.

All she needed to do was open the door and walk inside.

FROM THE WOODS, or further away, the owl hooted again. This was the first night Mary had heard him; now she had heard him three times in—how long? An hour?

She drew the baby tightly to her chest.

Flora brimmed in her arms. Small, but so much. An overflow of snuffling life. Or was it Mary's own feelings spilling as her fingers fidgeted to contain her, to hold her all? She bumped a palm over the baby's bottom and clasped the little foot tucked beneath, socked inside its sleeping bag. This little foot. She squeezed, and the toes paddled, stirring in her stomach the memory of the flutter, distinct and delicately convulsive—oh! there it was again—that had told her, five minutes ago, that Flora was alive.

Mary's thoughts flickered to Michelle and then to Eric, but she knew neither was right. Flora being here was nothing to do with them. The baby was a gift from her fox, and the thought made her mouth fall open. She drew a deep breath, sucked in another draught of night medicine. The air tasted clear and dry and tangy with green spice. She had to try to balance herself, her arms and legs and what they did with the things that spun in her head. In the woods, watching him slip from sight, she had felt certain she had lost him. But plainly, the opposite was true. All these weeks of comings and goings, bringings and takings, the egg, the nappies, the rag doll. This was the moment in which that collection of belongings, looked back upon from what she presumed to be a happy endpoint, lined themselves up into a new kind of sense. Because she could see now that what he had brought her, what he had laid at her door, more than any individual gift—yet presented most vividly to her in this incredible little girl she was squeezing—was the power to create a future. And it began right here at her back step.

Fine hairs on Flora's cheek stood alight in the moon like silvery reflective fibers. If Mary was careful, and leant in slowly, she could stroke the hairs with her own cheek hairs. "What shall we do, Flo?" she murmured, studying again the baby's sealed eyes, the stray yarn of purple vein. He had brought her, but he had not explained the rest or even said whether he planned to join them. Mary leant on the handle of the back door, sinking into it the weight of her own tiredness. She pictured her bed. How heavy she felt, her hot hand and the handle welding into one dull lump. It was the movement of the door that jolted her as if from a dream, but it had opened, really opened, and as she clung to it to keep her balance, it swung her inside. The idea had been to lie on the duvet with Flora, but now that they had entered the house, the bedroom seemed miles away, up stairs, around corners. So she carried Flora into the lounge. "Funny," she said as she felt behind her for the sofa cushions. "This afternoon I was imagining what it would be like if you lived here." Flora did not flinch or look to see where she was. She felt where she was, and that was happy. Mary knew this because of the way she nuzzled deeper into the warmth of Mary's chest.

She had the baby. He had brought her the baby.

THE GATE FRAMED the view down to the house, where a chink of light had sprung like a whisker-line crack in an eggshell. The light widened. A giant paw toyed with its corners, stretching it out. Then it stopped growing, and a human shadow fell through it. He waited for darkness to return the way darkness always returned, but tonight the light triumphed. A bright hole bitten out of the night.

Belly lowered, negligible crackle, into brambles. He drew his tail close. Long fur ruffled short fur. Body wriggled flatter. Just one ear left standing. Eyes half closed to the light that bobbed toward him. Giant cat eye. Its yellow edges fuzzed. He crouched his haunches. Thigh scripped on his heel. The light came through the gate: human Female with the loud bark. Walking asleep again. She dripped the wobble light down her path away from him. Going where she always went. Her den. Opposite end—

Safe to move.

He was so dab on his way. Worms flinched as he toed their lawn roof. He sniffed every pat of paw on the ground. He slooped up a string of chicken / chicken they'd left. Thought of the blackbird.

The grass stopped. Scuff scuff, clip clip, up, onto stone. A thrum came in his throat telling him. Bulldog. Squatting dark and lame in the house, with a healing thing on her head like the mastiff once wore. She was not going to bark.

He slinked along the path. He passed his dig and lifted a leg. No time for digging now. Quick spray. Remind them. *My dig.* Whoa. The hole was big and light, warm air falling out. Still and sticky with a cloud of sweet—the smell that fruits in their food dens. The vapors sprinkled his muzzle. His claws snicked the floor. Find the thing that made the smell!

He stepped up a ledge, a ledge, a ledge, pads muffling on the tufty stuff. He tunneled his own dens down under tree roots or into the welcome beneath sheds. But look what strange. Humans dug their burrows up.

His paws stealthed in single file.

At the top, which should be the bottom, his snout jerked left. Snared by the rush of sticky ripe. In the rotten pleasant air, the flavor bred and multiplied. Up another ledge. He opened his mouth and let his tongue snaffle the promises that swarmed his snout. He had nosed through all the passages to. Buried treasure! Same joy as finding a cached rat.

Loud growls flicked his ear. The infant breathed noisily. Liquid gurgled through her tubes. In this part of the burrow the ground felt thick, soft, akin to hutched rabbit. His claws curled in to check, but it was not rabbit. It was another dried matted fleece thing these humans liked. One low wooden hurdle to—

His feet sank and wobbled on her resting place. He pulled out a foot, a foot, a foot, ankles clicking with the strain. Warm, pelty, plump stuff surrounded him. He'd opened up a fleece-lined nest and jumped inside.

The human cub slept in a long sac, layered and downy. He sniffed at the nearest edges of her, where the sac lay flat and empty. Tugged at a loose fold of stuff, but. His top and bottom teeth clashed. He tried to clamp his jaws round enough of the stuff to get a proper grip. His lips slopped and sucked at the tucks and folds while he toiled to perk it up into a small scruff. He laid the side of his face on her chest, and she rolled her head, making room in her sleep for his ear. He pulled and dragged and lifted the sac. She landed with a squirrel thump.

He opened his jaws, swiped around his mouth with his tongue. Fluffy wisps of her cocoon had stuck on it, making him dry. Just sniffing her, the saliva came back. But he kept panting. Had to. Bunch up. Enough. Sac for a strong grip. Avoid tipping the load to the head end. She lay still, not trying to escape even when he parted his jaws. The time most made one last try. Escape-wise, carrying-wise, she was easier than a squirrel.

Bump, bump, bump. That was her, making that noise. They were going down, which was like up in his own earth, heading to the surface at the bottom.

Her head was first into the garden. His shoulders, paw, snout. Some strange new beast they made. He put her down on the grass. He licked her mouth and nose, and she tasted of she smelt. She was delicious. He licked the same place. Licked and. Too many to count, these licks. Her skin was pure sweet milk, and he lapped it up. He could lick and lick and the flavor would never go away.

Down the garden they went.

He pulled her through the hole he had burrowed under Mary's fence.

MARY TOUCHED HER head, felt behind herself for the arm of the sofa her head was leaning back toward. It all seemed certain. A mirthful choke escaped. With the best intentions, he had put her in an awkward position. She straightened her legs and folded a cushion between her head and the armrest. It would be wise to decide upon the most reasonable course of action from this position of exquisitely burdened comfort. The problem was that as soon as she examined the most reasonable course of action, it began to seem foolish. There was no easy way in which to return a baby in the dead of night. It was a path fraught with uncertainty. What would Eric and Michelle say? What would she herself say? She tried to envisage walking to their house, but even that was difficult: she was unsure if she should knock on the front door or back. To make matters worse, when she pictured either door opening, it was not Eric who stood there but Michelle. And at that point, the imagining gave out.

Her eyelids began to wobble. Not to sleep but to rest. It was the warm milk smell rising off the baby's scalp that made them heavy. That and the rhythm of her breathing, the wisp of a whistle in Flora's nose. Lie still or she'll fall, she told herself, even while she cubbied further into the dark hole of rest and the baby a warm weight on her dreams, telling her not to stir, not to turn, to keep them pressed safe.

She was not sleeping. She was only lying there with funny pictures in her head and her brain fuzzed with the effort of trying to stay awake. She was not sleeping; she could still hear the whistle. She had not slept, but time passed quick, slow, quick; she had no idea how late it was when her eyes slammed open in panic, and she bolted off the sofa to her feet, and one hand shot to her chest to clamp the baby's back. She had not slept; she had only slowly blinked.

Outside, the garden was exactly as she had left it, save the sky tinged with the promise of sunrise. And the snail, who had towed his long silvery string all the way across the patio and hidden it in the ragged grass. She and Flora were so unequivocally alone that the uneventfulness brought Mary to her senses, and she began to resent the fact that she felt guilty and that the guilt had pried her from her cozy snuggle. Eric or Michelle had lost their baby. Not the other way round. So they should come to her. Until then, she would keep Flora.

Mary sat quietly on the back step, scooping the empty part of the baby's sleeping bag into the gap between her legs. Now she came to think of it, how strange that Eric and Michelle were not here already. She stood again. From the lawn, the top half of their house, the part she could see above the fence, appeared normal. It did not look like a home devastated in the small hours by panic or loss. There was George's room, adjoining her own spare room, in darkness, and then sticking further into the garden, with the fan-light shut and the curtains drawn, Flora's room. Empty room. Mary began to smile. It was ever so slightly amusing to look at it with that knowledge, because now she understood that Eric and Michelle had no idea Flora had gone.

Oh, the relief. She had time in which to act, and she could still be the person who decided how to act. An early train called from the railway line, a short toot without rise or fall, like the cry of a child. If her neighbors didn't know they had lost Flora, at some point she would have to tell them. "Otherwise," she said to Flora, "I'll look like a thief." Surely there was another way to do it, beyond the absurdity of knocking on their door, the horror of them seeing Flora in her arms before they knew she was missing. She considered tucking the baby back into her cot. But, no, it was impossible to think she could get away with that, that two incursions might be made on the house in a single night without anyone noticing.

"What am I going to do with you?" she said to Flora. "Mmm? I said, What am I going to do with you?"

Flora smiled, a small perfect smile that swam from the depths to the surface of her sleep. It was a reply, a smile by choice. It was there, and then it wasn't. Her mouth, half open again and expressionless, seemed to deny all trace of what she had communicated. Mary scrunched Flora's hand inside her own and put it to her lips. "I could eat you," she said. From one hand or the other came the soft musk of fox.

Another door clicked.

Eric or Michelle, in the garden. Mary looked around, alarmed by the immediate removal of plans A and B. There was no way now to deliver the baby unobserved. No chance to exercise the privilege of the innocent and be the one to inform her neighbors of their negligence. From the other side of the white wall, she heard the metal foot of a chair claw the patio. Then again a quieter sound of furniture being shifted. Someone was looking for something with stealthy purpose, as you might hunt for a frog under a plant pot. Mary squeezed Flora into her chest until she felt their ribs wedge further into their interlocking clasp. Too late to sleep with her till morning. All their windows of opportunity had shut and locked them inside. The fences that wrapped around, the back wall, her own house . . . They were trapped in their box, waiting for their captors.

Mary strained for news from next door, but there was only a discreet commotion, a missable scuttle of tactful footsteps. If Eric and Michelle knew Flora had gone, they didn't want anyone else to know it. "What shall we do?" Mary whispered to the little red ear, flushed with heat and the intensity of their embrace. The idea was harebrained, but she wondered if she might, when no one was looking, roll the baby over the boundary. Once Flora crossed the line, she was their problem. Mary kissed her again. "You're not a problem, are you, darling?" she whispered, but she was interrupted by a low mechanical grunt of glazing sliding.

There was something odd about her neighbors' behavior.

If she, Mary, had woken to find Flora gone, she would have shouted the whole street out of bed and all the house fronts would have flashed blue, sirens wailing. Oh God, she was going to get caught holding their escaped baby, and all she had done was cuddle her. She touched Flora's cheek. She was thinking it might be prudent to step into the house for a moment when she heard Michelle scream. Mary twisted her head to look at Flora. Her eyes were still shut; her breath pooled in Mary's clavicle.

Every window of Eric and Michelle's house was ablaze. A door snapped open and shut. It was Eric's voice, calling "Flora! Flora!" in the same chirpy singsong he used to entice Tiggy home for milk. But Eric was calling more softly than that, as if he were embarrassed to discover how his voice sounded in an emergency. Ridiculously, he appeared to want no one to hear him, which undermined the idea of a search. Did they want this baby or not? Mary glanced at the little one again, in snug oblivion in her arms. There was something thrilling about the fact that she had started to snore.

Eric's footsteps disappeared in grass, and the next tentative "Flo-ra!" came to Mary from just the other side of the fence. Then she heard her own voice.

"Eric? Is that you?" Silence.

Obviously it was him.

"Eric?" she said again. There was still no reply, so she walked toward the place where his own call had risen and tried once more.

Eric's head appeared above the fence, his face blanched.

"I've got Flora," she said. He could see that, but she had to say something.

"Jesus fucking Christ, thank fuck for that."

The door clicked again. He looked away and then back at Mary, slipping her the words, "Wait there. I'm coming round."

"She's safe," he said, publicly addressing the back of the house. "She's safe."

If there was a reply, Mary missed it. The next voice was Eric's again, still talking to the house.

"Mary's got her."

MICHELLE WAS FIRST to materialize out of the darkness at the end of the garden. One leg, in mauve yoga pants, hooked itself over the wall, lashing as Michelle yelled "What the fuck?" She was less concerned about being heard now. A few strides and the woman had covered the whole lawn, Eric running to catch up. "What the fuck do you think you're doing?" Michelle was saying. Some of her spit landed on Mary's cheek, but Mary let it stay because both hands were holding tightly to her last moments with Flora, and nothing was going to take them away.

"Michelle!" Eric hissed. "God's sake!"

Mary hushed gently. "She's sleeping," she soothed, even as Michelle's knuckle kneaded her breast, and Flora was wrenched from her arms. Possibly owing to the change in body temperature, having been snatched from her warm rib nest, Flora's eyes and mouth pinged open. The wail that came out was not the distress cry of someone waking to an ordeal. Or perhaps that's exactly what it was—for the noise was just a weary, routine cry. She had tried her best, but she was back with her mother. As Michelle tugged her away, Flora snagged Mary's hair in her fingers and clung to the long strands as if she had been thrown a rope.

Michelle appeared not to hear Mary's cry of pain as she tugged the baby free. She did not say sorry. She did not say, "Thanks for keeping my baby safe." She almost certainly did not notice Flora's little hand fretting unhappily on her shoulder, a frizz of Mary's hair looped around the fingers. She just hoisted up her tunic top so that her breast, with a green sheen in the moonlight, gave Mary a funny, one-eyed stare, then slapped Flora on to it. Eric circled his wife and daughter firmly in his arms, as if in the course of the night he had lost and found them both. Mary watched them settle into each other, and even though her basket was suddenly empty, it was a relief, this peace.

"Call the police," Michelle said. She was looking at Mary, talking to Eric.

"What?"

"Call the police."

"Shall we talk about this inside, love," Eric said, patting the places where pockets would be. "I've left my phone at home." They were both dressed, Mary noticed, in similar outfits to her, the kind of clothes you wear when you think no human will see you. Eric was in Hawaiian-style board shorts. Between his waistband and the hem of his T-shirt, a pale roll of stomach shone. "Let's talk about this sensibly," he said, stroking Flora's head. "Is she feeding?"

"Yes, she's feeding. Of course she's feeding."

"Thank God for that. Thank God she's safe. Let's get her home. Let's get you both home. She can sleep in with us. Can't she? This once? Daddy's going to make everything OK." He looked at Mary. "Talk in the morning?" He began to turn Michelle's shoulders, to direct her back to the wall.

"I'll go and get a blanket, shall I?" Mary said.

"You'll go nowhere," Michelle said, looking up. "You stay right here where we can see you until the police come. Eric, the baby's fine. Get your phone."

"Darling . . . ," Eric said. But he had no words to follow, and the first blackbirds were beginning to sing.

"Do you want to come inside?" Mary asked. "There's a phone in the hall."

"Mary. That's—kind." Eric rubbed his eyes. "But that's not what we're going to do. Is it, darling?"

"Are you raving mad? She took Flora. She broke into our house, and she took her. One minute the baby's there, the next she's gone, and—*she's* got her. That's abduction. What kind of father are you, standing around in her garden, planning small talk tomorrow, happy to let this crank steal our baby and get away with it? You're a coward. Don't you Daddy me. You're a shit dad!"

"Darling! *Darling*." His voice slowed effortfully, as if he were trying to entice a child to reason while keeping calm himself. "That's not what happened, and we both know it."

A siren streaked down the main road, and the three of them looked at each other in panic.

"Just call the fucking police!" Michelle shouted. "Do it! Or I will." With one hand she rummaged in her pockets for her phone, and when she realized that hers was in the house too, she burst into tears. "I left the door open!" she sobbed. "I let her in."

So now there were two choices. Deny everything Michelle said. Deny it, because Michelle was unwell, and who would listen to an unwell woman? Tell the truth, as she knew it, because sometimes a crazy story is more believable than a realistic one. Mary was weighing all this, the decision complicated by the difficulty of explaining the time frame of the evening—how long had she had the baby?—when she looked up to see Eric watching her, waiting for her to speak. "What happened, Mary?" he said. "Where did you find her?"

She had no idea what she was going to say. And then, the next thing, Eric was replying.

"A fox?"

Mary nodded.

"You saw it?"

"Going into your place . . . The gate was open." Mary was unprepared for the wave of emotion that crested in her as she said the words aloud. She was absolutely swamped with pride. That he had done it for her. Done it out of love and kindness and . . . and . . .

something else she could not name and which only later she understood as belief.

"What? How? Wait. Where did you actually find Flora?"

"On the back step. I'd been for a walk in the woods."

"Oh Christ, not you as well."

"I couldn't sleep. I was heading back when I saw . . . it. Massive, it was. The biggest fox I've ever seen. I saw it go into your garden. I didn't see anything else. I hung around a bit. Thought the air would help me sleep. I heard an owl . . ."

"Get on with it, for fuck's sake," Michelle said.

"When I came back, there was something on my step."

"Not something, Mary! Our daughter!"

"Yes, but I didn't know that at first. It's not what you expect. I just saw the whiteness . . . I only realized it was Flora when I got close. I still can't believe it," she said. She tried to reach out to Flora, but Michelle steered the baby away.

"And she was on the step?" Eric asked.

Mary nodded. She knew it sounded unbelievable, but Eric was looking at her intently and nodding back. "Lying there," she said, "like a . . . parcel." Neither Eric nor Michelle spoke, so she went on. "I checked she was OK, and I was just working out how to bring her round when I heard Eric in the garden. Thank God."

"She was on your step?" Eric said again. "As if she had been left there?"

"I know it doesn't make much sense."

"I think it's starting to," he said.

Mary turned at the sound of a footstep in her other neighbor's garden. Eric was half stroking Flora's hair, half-examining her for evidence.

"She looks absolutely peaceful and unhurt," he said. "She has been beautifully taken care of." He looked at his wife and drew her head to his chest. "There, there," he said. "It's all OK now. She's safe.

You're safe. Those are the only two things that matter in the whole universe. It's been a horrible night, but it's over. Darling, we are not going to call the police. You know what the police would think? That we had done it ourselves." Michelle had stopped arguing, and Mary watched Eric take his wife's silence for assent. "It's OK, love," he said, pressing his mouth to her head. "We're going to get you help. Proper help."

"I still don't understand what happened," Mary ventured, feeling the pressure lift sufficiently to address Eric over Michelle's head.

He smiled at her, a smile full of sadness. "Something woke me. I don't know what. When I sat up, Michelle was missing. Not in bed, were you, love?" he said gently to Michelle's hair. "I checked George's room; he was asleep. Then Flora's—but the cot was empty. Michelle must have heard her cry and gone to feed her. But then why hadn't she put her back in the crib? I went downstairs"—he was weeping now—"and the kitchen was open. Not just a fraction. But like someone's blown a bloody great hole in the back of the house. I think that's probably when I saw you coming inside, didn't I, darling? I think you may have been sleepwalking."

Michelle ignored him and swapped Flora to the other breast. She seemed intent only on the baby.

"Right, but that doesn't explain how Flora came to be on my step," Mary said. She wanted to make Eric say what he thought.

"Why won't you tell us where you were, Mary? How you even came to be outside, miraculously finding my baby on your patio?" Michelle had woken up again.

"I was in the woods, like I said. I couldn't sleep. It was so hot. I came outside for air. Sometimes I do that—since Mark left." It occurred to her that showing Michelle weakness might ameliorate her desire for destruction. In any case, Michelle was hardly in a position to advance sleepwalking as a sign of madness.

Michelle looked at Eric. "I fed her and put her back in the cot," she said.

"Did you actually see the fox go into the house, Mary?" Eric asked. From the way he continued to brace his wife, he seemed to think that only his arms were holding her together.

"Toward the house. I saw it go toward the house." She was very tired, and only a huge mental effort prevented her from saying "him." She shrugged and then added, "Flora had leaves in her hair."

"Well, it makes no difference. You or a fox, it's the same thing," Michelle said. "Either way, you're responsible. You think I haven't seen you, always out here looking for them. Creeping around at night. I've even heard you putting down a pet bowl."

"That's not true. I've never done that," Mary said.

"I heard it. Once when I couldn't sleep and I was in the woods, I saw you flashing a light from your back room. Signaling at something out here. You let them sleep on your grass, on your shed. Look at this place!" she said. "Your garden's a jungle. They go in and out of your shed. I'm pretty sure I've heard you talking to them. Neville thinks you're feeding them. And you had all our stuff on your kitchen sill!"

Eric looked at Mary over his wife's head and mouthed a silent "sorry."

"Oh yes!" Michelle said. "Eric, do you remember when Mary babysat and we found those doodles of foxes all over my note? She's obsessed! We are so, so lucky that Flora's OK," she sobbed. "We're reporting this to the police. And we're calling that guy in the morning. What's his name? The one you liked the sound of?"

"I didn't like the name. It's a pretty corny name," Eric said. "But he knew his stuff."

"Who?" Mary asked.

"He's called the Fox Fixer."

CHAPTER THIRTEEN

It started as a single knock on a door in Mary's head. The inside echo of a car being slammed shut on the street or a clothes moth clapping its wings too close to her ear. Then the knock grew louder, and the hammering refused to let up. Betrayal. Her betrayal was waking her up, banging around in her head, hurling itself against the walls and windows of her mind, looking for a way out like a fly snared behind a blind. Buzz. Buzz. She had given him up, handed him over to Michelle and Eric, practically told them he was to blame, and all because she had felt, in that instant, so thoroughly loved.

The clock said she had slept for forty-five minutes. Somehow Monday was dawning without it ever having stopped being Sunday. Soon Michelle and Eric would wake—or maybe they had woken while she slept. Mary and her fox were only hours away from the arrival of the fox catcher.

Buzz. Buzz. Mary clasped her temples. She had told Michelle and Eric she had watched him enter their property. She had told them in a strange kind of boastfulness. She sat up, heard the stealthy electric whir of the milk float pause outside her neighbors' house. It was a vanity. Under pressure from Michelle's accusations, she had felt not so much the need to defend herself as to share her fox's high opinion of her: it was so at odds with their vision of her as a lonely woman failing on all the basics, whose relationship had unraveled because of her inability to take the leap of faith that nature intended. She tugged her joggers from the chair, and, seeing yesterday's knickers still inside, stepped into both at once. Quickly she pulled on a top, grabbed her lapsed gym bag, and began stuffing things into it: a change of clothes, a jumper in case the nights got cold, her phone for emergencies. He had come to their row of houses, looked into the windows, sniffed at the doors, studied their sounds, graded their smells and shadow, the human honeycomb. He had seen them all from the back. Not how neighbors see, with their muffled through-the-wall knowledge. Not how passersby, or learner drivers dawdling over their parallel parking on this quiet, tree-lined turning, see with a quick glimpse into a dull room. He had seen their lives lit up at dusk, when the insides of houses glow and all their dramas can be read.

He was the first, the only one, who believed she could do it. How unconvincing Mark seemed in hindsight, with his spurious assurances that she could do it *with him*, that her future became imaginable with his care. Only he—Rafael, she was thinking—it sounded triumphant—knew that this little stump of life she had, this dead end that never sprouted a new beginning, well, it could sprout. It had sprouted.

On her way downstairs Mary darted into the bathroom and scooped her toothbrush, toothpaste, and a dry bar of soap into the duffel. If she was honest, she had acted upon an additional consideration in telling Michelle and Eric. Her fingerprints would be all over that cot. From earlier in the day, when she had fetched Flora. In the kitchen, she gathered her keys and purse, laced her trainers over bare feet. She had thrown his life into danger. Now she was going to save him.

SUN STREAKED THE woodland floor, enormous fingertips dripping pale gold across hollowed twigs and burnt leaves. A squirrel clinging to the lime twitched his hood eyes at Mary and, as she climbed the wall beside him, snagged around the trunk in reverse. The sky burnt red, and there was much to be done.

First light had erased all trace of Mary's adventure. The paths she had made through this overgrowth in the night had vanished, and again she found herself battling nettles that bobbed about her chin. Since she discovered Rafael's hazel weeks ago, they had grown a foot taller, and the bindweed had unspooled its garlands by the meter. Walls, fences, and gates had disappeared under the greenery. The woods should have felt smaller, but the opposite was true. They had enlarged. They were a world without edges.

It was obvious to Mary where the fox catcher would start. When she reached the hole by the hazel, she kicked a few black feathers out of the way and lay on her side. "Hello?" she called into the mouth. It could be a dead end or the start of an underground mansion, as credibly deceptive as looking in a puddle and seeing a well. She wriggled closer. Way below, she could hear a grainy sifting. A worm cleaving damp clumps, the twitch of small lives. Or perhaps it was something heavier, further off, a distant tread through corridors she would never see. Was it him, answering her call from an underground turret at the outer edge of his kingdom? No eyes glittered. She had downed all the light with her face.

Behind her, a cough. One of those diplomatic, throat-clearing noises humans make when they hope to be noticed but are too polite to interrupt.

He was his own length away from her, looking down at her while his ears kept their duty.

Plucked by the wren, its squeak a taunt, its puff head tick-ticking this way that way, tugging his own head in circles. He could reach it at a jump. He could reach it at a jump but. Something crawled into his ear, and he shook his head, and the shaking made him—

"Bless you," she answered and began to crawl toward him. His eyes gleamed. Brown cloud streaked the orange, as if some sediment from the waterbed had been stirred. From this angle, his eyes had a glassy, colorless surface that domed protectively over those swirls, like an expensive paperweight. Mary knelt a moment, rubbed the twigs off her palms while he watched.

There was something she needed to say, but it was hard to say, so she kept picking bits from her hands while she waited for the words to come. She shuffled forward on her knees until she was close enough to see his nostrils flicker. "Thank you," she told him, her hands on her breast. In her life, she had never meant anything more. "Thank you. For believing in me. For what you did for me." His fur began to run through her tears. She sat back on her heels and opened her arms, waiting for him to step into her embrace, but his paws stayed put, and he lowered his snout to her. She dabbed at her eyes with the heel of her hand and looked down at her scuzzy top and joggers. "Yes, I rushed out as soon as I woke. Didn't even shower. But look, I've got a bag," she said, standing up and showing him the duffel. "Enough for a few days." It was implausibly fortunate to have found him so soon. They would be down the alley long before the fox catcher arrived.

"Oh no!" she said, seeing him sit with the sudden collapse function in his legs. He looked at her meaningfully and began to wash. "You can do that later. We've got to go." She shook out her legs, to show him what she meant.

When he still didn't move, she said, "Last night . . . oh God." There was no way round it. "I told them I saw you. I had to! I'm so sorry. They thought I'd taken her." His ears folded toward her quizzically. "Please forgive me. I was desperate, and not just that; I felt so . . . so proud of you and of us, and I said it without thinking. From now on, I'll say nothing. I know what it feels like to be betrayed." She thought of Mark, of Dawn stabbing her in the back, of her own mother's treacherous disinterest. "I would never hurt you," she said. "I've come to save you."

She raised her hands to tell him to stand, and he balked, let up licking his paw and looked at her, then back at the wren. "I'm trying to talk to you!" she exclaimed with rising panic. "Stop staring at that bloody bird and concentrate! You are waiting in the first place they'll look!" She kicked a fern in despair, and dry flecks and insects flew up from its crispy shudder. "I'm sorry," she said at last. "I don't mean to shout. I'm just so worried, and I feel responsible. If I don't get you out of here, who will?" Her palms were sticky with sweat, and with a pang she realized they had had their first argument.

LICK A PAW, pretend to wash an ear. Let the wren think he was busy.

MARY LOOKED AROUND the woods. Life was leaving all the collapsed straps of bulbs, taking the green. Yellow stealing in. Greener things climbing over the top. Some kind of life cycle had begun to close before her eyes. Nature's way of telling her, as if she didn't know, that this was all coming to an end. She could not stand here peeved and despairing while the leaves rustled and the birds whistled.

"There's a trapper coming," she said. "I'm so sorry to be blunt. He wants to catch or kill you. That's why I'm here. We can head to the gate together, then on to the park. We'll blend in more easily there. But we have no time to lose." She managed to keep her voice calm when she said, "We have to go *now*."

The pink in the clouds was beginning to disperse, and still he was rooted to his spot. "Come on!" she said. "Just leave it. There will be plenty of those for you to look at in the park. Let's go!"

TWO WORMS. TIED together. Lying neck to neck, a rich white band. Joined somewhere he could not see. Two worms thickening. Their tube bodies shrinking / stretching, as they piped obliviously. Rubbery rubbing, the grate and rasp of indigestible setae chafing. Liquid earth juicing outward. Rich soil odor damply rising.

He blinked. His eyes had begun to cross. Before his mouth taught him, worm scent tripped him. Male? Female? Yes, yes. Male and Female. Both at once. Every worm the same. Not like foxes. He lowered his snout toward the nearer him / her that was pressing into the further him / her that was pressing into the nearer him / her. Both doing both jobs. Sharing everything same / same. He let his snout prod the closest one. He / she must have felt his whiskers but kept throating away. He had tried this trick before. He pushed at the edge of them with a paw. Nothing could part worms busy with love. True fact. He hoisted them in two for one. It took twice as long.

They were still singing in his gullet when a magpie landed on a branch and the wren flew and the branch bounced. Jerking his head. The magpie's eye was a game of dare. She hopped to the ground, and he watched her strut. Muzzle swaying, tail up. Waiting for the right moment. Timing. Birds. All about timing.

"Come on!" Mary yelled. "Now!" She had never seen a magpie run. But at her cry, it started to sprint, its black legs clawing forward one after another. It dug out each pace, the back of its neck an oily glint, a reek of mackerel in its wake, and the message passed from the magpie's feet, iron toes cracking skeleton leaves, into his mouth.

"Oh, well, thank you!" she said. He had finally understood and was jogging into the thicket. She followed him, following her plan. It was a race to keep up on her hands and knees, twigs gnawing at her palms, ferns flicking her face, but though the stones and lumpy earth pummeled the bones of her knees, she didn't want to walk and be spotted. The path eased when she entered the bracken. A narrow trail gleamed within the rusty tunnel of leaves, and his paws lined up inside it. Each filled the space of the one in front, as if his hind feet would trust only his front feet's prints. At every step they released a vapor of wet musk, the puff of an invisible atomizer. Mary reached for the tip of his brush and held it. The tail gave a little throb as she squeezed; then he walked on. They were heading the right way for the gate.

After a few minutes, he veered off the track, and Mary watched him flick his tail while he rubbed his hindquarters against an old bedside table. The air flapped her face with a dark flag of scent. "Keep moving, darling," she whispered as he rejoined the trail ahead of her. The world was waking up around them. A van slowed on the street to her right, an engine turning over its thoughts.

He tipped his snout and let it hover side to side, cresting the scent waves. Crows lifted out of the trees above them, and when Mary understood they were cawing in honor of her and Rafael, her heart leapt at the unexpected validation of them as a pair. Mark had always seen himself as her rescuer, and a part of her—just a small part— longed for him to see her now. She had turned herself around. She was the one thinking ahead, organizing, chasing, saving. A sense of purpose pumped through her arms, and she sped up through a patch of spent bulbs and long grasses. One after another they folded their way through broad sheaths of flat leaves, cool and comfortable as cotton to her hands. Then a short way ahead he stopped.

A fern frond was swaying while all the fronds around it were still. He revolved an ear. The sway stilled but. Too late, Beetle! His feet were in the air. He snatched her from the stalk. His teeth crick-cracked the wing cases while he looked around to see if she had brought any friends.

"Concentrate!" Mary reminded him. "We don't have time for this." At best, his sense of urgency was fitful. She had hoped to tackle the trip to the park before the pavements thickened with commuters, but on her hands and knees, she had lost all sense of how far they had come, how much time had passed. When she turned to look behind her, she saw only the pale green shine of the path they had flattened. Ahead, the neat strip he was threading. Above—it was hard to see beyond the green. Somewhere up there a bird was making heavy work of a tune, its puff and whistle like the wheeze of a bicycle pump.

Mary rocked back onto her heels and scraped the hair out of her eyes with her wrist. Her hands were caked with powdered dirt. Dust lined all the cracks and creases in her fingers, and no amount of picking would shift it. She wiped her nose on her shoulder, smearing her top brown, and gave an exasperated cry at the sight of Rafael disappearing into a huge nettle bed.

When she came out the other side, Mary saw that they had reached the eastern end of the woods. A fragment of brick wall peeped through the ivy, laced with magenta roses. From one of the gardens on Drovers Lane a human was calling a cat for breakfast. She watched Rafael's ears fidget at the sound. They had reached the brink of civilization again. She turned to get her bearings and through the trees glimpsed the red gate.

"Nearly there!" she called. There were times when she had felt unsure they were going to make it. "Actually, it's this way," she cajoled, seeing him stalk instead toward a large oak. "Trust me. They are coming. Sooner than we know. We have to get you out of here."

From Drovers Lane they would walk straight to the park. Once there, they would make for the woodland section, with felled trunks, seats made out of stumps, and where the leaves grew so thickly it was impossible to see in from the outside. Mary focused on where they were going, partly to avoid thinking about how they were going to get there. She could hardly transport herself from garden to garden. They would have to stick to the pavement. What an odd couple they were going to make on their first public outing.

"This will blow over in a few days," she said, catching him up at the oak. "Think of it as a little holiday. What's the matter?"

He stood on his hind legs. His forepaws clawed up the trunk. She looked at his long, muscular back, but instead of turning to answer, his head disappeared into the tree. When he dropped to the ground, something jammed open his jaws.

She felt his eyes on her as she moved toward the oak. When she saw the hollow in its trunk, she looked at him for permission before reaching inside. Her hand paddled in a little nest, soft with the accreted slough of tree skin, until it found something hard. "How did that get there?" she asked in amazement. And then, seeing his fur thicken, "It's OK. I'm going to put it back." There was nothing unique about the egg, right down to the orange lion printed on its shell.

"The gate," she said, pointing. "See the gate?"

His STOMACH HIT the brambles. Whiskers batted silence to the bee jamming in the bramble flower irking his focus. A metallic clunking upwind. Death. He thought when he heard it. A clash no teeth can tear or crack. Noise tougher than superstrength Beetle case. Another clang. Heavy. Metal impact. Ringing in his ears. Making every other sound fade. In his head, the smoky fast growl that hit her. A gentle crunch. She was always gentle. The crunch was her, not it. Bones colliding, denting, flaking.

Close by, a clink. Said the mastiff had stood, stretched. Yelped ask to her human. The mastiff rattled. Sitting down. The rattle.

Took him back to the crunch. It was dark. Out together, working closely. You sniff that way; I'll sniff this. Your scent, my scent. Berries and spice. Our special defense. Put it on thickly. No scent spared. She wandered off to check—he never knew. What attracted her. Something good. Must have been something good. Her eyes glowed green when the giant eyes shone on her. He barked warning, but she didn't turn. One ear answered him with a flicker. Her last look she gave to the eyes that killed her. The growl went over her back. For no reason. Didn't even stop to eat her.

She was dead when he trotted to her side. He stood over her, licked her blood, her fur. Her one ear still spiked. But. Only for a bit. It didn't help. She tasted wrong. Berries slammed with metal. He waited. Barked but. She lay still. He had seen her do that once, running from a Doberman. She lay in the road. Trained her heart to barely beat. Playing dead. Not playing. Hiding to be free. When the dog stood over her, she leapt and snapped, fled. He found her back at the den. But she wasn't not dead / dead this time. She was dead / dead. Still he trotted to the den. Waited. First light he went to find her again. Thinking. The cubs should have been out. Could have been out. What if they did? They were so close to their time. Earth all ready. Everything dug deep and cool and nice. Burrows and tunnels and resting spaces. Two exits. Cover above. A roof made of roots. Big store of food. He went to check, but no cubs had come. Just she was flatter. He—. He saw her now in flashes like her eyes. Green eyes. Ear pricked. Lying. Flat. Cubs. He saw them, but not really. Cubs in his head. Cubs next year if life was good. Nights growing longer. Vixen soon. All this space and food. An ear furrowed at the Female crouching the other side of the tree. The mastiff yowled, and again the sound came.

He lay down his ear. It was only a gate opening.

THERE WAS PEACE crouching by the oak, looking up at the tall stories of its trunk, a song on every branch, each leaf exercising its will. The world was going about its wild business, with no care for Michelle and Eric. From Drovers Lane, Mary heard the high-pitched beeping of a vehicle reversing. At last Rafael seemed satisfied that all was safe and got to his feet. But he kept his body low as he regained the trail toward the alley, and his tail stretched out behind. When he disappeared between two bushes, Mary followed him, but he had gone.

It was unclear to her which of them had lost the other. Further along the path he still hadn't reappeared, and she began to worry that he had simply tolerated her company until he could shake her off. Here the vegetation grew thickly, light greens snagging on dark, ivy and bindweed in a race to the light, and Mary stopped seeing the gate. The woods were full of the rub and squeak of birdsong. But there was no sound of him. All she could hear was the low churn of the basement conversion at the end of her road. They were creeping down Hazel Grove, those conversions, with their rolling and rinsing, their all-day, all-week drilling and digging, their conveyor belts shunting, for several hundred quid a cubic meter, apparently limitless earth.

She could not say how she became aware of him—but one minute he was ahead of her, and now, magically, he was behind. Well, magic was just a word for things people don't understand. His paws on the brittle leaves were as quiet as paws in snow, and his back and tail were elongated into one roll of muscle. "OK," she whispered, crouching. "I understand. You've got a different plan. So share it."

He revolved on the spot, then headed under the canopy of two neighboring hazels whose branches had grown so tall that their weight pulled them horizontal, making a sheltered den between the two main trunks. He waited politely at the opening. Fallen hazel sticks covered the floor, crisp layers of old leaves, the dusty remains of catkins, an old yogurt pot. A thorn prickled Mary's knee through her jogging bottoms as she crawled inside. The whole place smelt strongly of him, and the smell drew over her like a heavy skin. She submitted to its weight while he folded himself beside her. A hedgehog lay flat on the floor, with just its head intact: a sort of small decorative rug.

Although she felt the immense affirmation of having made it to his home, now Mary looked around and saw the futility of their attempted, for want of a better word, elopement. It had taken her the whole journey to work it out, but he was not trying to escape, was he? If anything, he looked as if he was about to go to sleep. She had absolutely no power of control, or even barely of suggestion, over him. It had been madness to think she had. For a while, their two plans for the day had coincided, that was all.

"Only one person here is running away," she said.

He looked up at her heavy sigh, and for his benefit she made an effort at cheer. His muzzle expressed perpetual benevolence: the black hairs sketching the line between upper and lower jaw were the side strokes of a crayon smile. "What would I do without you?" she said.

She wondered if this was his main residence or if that would be the hole under the hazel. She was pretty sure her shed was a sort of summerhouse, an inside/outside space, as the property experts said. But this place was not an earth; it had no tunnels. It was more like a napping den. Maybe there were morning and afternoon napping dens, sunny ones and shady ones. A leaf fell from a nearby maple, and she watched his snout pursue its decline. When it landed, his shoulders relaxed, and he dug himself lower into the woodland floor.

The den was filling with her scent. His snout twitched at sandalwood and Beetle, the expulsion of an egg giving her a peppery grind, a clear, salty yolk leaking—

His warm tongue lapped at her arm. He was licking the ooze from her insect bite, and when he had finished, she reached round slowly so as not to alarm him and touched his back, fingers probing the cloak of thicker fur on his neck and shoulders. His hair was shorter than she had imagined, and beneath it the muscle relaxed and twitched against her touch in permanent tension. He had soothed her arm, and she found the act deeply touching. It was the kind of care she supposed he would take of a mate, and the thought made her look appreciatively around the space. In her garden, he was always the one to disappear, to bring their time to an end. If it didn't sound so naff, she would call him Houdini. "What about Flight?" she asked. How silly that it had occurred to her only now to seek his opinion. "That would suit you, but it's not very namey."

"I'm so glad I found you," she said.

The fur grew in bushy arches around the top of his eyes, and he seemed to adjust a brow.

"All right. I'm so glad you found me," she said, laughing. She let her hand explore the coarse coat of his back and heard a noise like a chirp.

"I do love you," she said.

The marvel was, it was as easy to say as to think. She stroked him again, and her words spurred another chirp. It was a noise of pure happiness. He turned his muzzle to her, and she felt a weight on her knee. Looking down, she saw that he had rested his paw and was lying there, paw on knee, as if their arrangement were the most natural thing in the world. She felt her ribs, her stomach, her pelvis relax, as if some inner belt had unfastened. She was letting happiness loose.

When he shifted his weight, she glimpsed the remains of an old mattress beneath him. "What is it?" she said. Something was wrong to make him stand so suddenly. She peered through the gaps in the leaves and saw a pigeon labor on a skinny branch, shaking out each wing as if it was wriggling into a gray suit jacket. It could have been the flapping that disturbed him or the heavy clatter of the building site on Shepherds Bridge Walk.

He returned to the mattress and pressed himself deeper into it. All four ears were pricked. Human male voices drifted downwind.

She was so close to him, she could feel every muscle prepare itself in continuous decision. She thought she heard Mark, but she knew this was just her fear searching for its worst form, because she could see only one human. Through the gaps in the leaves, she pieced together fragments of a male standing with his back to them, a garden length away. In their den, they kept each other updated through the tension of their bodies. The male was stepping backward. Mary saw a waist, an arm. Black vest. One hand. Black gloved. He was talking, but she could not pick out words. She dared not move. Her mouth opened, and the air entered silently. The man kneeled. A bald head came into view. He looked over his shoulder, and she caught the word "activity." If he turned, he would see her eyes. She killed her headlamps.

The voices drifted away. Her fox's breath slowed through the mattress, through her legs against his flank. When she next looked, his eyes were a thin gleam, his tail pegged beneath his snout. It had been a long night. There in the warm, with the humming dimming, she laid her head on his shoulder and slept.

CHAPTER FOURTEEN

She woke to find herself alone in the den. Somehow he had levered his body free, wriggled from beneath her, and replaced her head on the mattress while she slept. She had played this thing all wrong. It was impossible to live together in his world. How she wished she had tried to take him into hers. Now she would have to go home and pretend sympathy to her neighbors and their fox catcher.

As Mary climbed into her garden, she looked up at her house and saw that the lounge sash was slightly raised, which was not how she remembered leaving it. Most of the window shone green and leaf-dappled, while a lower strip divulged the discarded mail that fluttered on her table. She walked slowly up her lawn listening to the music grow louder. At the edge of the patio, coffee rose in her lung. The scent poured from the house through the open door.

Mary was still staring at the space where the door should have been when Mark stepped into the kitchen from the hall. He was wearing a concerned expression, as if he had come to investigate a mysterious noise, as if her appearance here were the mystery, and his a function of normal household security. When he saw her, his inquiring look cracked into a smile. "You're safe!" he said, moving toward her. "Thank God! Where the hell have you been?"

It was the wrong question. The wrong person asking the question. Mark was in her house, with the back door open—because that was how he got in? Or because he knew that was the way she would come home? He leant into the frame, a slab of tan forearm planked against the wood. Mark was the doorway now, eyeing her as if his name was still on the mortgage. She let the surprise of seeing him settle in her stomach. Maybe this was how spiders felt when they came home to find company waiting in the web.

"I went for a walk. In the woods," she said, in a voice she hoped would disguise her unease. When she was small, her mother liked to scare her with a story about an old school friend who had watched helpless while an intruder fatally stabbed her husband. Afterward, the killer turned to the woman. Fearing for her own life, she said the one thing that came into her head and offered him a cup of tea. It was the brilliant, unfazed ordinariness that disarmed him. They drank it together while they waited for the police.

"Have you been here long?" she asked, meaning to defuse his threat by submitting to the version of normality he was trying so hard to create.

Mark opened his arms and pulled her toward him. "You had me worried," he said into her hair. "Empty house, the door not double-locked . . ."

Mary heard the sole of her shoe prevaricate on the lino with a sticky stammer. Was it safer outside or in?

". . . The lights blown and the oven clock flashing as if the power had been cut," Mark was saying. "You hadn't brushed your teeth. House reeking something rotten . . ." Six months apart, in which she had traveled as far from him as she could. She had bought him out. Wanted nothing except the chance to recover from him in solitude. Their relationship, such a strong arm around her. But wherever she went, he was there too, stalking her periphery. And now he was actually in her house, had been the one to invite her in, and even though she knew what he was doing, even though she recognized his old trick of deploying consideration as a means of control, she asked in the most casual voice she could find, "What brings you here?"

"Eric. Called me this morning," Mark said as his biceps wrapped her in a hard jersey clench. "Said he couldn't get hold of you on the phone. No answer at the door."

Mary tried to find daylight, but by squirming she managed only to nose further into Mark's chest. She opened her mouth to breathe, and his T-shirt furred on her lip with the movement of his muscles: he was roughly forking through her hair. As he worked, her view enlarged to a sliver of light between his sleeve and his ribs, through which she saw that the oven clock had been reset to 14:31. His hand picked over her head, flicking leaves with a dry crackle onto the patio behind her. The fumes of sandalwood cologne were so stifling she assumed they rose from both their bodies. "What have you put in your hair?" he asked. "It stinks. Some sort of organic mask?"

"What do you mean, Eric called?" she said, trying to push herself free of his chest. "Why would Eric call *you*?" She tried to liberate a second nostril, but his shoulder flexed against her skull and involuntarily her hand found his back. His body felt different, but something about the structure of the embrace, the clamp of his chin on her scalp, the rhythm of his breath against the movement of his fingers, treading small steps along their old path down her spine, made her feel as if she had returned from the woods to a different time—about a year and a half ago—when Mark, unraveling at her refusal to commit, had begun to grow angry. She thought of New Year's Day. It was such a commonplace to say that you had made someone angry. But she didn't mean she'd got to him that once. For months she had worked away at calm and steady Mark until she had altered him, turned him into something he wasn't. And he had done the same to her, made her weak and defensive and desperate with his relentless cornering of her. They were both to blame, she thought, lost within his dark embrace. They worked on each other's tender spots like acid.

She pushed him hard in the chest.

"Hey, easy! What's the matter?" he said, regaining his footing. Somehow he had managed to hold on to her shoulders, and he gripped them more firmly. "What happened was Eric phoned. He was looking for you, to talk about last night. He said he knocked several times. Then he asked me to try. That was about eleven. I've been waiting for"—he glanced at the oven—"three hours. What am I thinking? You must be thirsty," he said, releasing her.

For the first time, perhaps because it had started to spin, she registered the washing machine, its whir of apple-green cotton.

In spring, after Mark moved out, Mary had rearranged all the cupboards. But now she saw that the first door he opened was the right door. In his brief occupation of her kitchen, he appeared to have rehabituated himself. He withdrew her favorite mug, the one they had bought from a potter in Crete, spun the stove knob to off, and poured out coffee. "I hope you don't mind," he said, handing her the cup. "I opened a few windows. It smelt weird in here. Kind of pungent."

She kept her bag on her shoulder and her nose inside the mug, staring at the white crescent of its base, hoping to find an answer. But the cup was just another burrow that didn't go far enough. "Eric?" she said, and he frowned at her, leaning back against the oven with one foot crossed over the other in the old way. "What did he say about last night?"

He licked his finger and rubbed at a coffee ring on the worktop. "That a fox entered their house and took Flora. You found her. Michelle was pretty hardcore."

"He said a fox took her?" she asked. "Definitely? I mean, not did he definitely say it, but is that what he definitely thought happened? Because I said I saw one go into their garden, but I don't think it could have taken Flora." He could. She knew he could. But she wasn't going to make that mistake again. Tiredness washed over her. She let her eyes close in turns, watching Mark through the open one, certain he knew more than he was saying. She swallowed the last of the coffee, and the china mooned her own face back at her.

Mark opened his mouth and shut it again, as he did when he was thinking carefully. Then he said, "I'm going to run you a bath. Get you a bit more human. After your bath, I'll explain everything."

THROUGH THE CEILING she heard the plug clang into place, water clatter on the bottom of the tub, and then quiet to a steady gush. Sweet, calming rose floated into the kitchen: her favorite oil. Quietly Mary followed the scent to the hall, past Mark's rucksack, hung on the newel post where it used to hang, up the stairs. From the landing, she eyed a slice of Mark's back through the doorway. He was leaning into the bath, swishing the water. A towel lay folded on the stool. Next to it a flame wobbled in a jar. She had seen the candle before, but it took a minute to place it. Three Christmases ago, he had given it to her in her stocking, and she had buried it in her bedside drawer.

He was still leaning over the bath, crooning to the music. Swirls of steam rose from the water, and his birthmark glimmered slickly. It seemed to suggest itself as something to aim for. Because, after all, she had a legal right to defend her property against intruders. Calling the police was out of the question; Michelle would see the patrol car, and she, Mary, would end the day as a baby snatcher. She pictured the heavy base of the lamp in the spare room. The bathroom clouded with vapor. Moisture speckled the ceiling where the paint had begun to blister and where a pair of tiny folded wings shadowed the base of the porcelain light. God knows how a moth had got in there, because the shade was stuck flush to the ceiling. He must have flown to the light, stolen in, and found no exit.

"How did you get inside?" she asked.

"Spare key," Mark said, over his shoulder. By now he would be flopped over the edge of the bath. "I see you keep the back-door key in the little pot still."

"What?"

"The pot on the draining board."

"What? You used your old key?"

"Yes." He sounded surprised. "You didn't change the locks."

"I didn't know I needed to," she snapped.

"It was an emergency, Mary," he said. "I had no choice."

"Emergency!" she scoffed. "For who? Well, come on, if it was an emergency, what did Eric say? What danger am I in?"

"Bath first, Mary. You need to get back to some kind of . . ." He frowned. "Normality, I suppose. Then tackle the . . . tricky things." He fussed at an imaginary leaf in her hair, took in her muddy track-suit trousers, the thick rim of dust around her ankles. "You look a state. Beautiful. Extremely sexy. But a total mess. It's going to be OK, you know. I'm going to make everything all right." He moved toward her, and his hands closed lightly over her elbows, his thumbs rubbing her arms. "Try to remember how we were. When things were good. Trust me. Like you used to trust me."

He tugged at the hem of one sleeve, and the neckline of her top scooped her shoulder. She had no memory of dressing, but now she registered the absence of a bra strap. He bent her arm upward, and she watched her own hand offer a limp wave. "It's OK. I can do this," she said. He was holding her elbow and maneuvering it back up inside her sleeve to the armhole and then inside the body of her top, and she was surprised to find his look of concentration endearing, like a parent patiently undressing a child.

"There we go," he said, waggling the empty sleeve. "Not too difficult, was it? Oh, Mary! Your arm!" He ran his fingers along the scratches and fine crusts of blood. "They're not deep," he said, more to himself than to her. "How did you get them? You're absolutely covered." He touched her cheek, and she felt a sudden sting.

"I told you. I went for a walk in the woods," she said.

"Jesus." He stepped back and rubbed his face vigorously with his hands. "All right. The bath will help," he said, returning to address the other sleeve. "It will help everything." Soon her second arm hung down inside her top, pulling it across her chest like a straitjacket.

"I can manage from here," she said.

"It's OK. I'm not looking." He held her gaze to prove it.

She trawled his warm blue eyes, not glancing away even when his hands on the hem of her top began to lift. She pulled in her stomach. He was going to lift it all the way, wasn't he? She kept the question out of her eyes, and his face looked back oddly serious and immobile, apart from when his knuckle bumped her nipple, and then he smiled.

The top hung around her neck like a scarf. His hands clung to the fabric; his wrists rested on the way-post of her collarbone.

"It's OK. I've got this," she said, trying to take the top from him.

"I told you. I'm not looking."

Her whole body trembled on the line of its decision. She did want to get in the bath. She did want to be taken care of. For a short while. She did want everything to be OK, to be the acknowledged bystander of an unexplained crime, so she would not have to hide from her neighbors and herself like a guilty thing. She did want to feel another warm body close. Could she take what she wanted and leave the rest? The remnants of Mark's power still, slightly, fascinated her. Partly, she tried to persuade herself, because she wanted to discover how far she had strengthened too. Could she resist him? She looked at the vapor glistening in tiny beads on the beginning of his stubble. The candle, scent, music . . . In a few hours, he had created an impeccable home within her home. It resembled a historical reenactment, in which every detail was exact, and the exactness was precisely what betrayed the artifice.

Mary was thinking all this through, thinking how to play her part in this drama, when Mark flipped the top over her head so that she was naked from the waist up, watching him stare at her breasts. "I'm going to leave you to have your bath," he said.

STEAM HUNG LOW as she stepped onto the landing, hair dripping down her back. Now she had left the safety of the locked bathroom, she had the feeling that Mark had turned the house into a trap, and she was his quarry. She pulled the towel tightly around her chest. He had changed the music. It was Amy Winehouse now. They'd listened to her the night they met. Maybe Mark was running through the greatest hits of their shared life. He was trying to lull her with comforts and care into accepting him back, with his foibles and his excessive domesticity, his compulsive everything has its place and your place is my place. How quickly all those small controls were reasserting themselves. It was those, rather than the occasional explosions, that had most cowed her: the obsessive scheduling of their social life, which was in practice an intolerance of any independent friendship, the advice about what she could and couldn't eat, screwing lids and windows too tight so she had to ask him (weakly) to open them. She gasped for air, but all she could taste out here on the stair was rose. The scent tucked over her drowsiness, made her woozy. Somehow she had to keep her brain sharp.

There was no sound of Mark. She would dress, then find him.

In her bedroom, she made for the wardrobe.

"Knock, knock." Mark was already in the room when he said it. "I brought you this." He set a glass on the bedside table and left.

The goblet was chilled and clouded, which made her question how long it took to cool a bottle of wine. How much planning had gone into this? The bowl wobbled heavily to her lips as she thumbed the hangers. She knew the effect she intended—self-possessed, authoritative—but not the exact piece of clothing. She took another sip and reached for the stripy shirtdress.

"I used to love you in that," he murmured.

His mouth was so close to her ear, the movement of his lips touched her as pure heat. She glanced down and saw his leg locked into a bend, taking the strain of his effort to lower his body to her height. His tanned shin gleamed along the bone to his ankle.

"You forgot to dry your back," he said, wiping away a droplet with a finger slipped inside the towel. She was still holding the sleeve of the shirtdress as the finger inched along her back, then dipped under her arm. It moved as if on cruise control, maintaining its speed despite the ascent even as it climbed her breast. When it reached the peak, it slid down and tapped three times on her nipple. "Can I come in?" Mark said in a funny voice.

She let go of the dress and made a noise that was not a word. His mouth was on the back of her neck. With her free hand, she tried to bolster the place where the towel was fastened, but his hand caught hers first, and the towel slid down. It clung to the curve of her bottom till he retracted his hips to give it free passage to the floor. It had been such a long time.

She heard him spit and lick, then a hand reached round, and he began to soak her left nipple, his saliva shining down her stomach like a snail's trail, until his signet ring snagged on the fringe of her pubic hair. She turned into him, reaching for a body to hide inside, wanting him to be where she could see him, but he gripped her wrists and took a step back. "Relax," he soothed her. "You're going to enjoy this."

He bent her arms behind her back and held them there, as if his hands were cuffs. Dream on, Mark. Don't you know it's the other way round, and as soon as I'm done, you're out of here. She watched the top of his head descend. It bobbed around her belly button while his tongue fought its way through the overgrowth of her bikini line. She had not kept on top of things, and a sort of rewilding had gone on. She had slept for a hundred years, and he was scything through the forest of thorns. He freed her wrists, and his hands slid down to her hips.

She reached for his hair while his tongue pushed up inside her, but there was no hair to grab, only hard scalp. The way her hand idled there, coaxing the top of his head, she had the sensation she was petting a dog. She sucked up the last of the wine and shifted her feet a little wider. Mark's forehead wrinkled, his eyebrows laboring upward. He was wondering how he was doing, how much longer he had to stay there for. As long as I want, Marky. A flurry of arrhythmic clapping out on the street pulled her gaze to the window: a group of kids ambling home from school. She clapped both hands on the sides of Mark's head, practically boxing his ears, and thrust down. Whose house is it now, eh?

When he finally got up off his knees, his lips and chin glistened, and she smirked because she had left her mark on him and the sight of it, of his subordination, thrilled her.

"Come here, you!" He snatched the empty glass from her hand so the base clipped her fingers, and tossed it out the open window. His hands reached behind her and inside her thighs, and she felt her feet leave the floor.

"Put me down," she told him. When he did not, she bent her mouth to his neck and bit him.

"Hey," he said, dropping her on the bed in surprise. "No nasty stuff. OK?"

She clasped his neck with both hands and threw her legs up. He was broader than she remembered, but she hooked her feet around his back and latched her ankles. Try getting out of that one, Marky. His back rocked, obeying the downward kick of her heels. He was still wearing his underwear, and she could see, as his backside rose and dipped, rose and dipped, a fragment of his old bluechecked boxers. He was the same Mark as ever. And she was the one who had changed.

HE WAS STROKING her hair when she woke. "I hope you don't mind," he said. "I didn't want to leave you."

"It's a bit late for that," she said, propping herself on an elbow. "What the fuck are you doing here?"

Mark looked astounded. "You don't mean right now, I take it?" he said. "Because obviously I'm here having made love to you and having wanted to hang around to see you afterward."

She snorted. "I think you'll find it was the other way round. Let's cut to the chase, shall we? What are you doing in my house?"

"I already told you," he said. "Eric was worried."

"But you haven't told me what he said. Whether Michelle called the police, what they plan to do. Whether they blame me. I need to know."

Mark reached behind him for another pillow and plumped it under his head. "As I understand it," he said calmly, "it's perfectly straightforward. A fox took the baby. The baby is OK. I don't think anyone—not Eric, not Michelle, not the police, and certainly not you—needs to hunt around for alternative explanations. Do you understand what I'm saying?" He rolled toward her and kneaded her tummy playfully. "You saved the baby!" He grabbed her hand and flopped it in the air in triumph. "You found her and kept her safe!"

She snatched her hand back. "Is that what Eric said?"

"Eric and I have had a long conversation, and these are the facts as best we can establish them."

"What the hell does that mean? And what does Michelle think?"

"Michelle is out of consideration here. She has postnatal depression. She'll be OK."

"Oh," she said. "I thought that might be it. Poor Flora. Poor . . . them. But, I mean, does she believe that the fox did it?"

He ignored her question—or perhaps he thought he was answering it—and said, "Sometimes, Mary, people need to agree a way to tell a story for everyone's benefit. Do you understand? Relax. Act normal. It was pretty stupid to run away. It made you look guilty. But no one thinks you're guilty! Just—don't do it again! OK?"

"So let me get this straight," she said slowly. "Eric called you because he couldn't reach me. This alerted you to the possibility that I was in trouble?"

"Yes, but I already knew something was wrong," he said. "Monday morning and you hadn't got ready for work."

"What do you mean, hadn't got ready for work?"

"No big deal. Only that normally you get ready, and today you didn't. Did you?"

"How would you know?"

"That's the next thing. Now. Stay calm." He reached for her hand again. "I live over the back, on Ashland Road. I thought it would freak you out if you knew. I did want to tell you. Well, did want to show you. I don't make a habit of spying on you, if that's what you're wondering. I just noticed that you didn't appear in the window this morning. We usually brush our teeth at the same time."

"What?"

"Can we focus on the important things, Mary? There's a lot to get through. So, first things first. The baby is OK."

"I know that."

"Eric has reported the incident—the fox incident, I mean—to the police and the council. And he's hired what he calls an eradication professional."

She bit her lip. "I know that too."

"You don't know the best part," he said, patting her hip. "I gave you an alibi."

"An alibi?"

"I told them you were with me last night, that you found Flora when you went home. I think they were a bit surprised to hear we were back together."

"So they really thought I did it?"

"But I've fixed it for you. It's genius, Mary. It's literally the perfect alibi. Here's your way out of this mess. My flat's over the back, you see. It's got a gate to the woods. You got there without anyone seeing you. We hooked up after the barbecue on Saturday. Thanks so much, Eric and Michelle, for making it happen. Are you following me?"

She nodded.

"Last night you came to find me. You should have seen their faces."

"Which house?" she said.

"You're missing the point, Mary. I know what you're thinking, but it's not like that."

"Which house?"

"The one behind yours. Top flat. I can show you from the spare room. I know it's weird. I almost didn't take it, thinking it was too weird. But the location is great. It's only . . . Well, I'm hoping it's only temporary."

"I knew it!"

He started drawing down her flank with a finger.

"Do you see," he said, "how things need to go if we are to keep Eric and Michelle off your back? I am your alibi. I am your way out of this mess. We stick together."

She did see. "Aren't you going to ask me if I did it?" she said.

"Nope. I'm . . . *we*—are going to make love again, and then I'm going to fix you something to eat."

It was night in Mary's dream. She dreamt she was walking down Michelle and Eric's lawn to the back of their house, past the giant barbecue, the squatting bulldog lamp. She dreamt she climbed the stairs and found Flora in her cot, and that she took her, then changed her mind at her back step and laid the baby there instead.

When she woke, she dressed and followed the smell of melting butter downstairs. Mark was at the oven, shaking a frying pan. Mary was fairly certain that when she woke for the first time today her kitchen had not contained the ingredients for an omelet. Outside, the sky was beginning to deepen. The oven said 21:13, but day and night were all one thing now. It was Monday when she woke this morning. When she woke before that, it was Monday too. It had been Monday for such a long time.

He turned to her and smiled. "Baby, you're up. Look, there's something I want to say."

She made to interject, but he lifted his hand for silence. "Let me speak. Please? The last few months I haven't stopped thinking about you. I've turned over all our arguments, the worst ones, all the things that went wrong. I have changed." One bicep twitched, but he wished her to understand that he meant more than that. "I don't want kids . . ." When he saw she was about to interrupt, he danced across to the sink and began to open and shut the cupboard with a grin. "Look, Mary! I was such a git about that. But see? No child lock!"

A corner of Mary's mouth lifted. In that swinging door she saw their past and present selves flip. They were as far apart as they had always been, just in opposite places.

He looked relieved when he saw her smile. "New Year's Day,

though, Mary," he said with a wince. "We have to promise never to go there again."

"I'm not going there again. *There* is always in my head—the things you said."

His eyes widened, but he clamped his lips together. "I'm sorry," he said eventually. He waited for her to speak, and when she let the silence stretch, he asked, "Aren't you going to say anything to me?"

She shrugged. He had only been here a few hours, and already her words were locked inside her mouth again. The loss of control, the violence of that argument, obliterated everything she might say.

Mark frowned and checked his reflection in the window. "You have got to be joking!" he said and leapt to the door with the omelet pan.

"What are you doing?" she shouted after him. But he was already outside.

"Here, boy! Here, boy!" he called softly. He was crouching at the edge of the lawn, one hand in the grass to steady himself, the other extending the pan.

"Mary, don't move," he whispered. "I want to see how close it will come."

He, her fox, was standing on the lawn in front of the shed, half formed in the half-light. She sensed his puzzlement in the tension of his body.

"I thought that was my dinner!" she hissed.

"Ssshhh. I'll make another one. Here, boy. Come to Uncle Mark."

She shook her head vigorously, but her fox took a step toward the eggs. Mark slowly unfurled a leg from his crouch. What was he going to do—bludgeon him with the fryer? Mary cast frantically around the patio. Sorry, Mr. Frog, she thought, as she kicked the watering can to the concrete with a clatter. "Sorry," she told Mark. "I didn't see it."

When they looked down the garden again, the fox had vanished.

IN THE LOUNGE, Mark put the plates on the table. Two chairs had miraculously appeared—from upstairs or his flat. "Do you know what I want?" he said. "I want us to sit here and look out the window, just like we did when we first moved in. Remember? Hello!" He bent under the table. "What are you doing there?" he said, straightening the hen doorstop's gingham comb. "This chicken seems to have taken 'free-range' a bit too literally." He ruffled the tail feathers and sniffed. "Phew! No offense, but it could do with a wash." He toed the hen to the door. "I always thought you hated that doorstop. It means so much to me that you kept it. Soppy thing."

"I feel bad for the fox," she said to this excessively doting Mark, whom she planned to let wash up. Whether it was the sight of him out there, a shadow riffling the fringes of her garden, less substantial-seeming than before; or whether it was a sense that this pact of Mark and Eric's had created a sort of ghost fox, a thing they agreed upon that was not really what he was . . . a pretext, a cover-up for Michelle and for her, for the supposedly weak women they thought they needed to protect: for some reason, the events of the day gave her the feeling that he was beginning to fade. She felt desperate to talk about him, as if talking about him would give him substance.

"He likes eggs, you know," she said sadly.

"Who?"

"The fox. There's a tree. It's got a hollow in the trunk, with eggs in it." Mark raised an eyebrow, so she carried on. "He would probably love omelet."

"Bizarre," Mark said, glancing outside again. "Jesus Christ!"

"What?" she said as he raced to the back door, but by the time she reached the kitchen, he was already returning.

"It's gone. I can't believe it came back. Why would it do that? What's its problem?"

He was defiant and brave and alive, and no eradicator was going to outsmart him, that was why. "I found the eggs yesterday," she said, to change the subject. "When I went for my walk."

He looked at her, concerned. They had retaken their seats. "You went for your walk today, Mary."

"Today, then. Nestled in this hollow."

"Well, that makes sense. That someone's feeding them." He thought about her story for a moment. When he finished swallowing, he asked, "Which tree?"

She shrugged again. "Big oak at the eastern end. Near the alley."

He looked out of the window again. "I don't fucking believe it," he said. He walked to the window and laid a fist on the wrinkled pane. "It's watching me from the shed."

She went to join him, and her fox's tail lifted as he registered the sight of her with Mark. She knew he would be worried about her, but she hoped he could see how far she had come with him, how well he was saving her.

"All right. What do you want?" Mark said, staring ahead. And then, because it was irrational to hold a conversation with a fox, he turned to Mary. "I don't understand. I tell it to leave. It leaves. Then it comes back. It goes, comes back, goes, comes back. Why? Why is it so fucking insubordinate? It's playing some kind of psychological game with me. Loitering out there like a *stalker*!" On that word, he thumped the glass.

"No, Mark," she shouted, running her fingers down the wrinkle to feel for damage. "That's my window! And this is my house. You have to calm down, or leave." Her fox stayed put; ears, snout, tail, all his extremities stilled. He was watching to see what Mark would do next. In the dusk her own face glowed back from the glass, next to Mark's glowering fury, and she knew that Mark would see any sign she made. So she waited till he stormed out of the room and the back door slammed before she lifted her palm to the window and shut one eye, to let her fox know that she was with him. With him in the way that counted. He vanished over the wall, and she watched her former fiancé, she supposed she should call him that, walk slowly to the house, turning every few steps to check he wasn't being followed.

"You know where we'll be in ten years?" he said when they finally sat back at the table. "Eating our tea in a hole out there while they make themselves at home inside. We need to fill our plant pot with stones again. By the way, you're right about someone living next door. He's out there, calling his dog." He put on a creepy whisper. "Roxy, Roxy."

"I know I'm right. But why does everyone hate foxes?" she said. "At least they look you straight in the eye. Unlike squirrels. Squirrels turn their heads in order to look at you sideways."

Mark raised an eyebrow. "There's dozens of them out there. How long till they realize that we're more scared of them than they are of us? You just saw that huge thing in the garden. The one at the barbecue was even bigger. And they don't know when to stop. Yesterday Eric had to bury the remains of their cat, and he said that he's already had to rebury it. And the second time there was less of it. That's how civilized they are."

"You don't know that's a fox," she said. "And anyway, there aren't dozens. I only see one."

"You probably think you're seeing one, but really there's loads."

"Or you think you're seeing loads, but there's one, and all this fuss is for nothing."

"All right, then. What does the one look like?"

She thought about this. "Well. His coat is reddish brown. Redder in the sunlight. There's a white tip at the end of his tail. His shins are black. One, the front left, has a white rib on it. He has a broad face, a white chest . . . He's big. Look. The point is. I could describe you like this—close-cropped hair, blue eyes, six foot one, muscular." He smiled when she said "muscular"; until then she had given no indication that she'd noticed. "But there are loads of men who answer that description. All I know is, when I see him, I know him. Anyway, I don't think the fox could have done it," she said. "I wish I hadn't said I'd seen him. Do you know what I think? I think Michelle did it."

Mark rubbed his eyes. He had his own ideas about what had happened. "All things are possible," he said, beginning to clear the plates.

"Think about it," she called as he headed to the kitchen. "Were there any signs of a fox in the house?"

For a while she listened to the dutiful clatter of the washing-up, the scrape and ping of the bin. When he returned, he had something on his mind. "Hey. This has been bugging me," he said, stroking the back of his head. "You haven't mentioned my hair. What do you think? Do you like it?"

"Yes, though I didn't know you had a birthmark."

He laughed in surprise. "Do I? My mum always said I had one when I was born, and then I guess my hair grew. Does it show?"

She pushed back her chair and stood. "Turn around," she said. "Bend your knees." He put his hands on his thighs to steady himself. "So there are a few marks. Here." Mary placed her little finger on the smallest. "One." Her ring finger settled into the next blotch. "Two." Without straining, each digit tapped a stain. "Three, four." Then her wrist rested on the largest mark. Her hand fit so perfectly, it could have made the print. She drummed her fingers on the back of Mark's head. She could handle him.

CHAPTER FIFTEEN

The next morning, Mark was already showered when the light broke around the edge of the blind and woke Mary. She watched him through slitted eyes, his head bowed over his shirt buttons, pale blue cotton stuck to his shoulders where he had dried in a hurry. He fastened each cuff, then busied himself at the shelf that used to be his. She heard the clunk of glass on wood; then the cologne's drift of sandalwood began to engulf her. Maybe Mark heard her sniffing, and that's how he knew she was awake, because he turned to face her with a grin. He was holding the little wooden puzzle. "Less than a minute," he said, tossing and catching it lightly. "Still got my touch. God, it's so nice to find some of my old stuff here. Like you knew I'd be back. Like you wanted me back." Time and again Mary had thought the same. Even two months ago the thought had been a comfort, but hearing the words in Mark's voice struck her as an enormous trespass.

"Mark," she said. "This isn't right."

Less than twenty-four hours since she found him in her kitchen, he appeared to have moved in. He came and went with his old keys.

He had mown the lawn, shopped, tidied, begun to rearrange cupboards. The truth was, she had needed Mark, needed his negotiations with Eric to erase the suspicion that she might in some part be responsible for Flora's . . . misadventure. But all the while Mark was here in her house, her fox was living in exile. And so was she, from the life she wanted, the one that would deliver on the happy promise of those days before her neighbors' barbecue, when she felt she was in a relationship that was going somewhere. She shut her eyes—just to see in her lids the color of his fur.

"I need you to leave," she said. "I mean, have some breakfast, but, you know, don't stay here, today, tonight, tomorrow."

Mark turned from her and rested both hands on his old wardrobe. After a moment he tilted his head sideways and stiffened, and this minute seemed to last forever, while he contemplated the long streaks of coffee, placed a hand at the top of the stain and stroked his fingers down till the runnels of their old fight ran dry. The action seemed to mollify him. He replaced his hands on the wardrobe and bowed to the door in an odd upright prayer. Then he lifted his head and smacked it hard on the wood.

"Mark! Stop it!" she cried as he tipped his head back for a second crack. "Please!"

He stayed perfectly still. Only his shoulders moved, rising gently with a long intake of breath, then slowly sinking, before he faced her calmly. "Last night, when we talked in the kitchen, I thought that was us getting back together. Why did you let me think that? Jesus, I came here to take care of you, Mary. To keep the house running. Do all the boring stuff while you put your strength into getting better. I thought . . . I think you need that."

"But there's nothing wrong with me," she said. "I'm just exhausted, that's all. And anxious. I've seen the doctor," she said quietly. "I need to rest, give myself time. I'm loads better already."

"This new boyfriend of yours," he said. "I mean, where is he? If he's so special, why isn't he here looking after you?"

There was not much Mary could say to that. He was not here because Mark was here. She gave a shrug and watched Mark walk slowly to the blind. He whirred it upward, releasing an angry buzz. Her poor fat fly had been woken again. And then the whirring halted. Mark flapped the fly toward the open air, and she thought, as the buzzing faded, how typical that was. The way his anger transformed itself into practicality. "Wow. This will interest you," he said warmly. "Come and look."

It's happened, she thought. The worst has happened. And I'm going to have to see it here with Mark. She steeled herself against the sight, so that while one foot, then the other moved, she began to picture her poor fox, his body in the road. He would be outside her house. Of course he would, because . . . "Oh my God!" she said, when she reached the window and finally saw, rising out of Michelle and Eric's hedge, the sparkling *For Sale* board.

"I wonder what they put it on for," he said.

After Mary had showered and dressed, she crept downstairs. The rucksack had gone from the hall, and as she rounded the banister, she saw it in the kitchen, on Mark's back. His breakfast bowl was already slippery with suds on the draining board. But he was busy on his phone, and when her presence did not distract him, she felt relieved he had chosen to make this easy. Then she got close enough to see that the phone in his hand was hers.

"Give that to me!" she cried. She tried to grab the mobile, but he shielded the screen with his half-turned body. "Give it!"

"You've got fourteen missed calls. Nine from me yesterday," he said bitterly. "Three questions, OK? Give me three questions. I won't ask more. I promise."

"What are you talking about? Don't be stupid. Give me the phone."

He held it behind his back. "One, who is he? Two . . . Two, what does he do? Is he better looking than me? OK, if you don't want to tell me, let me guess."

"Give it back, Mark," she yelled. Her right hand curled into a fist.

"What car does he drive? Where does he live?" He was nodding his head at every question. "And why isn't he here when you need him? That's what I keep coming back to. Where is he?" His face brightened. "I mean, there were only my clothes in the wardrobe," he said, then countered himself. "But someone's been using my after-shave."

"Now!" she said, mauling his hand.

He slammed the phone on the worktop. "It's pointless anyway. You've deleted everything."

"And your keys."

Mark rooted around in his pocket and lobbed them next to the phone. "Don't you keep them on the little orange ribbon?" she said.

He looked at her, staggered. "The ribbon's mine. You gave it to me when we moved in. Anyway, it's at home. If you want it, you'll have to wait till I see you next." A tear rolled down his cheek and splattered on the lino. She touched his arm non-committally.

"Change your mind," he said, reaching around her waist. "I'll take the day off work again. I'll cook for you."

She shook her head and unbolted the back door for him, wondering if the front door would ever be the main door again.

"I lost one a bit like this," Mark said, picking up the shoe from the sill. "Yesterday, when I saw it, I thought you somehow knew that and kept it for me. I obviously got that wrong. Deluded fuckwit that I am. What is all this junk anyway? I have to say, I am struggling to understand the mind-set of someone who keeps a filthy shoe on a window ledge."

"How do you lose a shoe?" she said, dismissing his jibe.

"It was nicked from my fire escape by some idiot mindless enough to take only one. Mine was brand new. Unlike this," he said, putting it back.

"Take it," she said. "See if it matches."

"Mine were blue."

"This one was blue!" she said triumphantly. "Have you lost anything else? Boxers?"

Mark shook his head, baffled. "I've tried to help you, Mary, but you're probably a bit beyond my reach." He was turning to go. "Er, stay indoors, yeah?" he said, seeing her move to follow him. He nodded toward Eric and Michelle's. "For your own sake. Keep a low profile for a couple of days."

With Mark strolling through it, the garden looked unsettlingly different. He kicked at a dandelion clock the mower had missed, and the seeds sprayed in the sun like sparks from a bonfire. In the middle of the lawn, he stopped. Mary shrank back into the door frame. He was checking that she had obeyed him. He looked at each rear window in turn, and when he saw she wasn't there, set off again. She lost him briefly, in the blind spot made by the house wall.

Before the shed, Mark bent to one knee. The rucksack slid off his shoulder and landed on the grass. Mary heard a dim, metallic jangle. She was running down the garden properly then: even in the shade of the lime, the thing had a nasty glint.

Mark picked up his bag and swung it over his shoulder, and when he saw her coming, he adjusted his posture to relaxed and let her reach him. The thing was an unfriendly hutch. A hutch without the wooden bits. He gave her no chance to ask. He said, "I should have mentioned the trap, but I didn't want to worry you."

"Trap? You've got to be kidding!"

He glanced up at Michelle and Eric's closed curtains. "See." He knelt and made his fingers walk along the grass. "Here comes a fox.

Sniffs something nice. A paw treads here, and down goes the gate. Only it hasn't done that, has it?" He rattled the door with a frown. "I have serious doubts this is going to work."

"Who the hell put it in my garden?"

"Eric's man. The Fox Fixer. Er . . . Andy. He was here yesterday, while you were sleep—" He interrupted himself. "Eric said you knew about this. Michelle cleared it with you?"

"I knew someone was coming to look, but no one said anything about traps. I'm not having a trap in my garden. Ugh! What's that?"

"Dog food. That's Andy's. And an egg. I've just put that there." He managed a grin. "After what you said last night, I thought they might appreciate an egg."

"It can't stay here. You'll have to take it away."

Mark glanced again next door. His top and bottom lips were oddly offset, and the misalignment gave the appearance of anger only partially contained. "I'm not taking it anywhere," he said equably. "The fact is, I persuaded them to try the traps because a nonviolent solution seemed important to you. Michelle was all for ordering the hit. Andy can kill twenty in a night."

"But they don't have permission!"

"Andy does. He gets police clearance."

"Well, what about permission from neighbors?"

Mark laughed. "They're not pets, Mary. Look, I've got to get to work. If you want traps removed, you'll have to ask your boyfriend to do it. In fact . . . as a friend, Mary, I think you should ask him to come and stay with you."

"He's coming later," she said, leaning across Mark to activate the door of the trap. "OK. I see how you do it. Where are the others?"

"It would be good to think you might put some food in your fridge, or keep the house tidy."

She gave a big sigh. "You said 'traps.' There's more than one, isn't there?"

"I don't know. Andy set them." He rubbed at his forehead. He was such a bad liar.

"I thought you were there too."

"Only for a bit when Eric was busy with the kids. Look, I've got to go now. I'm already late."

"What will they do if they catch him?"

"Him? You mean the foxes?" He shrugged. "Some kind of humane disposal?"

MARY NEEDED A watching place. She made for the house but then swerved toward the Tangle Wood fence. The shed, the overhanging lime branches, meant that from this angle she had no way of seeing the crumbling rear wall Mark had just jumped off, and Mark had no way of seeing her. She sidled along the fence to the gap beside her shed. He had escaped this way often enough, so why shouldn't she? The space was so tight, the splintery slats pressed against her cheek and knees, while the shed pinched her back, and her hands patted desperately for a way out. She could scarcely believe it when her fingers, instead of hitting the fence, disappeared through it. The panel stopped. She had found his hidden doorway, and it was just large enough to squeeze through.

Next door the grass had grown as tall as grass could. It feathered at the tips into hundreds of little ears, which reminded Mary that she needed to keep very quiet. She knelt and the little ears tickled her shoulders. Rafael's scent clung to the stalks, and the greenery was thick with his musky promise. She sat back on her heels and swallowed down a strong dose of fox. From here, two yellowing trails cut diagonally through the garden. They made the shape of an arrow at whose apex she crouched. One path led to the house, one to the woods.

Mary chose the second. Calluses had begun to form on her hands, and thick gray skin crinkled the underneath of her knees, so she padded along without great discomfort. Each tread disturbed a rich swarm of musk. The Tangle Wood garden went on forever. The long grass spilled into the woods; the woods spilled into the garden. There was no wall. Eventually, something square and solid emerged from the grass a little way off. As she approached, Mary saw an old chest of drawers had been dumped and brambles grown up around it. While she paused in its cover to work out her route, she heard a sigh and, peering around her shelter, caught a glimpse of pale blue shirting.

Mark had gone no further than the other side of her wall. And now she understood why. Although he faced her, he was visible only from the waist up, his lower body obscured by a second trap. They had put this one directly behind her shed! Now she understood his insistence that she stay indoors. She was not meant to find these. The little vertical door remained in the open position and next to it lay the cause of Mark's frown: a half-eaten rat.

She pulled her head in sharply and bunched her hair out of the way as Mark stood and looked around, shielding his eyes from the shafts of sun that slit through the canopy. At last he turned, his red backpack bobbing toward Ashland Road, his road, as she now knew it to be, and the clearing. She waited and, after a while, Mark doubled back, then veered toward the far end of the woods. When the greenery covered him, she slipped out. The second trap was stiffer than the one she had closed in her back garden, but after several tries, she joggled it shut.

She moved quickly to the clearing, staying low behind the nettles, and found the third trap, which they had left, rather unimaginatively, next to his hole. This time the mechanism slid shut with no resistance, and she was thinking how easy it had been, wondering how many more traps she would need to disarm, when a crow cawed overhead, clearly intending to give her away. She ducked into the canopy of the hazel and hid behind its trunk, just as Mark began to rematerialize from the greenery. Mary tucked in her head and waited as his footsteps crackled toward her. One espadrille loomed so close she could see the canvas faded over Mark's big toe, a thread of frayed rope, a trodden heel. How long she stayed there she had no idea. Eventually, the footsteps faded into a thin crunch, a sound like snail shells breaking. Then the catch on a wrought-iron gate. And still Mary waited.

Long minutes passed before she dared to crawl out.

It took a while to spot the fourth trap at the far end of the woods because someone had buried it beneath a mound of leaves. As she drew close, she started at the frantic plink-plink of claws on metal. A dull, dread ache spread through her arms. Heavily she pulled a thick branch from the mound. She had to be quick. She yanked at sticks. Leaves tore in her panicked hands, and then through the foliage she caught a flash of ginger. Any minute Mark would return with the Fox Fixer. Or alone, which would be worse. Because this was the kind of glory he preferred not to share. Mary checked behind her. Must free Flight. Seconds disappearing. The crow cawing. She grabbed at the branches that jagged in the trap's mesh. She tugged the largest free and jumped back in fright as Neville's cat leapt at the side of the cage, his teeth slitting out of the gaps.

CHAPTER SIXTEEN

It was a still afternoon. A magpie flew down from his lookout at the top of a sycamore and landed with a clack on Mary's kitchen roof. The bird began to walk with a nod and a shuffle of tail feathers, a spill of emerald ink slicking his wings. He scritch-scratched down the tiles to the gutter, into which he directed a disdainful peck. Still no rain. Then he swooped to the laurel, snaffled a bug from the glossy leaves, and caught sight of himself in Mary's kitchen window.

Well, now, this must be what normal life felt like, Mary thought, though it felt much better than anything she had previously thought of as normal. For the third time, she popped the door of the fridge. The snug of chicken breasts that strained against their plastic sheaths, the scrolls of fresh pasta, prime cuts of beef, game burgers, and artisan venison sausages, tower of packaged berries, and stacked cartons of milk, all individually pleased her. But what really amazed her, the sight she kept opening the fridge to admire, was its collective fullness. Both drawers of the freezer were also rammed. And still she experienced a small crease of anxiety: Was there enough?

She had laughed when the cashier announced in a bored voice,

"£355.28." Far from boring, the amount was triple anything she and Mark had spent on a single shop, and the cost proved her total abandonment to her decision. It was a vindication to wheel the trolley outside and realize that the only way to get all the bags home was in a taxi. More money! The day had been wonderfully expensive, and the house, bursting with sunshine, seemed to ripple with the freshness of the experience. A breeze came down the hall through the open door, picked up the hopeful scent of rose from the vase on the sill. She was so excited, she lifted her fox's magic egg again, and her heart fluttered at its lightness. That was how she felt too.

In the seven hours since Mark had left, Mary had shopped, vacuumed the ground floor, tucked her gran's blanket over the sofa, pummeled the cushions, removed breakables from low shelves, undone Mark's changes to her kitchen cupboards. She had almost forgotten the locksmith, when he called from the hall to say he was done; it was in the nature of Mark's practicality to have made a copy of his house keys. Mary settled up, then double-locked the front door. The heavy new levers shifted into place with a satisfying clunk. It was twelve minutes past three. She had approximately two hours in which to ready her home and herself.

In January, when Mark moved out, Mary had felt too depressed to tidy. Then, as the house became messier, she felt too late to tidy. But today she was wiping, rinsing, and sucking away all trace of him. After months of wondering how to find it, here was her new start. She hummed along with the drone of the vacuum, nozzling the skirting boards of the study, marveling at the way each task, once completed, supplied energy for the next.

After she had tidied the desk, Mary sat on the floor and began to shelve the books from the boxes that she had halfheartedly filled at Mark's insistence, back when he'd been concerned by her failure to pack. (This was before she told him about the inheritance.) As a promise to her future self, she slid *Pride and Prejudice* into the top

left-hand corner. One day, when there was time, she would alpha-
betize. Then she lugged the vacuum to her bedroom. Dust and coins
and buttons rattled up the hose. When she was done, she stuffed
Mark's leftover shirts into a bin liner, along with the wooden puzzle.
Her eye fell on the bottle of cologne.

The clothes were going, so the cologne should go too. She picked
it up, and the liquid slunk into an amber triangle in one corner. She
had the feeling that this whole story of Mary and Mark would
finish only when she reached the end of the bottle. With her wrist
laid over its neck, she flipped the flask and took the draught, with her
eyes shut, in the spirit of an injection. The fluid scarcely covered the
glass base. This thing was nearly over.

At the back of the house, she drew the blinds. Then she quickly
showered and fetched her navy dress. He had seen it before, but that
was actually a nice thought. She put it on and, for the first time in a
fortnight, checked herself in the mirror. How thin she looked! As she
stood there, the discovery hit her twice, the second time because she
realized what a bad state she had been in not to have noticed sooner.
Well, that was all about to change, she thought, picturing the fridge
and tightening the waist tie behind her back. The action produced
a crackle in one of the pockets, and, when she investigated, she found
a thin stiff leaf, the color of autumn. It took Mary a moment to
remember how it had got there, that she had picked it up from her
bedroom floor the night she'd left her house open, and she smiled at
the memory of that evening, the babysitting, the airy way her home
had smelt when she walked inside. It cheered her to think that the
two of them had a history, as well as a future.

It was half past five when she went down to the kitchen and
flicked the heat under a pan with a knob of butter. She sliced onions
as finely as crisps, according to the recipe in her *Basic Italian Cooking*, and let them soften. She grated Parmesan, chopped ham, then
began to crack the eggs. At number eight, she hovered over the bowl,

suddenly uncertain that the recipe would work on this scale. It was perfectly normal to be nervous, she soothed herself. This was the first time she had cooked for him. She cracked the last five eggs into the slop of yellow blobs. He would want for nothing.

An odor of buttery onions began to seep from the edges of the pan lid. The late sun streaming through the back window gave the steam the appearance of a thin cloud as it wafted its news out of the door and into the garden. Mary stepped back to take in the room's productive haze, and the notes of a made-up tune came to her. She started to sing. Something strange was happening. The place was beginning to feel like home.

She had no way to tell him what time to arrive, but she knew he would come. In the lounge she puzzled over the table, unsure how far to go. Finally, she set down Granny Joan's place mats. They were printed with pictures of grouse, which she figured he would appreciate. She lit Mark's candle on the mantelpiece and deliberated over cutlery before laying two places, mainly for symmetry. And then the alarm sounded, summoning her to the oven, just as a movement in the window caught her eye, and she saw that he had already arrived and was watching the house from the shed, no doubt smelling—

EGGS! his tail said, as it swirled in the air.

She stepped onto the patio at the same time as he snapped into a run, and in a second they stood before each other. "Darling! You came!" she whispered—she did not want Eric or Michelle to hear. "I knew you would! And this time, I'm not letting you go."

She skipped into the kitchen. "Dinner's almost ready. I was just letting it stand." His right ear flickered, detecting the new brightness in her voice, but he faltered on the step, his tail an upward curve. Mary tightened her ponytail, tipped her head to show him the dark yes inside her ears, but he still delayed. His hesitation bewildered her. At last she gave a relieved chuckle. "Ah, don't worry about him! He's gone. And he's not coming back."

Fox trotted inside, and she closed the door behind him.

"How hungry are you?" Mary asked as she halved the omelet and slid the smaller piece onto her own plate. The splintering sound she heard was the scratch of his forepaws on the worktop, gouging the pine while his ears stiffened into points. This was why kitchens had breakfast bars, she thought. To make cooking sociable. "It's frittata," she told him. "Like omelet, but more special." A feeling of immense emotional prosperity surged in her as she walked down the hall with the plates, his claws click-clacking at her heels.

EGGS.

"We're in here," she said. But when she entered the lounge, perhaps because she wanted to put herself in his place, a new worry hit her. The room smelt overpoweringly of chemical lemon and the musty blowback of the vacuum. She rested the plates on Granny Joan's mats and went to raise the sash, unlocking the safety catch in order to lift it right up. The warped pane whisked a few dried leaves into its vortex, and she gasped. "Oh no! Sorry, Mr. Spider." His web clung to the frame in sticky strings. "Can you mend it?" The poor fellow had lived there for weeks.

She turned to Fox, who stood sentry-like in the middle of the rug. "I'll bring some water."

The door sloped closed behind her and softly rebounded as if it had heard an enemy and jumped back.

He followed the movement with his muzzle, but it fizzed with astringent vapor. The sound of water in another part of the cave bent back his EGGS ear. He tried to take in the new EGGS information while nosing for old. The den was different. He whiskered the fleece on the sofa, swept a crease with his tongue for the papery wings of a clothes moth, a Beetle leg. The matted old sheep fleece he used to.

Here. A trace. He rubbed his body in the place to make his stale tracks fresh tracks.

Mary came in with the water.

"Oh good, you found the blanket," she said. "I hoped that would make you feel at home." She toed the hen doorstop back into place and smiled as he cocked his head at it. "I hate that thing. I was going to chuck it out, but then I remembered how much you liked it. Now, as Granny Joan used to say, *Mia casa es tu casa.* You know. Everything is the same as before. Only better. Relax." He stepped toward the foot of the table, the leg of the chair. "All those legs. What creature is this, eh?" she said. He waited uncertainly. Watching him wasn't going to put him at ease, so she stepped onto her own chair with both feet, then lowered herself into a crouch, a kneel, and finally sat. The thicker fur of his brow scrunched a little, but the demonstration served its purpose because in a leap he was on the chair where Mark had sat the night before, circling furiously, his claws tapping at the wooden seat as if they were punching in some sort of entry code. When he finally landed his brush, he opened his mouth, and his tongue fell on the table.

He probed the plate, the knife, the fork with his muzzle. She had expected him to dive straight in, but all the stainless steel seemed to inhibit him. "That's just for decoration," she explained, seeing now what idiocy it was to have put out cutlery. She pushed her own aside and grabbed the omelet with both hands. "*Buon appetito,*" she said, biting off a chunk. "Mmm. Seven out of ten. It could have done with more cheese, but it's not bad. Not bad at all!"

She rolled her eyes as Eric shouted next door. "Someone's in trouble," she said, feeling smug. Fox's snout drummed the rim of the plate on the wood, banging and clattering and shoving it around as if he were teasing prey. Finally, he tilted his head, opened his jaws, and clacked his fangs against the china. She reached over, meaning to slide the omelet onto the table, but he shook the plate so vigorously that the china crashed one way and the omelet flew the other, and this time he pounced. His tongue scooped, and he jerked his head to toss the frittata further back into his mouth. Several smaller lumps broke off and fell to the table, and he washed them into his jaws with his tongue. He was already licking his lips while Mary took her second bite. She broke her own dinner in two and pushed the larger piece across the table. It vanished in seconds. Then he sat there, his beautiful white chest rising and falling, calmly waiting for her to finish, making no attempt to rush her or to get down, and she thought again how polite, how well brought up, he was.

"I wish I knew more about you," she said.

Silence.

"Where you grew up, your family . . ."

He bent an ear to her while his muzzle examined the space in front of him for overlooked morsels.

Well, what could he say? That he was one of several boys, the eldest, largest, and his mother's favorite. That he was first to learn to hunt and did all he could to help her with the chores. The fact was, Mary knew what sort of child he had been because she saw what sort of an adult he was. She edged her hand toward him. He watched its slow approach across the table with swaying muzzle, ears tapered to his head, claws extended. At last Mary's fingers tweaked the soft hairs that broke over his toes. His claws retracted, a gesture of invitation which she answered by lowering her fingers until the full weight of her hand lay on his paw. He did not flinch even as she squeezed.

WHEN MARY RETURNED from taking out the plates, Fox—the name had grown on her and now sounded appropriate and respectful rather than abrupt—stood at the back window with his forepaws on the sill. A shaft of late sun lit the top of his head, edging the summit of his ears in soft gold. "That's where I first saw you,"

she said, going to join him. "Do you remember?" His outline that
day blazed in her memory in russet ink. She had been so scared of
him, not understanding, as she did now, that if she shared her world
with him, her world would grow. For weeks she had wondered what
he had come for, but tonight, standing beside him, alive to each nervous leaf, the tireless chit-chat of the wrens in the laurel, everything seemed so clear. The messenger and the message were the same
thing. He had brought her comfort, company, happiness, an imaginable future. He was a kind of faith, and the answer, like that fox-
face sign in her old school maths book ∵ was just *because.*

He flopped his tongue onto the sash cord and scooped up
the spider. "Oh no! Was that really necessary?" she cried. After all
those eggs, he surely could have done without a spider. "Look, let's
make ourselves comfortable," she suggested. She led the way to the
lounge end of the room, closed the wooden shutters, patted the sofa.
"I promise I won't go on about him all night, but I've got to tell you
what happened with Mark." By the time she reached the part where
she ordered her ex-boyfriend to leave, admittedly slightly more dra-
matic in the re-telling than in real life, Fox jumped onto the cushion next to her, his eyes flecked with encouragement, a hint of musk
beginning to bloom.

"Anyway, that's it now," she concluded. "He can't come back. I've
changed the locks. And I'm thinking of building up the back wall."

Fox raised his muzzle quizzically, so she said, "Oh no, I'd never
make it too high for you. But . . ." she felt her eyes widen in excitement, "I want it high enough to keep *him* out. I've told him it's
over, but like I said, he is still living behind us." Fox nodded and,
lowering himself into the sofa, stretched a foreleg in her direction.
His muzzle stooped to rest upon it, and he looked at her along the
line of his snout.

"Listen. You don't need to go anywhere else. You can have whatever you want," she told him. "Anything you want to eat, anytime.

Just tell me when you're hungry and . . ." She gasped and jumped to her feet. "What an idiot! I forgot your pudding!"

"It's shop bought," she apologized as she carried in the apple pie. But he didn't seem to care. The idea had come from that documentary she and Mark had seen, in which people fed foxes jam sandwiches and fairy cakes. In every other regard, her relationship with him was unlike anything she had seen in the program. Those people were delusional. What the two of them had, in contrast, was real. Food was a necessity, not motivation or reward. Was it reasonable to look at other households, other balanced human relationships, and say, well, he or she comes home each night just for food? Of course not. Humans who lived together often ate together. It was a practicality of any shared life. Besides, when he arrived today, he had no idea she was cooking for him. He ate half the pie, then pushed the rest down the back of the sofa with his snout.

"You're quiet," she said after a while.

He made no answer, and she felt herself redden. She had never asked anything like this before, of anyone, and her mouth began to dry with nerves. She cleared her throat. "So there's a conversation we need to have," she ventured. God, that was the kind of thing Mark would say! Well, she refused to feel self-conscious for using the word "conversation." It bewildered her that some humans were embarrassed to talk to animals. She had once seen a famous environmental campaigner interviewed on TV, and he had confessed to resisting the urge to talk to sheep. It was the resistance rather than the urge which she found stupefying. Such shame was madness.

Fox nudged his muzzle up and down his shin, which meant she should continue.

"Remember I told you there would be traps in the woods?" she started. "Well, as you may have seen, they are all over the place. I have no idea how dangerous they are to you. Whether you spot them a mile off and avoid them. The thing is, I deactivated them this morning, but the fox man—or Mark or Eric—will reset them. It's impossible to keep an eye on them all day. I can't guarantee your safety out there. Besides, sooner or later, they'll know it's me and resort to something more . . . extreme."

He was still listening.

"So this is my idea." She took a deep breath. "Are you ready?"

He gave something like a nod.

"Move in with me."

Both ears leant back, and he made a series of quick blinks, not proper blinks, but a flickering of eyelids.

"It *is* soon," she said. "I'm sorry to be brutal about it, but it's a matter of life or death. Ignore it. That's Eric filling the bin," she tutted, as he fussed an ear at the clanking of chains outside. She waited for an answer, but Fox hooked his snout over his tail, so she could see the murmurings of his nostrils, and began to lower his eyelids. It was barely ten o'clock. Poor guy was tired with the effort of avoiding the traps, the emotional weight of the evening. She understood that, but it troubled her, this quietness. There were occasions when she could hear his thoughts as clear as day, and others when she longed to hear them, but he may as well have been switched to mute. With a sinking feeling, it occurred to Mary that the closeness of his thoughts to hers might depend on her own sense of their proximity at any given time. For all that they were embarking on a serious advancement of their relationship, she felt foiled by his remoteness. In her worst moments she wondered whether it wasn't her need powering him. But she reminded herself that these were only the doubts of a sensitive person's firm belief.

She left him where he lay and went to fetch the airbed. She had inflated it in the spare room, imagining he would sleep there. But now that it was growing dark, she saw the impossibility of going to bed in the usual way herself: he was sure to wake at some point and wonder where he was. So she heaved the mattress on its side. Clinging to it with her arms spread wide, she dragged it to the landing. At each bump down the stairs, it cuffed her nose, so that by the time she squashed the thing through the lounge doorway, sweat pooled under her arms. She glanced at the sofa and was pleased to see that her housemate had tidied himself into a spiral and entered a deeper, more comfortable phase of rest. She lowered the airbed quietly to the floor beside him.

Mary knew that these moments, when he slept during her waking hours, were crucial to the plan's success. She had no idea what time he usually ate, and she wanted to be ready. No one could bait him on a full stomach. She thrust a pork fillet into the oven, half a dozen chicken thighs, a handful of burgers. Even though she was the one cooking, she had the funny sensation that he was looking after her. She honestly couldn't remember when she had ever felt so . . . domesticated. Afterward, she rummaged in the understairs cupboard and found a large sheet of cardboard, which she tore into mats. She hoped he would use them as toilets, and she planned to communicate this delicate matter to him when he woke. She performed a few other administrative necessities—unplugged the broadband and landline, switched off her mobile and put it in a drawer—before turning to her own bedtime routine.

How strange all her regular jobs felt. To brush her teeth. To undress. To pull her nightie over her head. These usually thoughtless tasks struck her as immensely bizarre now they were carried out while Fox slept in the house. She performed each slowly, to prolong the sensation of strangeness. Were these rituals really all necessary? she wondered.

When she headed downstairs to the airbed, she walked right into his burnt licorice aroma, as tangible as if he had popped up a tent inside her lounge. A sigh of relief escaped her lips because she knew then that he wanted to be here, that he was making the place his. She sat beside him on the sofa, laid her hand on his head. Immediately his ears began to fret at her palm with sharp flicks. His mouth parted, allowing her to wipe a dribble from his lower jaw with the hem of her nightie. She stroked his head, and the gap between his jaws widened to release a small, unconscious chirp. How silly she had been to worry that he was quiet. In silence, such intimacy. She straightened the fingers of her right hand and tapped the tips on the points of his teeth. He didn't seem to mind, so she fed them slowly into his mouth, dabbing them along his throbbing tongue while his sharp jags made their way down her fingers to her palm. He panted slightly in his sleep, but his jaws stayed open. "You're the best thing that's ever happened to me," she said. She waited, to see if he would contradict her, but his mouth did not close. Because it was the truth.

FOR THE NEXT few days, Mary and Fox lived a fitful life divided into small segments of repetitive activities. They napped, they rested, they ate, they sat and chatted, and, mostly, they watched—each other, the gilt wings of the clothes moths, rich from all Mary's jumpers, and sometimes the world left to them through the streak of day between the shutters. Any negligible movement was breaking news for them. Each time Mary shook her duvet, Fox leapt to snap at specks of falling dust. When she scraped balls of hair from her brush, she flicked them to the floor and let him chase them, skittering over the boards till he caught her hair in his claws.

So what if the sheets of cardboard proved hit and miss? She had done worse things for love than clear up someone's mess. As for chewing through electrics and other scaremongering, there was no such danger. He was considerate, sociable, and civilized. Although he disliked TV, occasionally she read to him. And often they listened to Flora crying through the duck-egg wall.

There was only one victim of this honeymoon period. On returning to the lounge from another long stint at the oven, Mary found the hen doorstop on its side, the gingham split open and the floor rolling with hundreds of tiny polystyrene beans. "I see," she said simply. Fox stretched his jaws in reply; a few of the white beads had stuck to his tongue. He swilled them down and she smiled. The last traces of Mark were vanishing.

CHAPTER SEVENTEEN

It was into this paradise that the outside world stole. Fox and Mary were reading together on the airbed when the first rap came. Few visitors knocked at Mary's door, and those who did so tended to knock on her neighbors' doors as well. Charity workers, men selling dishcloths, touts for window cleaning or God. She slipped into the hall, shutting Fox in the lounge, and crept to the peephole. The man faced her squarely through the glass. He was much younger than she had previously thought; his head was not bald but shaved. She suppressed a derisory snort because apart from his youth, he was a cliché of death. He was wearing the black vest and gloves again. Even the 4×4 she could see in the street—she assumed it was his— had black tinted windows. Evidently, he luxuriated in the deathliness of his profession, because embroidered on the flap of his breast pocket were a paw print and the words *Fox Fixer—Pest Assassin*.

He knocked again and smiled, readying himself to make a good impression. Actually, he made poor viewing. Mary watched him remove a glove, scratch at a rash on his neck, check his watch, put away his smile. Why did he think she would help him? He had no power to act on her behalf. He wanted to impose his vision of city life on others, that was all. Mary waited for him to leave. Shortly afterward she heard Eric and Michelle's door close and guessed he had gone to report his findings.

She knew she needed to prepare for the likelihood that the Fox Fixer's visit was only the beginning. All it would take was for someone to peep into the hall when Fox happened to be there, and the two of them would be discovered. She found a large knob of Blu-Tack in a kitchen drawer and dotted balls of it around the letter box. The flap held even when she tried to open it, but as a precaution she sealed the top with packing tape. The activity calmed her, so she kept unwinding the tape, round and round the entire door frame, until the reel was empty.

It was hard to sleep after that. Maybe sensing her restive mood, Fox lay awake too. They had discovered that he liked to watch her play Patience, his snout following the flip of cards on the mattress. So now she reached for the deck to help them settle. Sleep came fitfully. Twice he woke her for food, and when she was finally dropping off, another knock roused her. This time her name in Eric's voice came muffled into the house. She dragged the duvet over her head.

Was it the next day or the same day when the black 4×4 pulled up again? Fox heard it first and sprang to the crack between the shutters. Then came the sputter of the Fox Fixer's two-way radio up their path. The relentless pressure and harassment were beginning to take their toll, and Mary burst into tears. "This is a siege!" she cried, hanging on to Fox to stop him going to the door. "Why won't they just leave us alone?"

She buried her face in the fur on his flank. It amazed her, how much of society's organized censure it was possible to provoke simply by living quietly in their own home. She knew she needed to rest. Yet the onerous cooking schedule, worry over how long she could make the provisions last, and, above all, concern about a new behavior she detected in Fox, which was a kind of listless aloofness, made it difficult to rest for any length of time. "This world really doesn't understand wildness, does it?" she said, stroking the white rib on his shin. "Society wants us all shut up in our hutches." On the other side of the wall, someone was moving around in Tangle Wood, and Fox's right ear twitched at the sound. Don't worry, the ear said, I'm not going there again, and with a twinge of horror Mary realized that these days she never heard Mr. Farnworth's dog. Roxy indeed! Had he really called Fox that? What an insult—when Fox's body and demeanor and size were so comprehensively masculine.

NOW THEIR LIVES broke into smaller segments. The napping, resting, eating, idling, and watching could be snapped at any moment by the rap of an unwanted visitor. Once, the Fox Fixer trespassed in their garden to hammer on the kitchen door. They watched him through the gap between the rear shutters. Another time, he dropped off an assistant, who sat on the little wall by their front door for hours, waiting for Mary to surface. The postman knocked, then the postman and Neville. Their persecutors trailed their slowing engines, starting engines, crackling radios, and crepey soles through Mary's sleepy ear. Every car that stopped in the street felt ominous. In the pop-pop of an exhaust she heard gunshots. When the police helicopter hung over the house, shaking its walls, she imagined a giant drill descending from its belly and coiling into her roof. Why was everyone so predatory? And how long could she and Fox stay stuck in this burrow? One dark sleep she was woken by a scraping sound and leapt from the mattress convinced that the police were digging through the air vent to winkle them out. Not even Fox could reassure her: her eyes went to the sofa, then under the table, where he spent happy hours shredding the gingham hen, but she was alone in the lounge.

With her heart in her mouth, Mary darted to the hall, only to find that Fox and the noise were one and the same. He was on his hind legs, clawing at the back door; these days she kept it bolted. Twirls of peeled paint lay on the lino, and she gave a great sigh. It was not relief she felt; it was only more fear. Persevere, she told herself. Fox would adapt. The path to freedom for both of them depended on Mary holding her nerve until it was safe to venture outside. She rested her hands beside his paws on the door and began to claw her fingers at it too, to show him that she was also desperate to taste fresh air, but her frenzied scraping only made him more agitated. He curled back his lips and showed his teeth: if she didn't know him better, she would have found the gesture threatening. "We are more than halfway there," she promised, picturing the emptying fridge and freezer. Oh, how she hoped they were more than halfway there.

He gave a bark, and she felt suddenly stricken that his noise, if it escalated, would give them away. A bark could be passed off as a dog. But what if he bayed or unleashed one of those bloodthirsty screams that foxes are said to make? He had never done that because he was happy. What if she kept him inside and he became unhappy? "Just a few suns and moons," she told him. "That's all." But the truth was she had no idea how long they would be holed up. She resolved to ration her share of the food.

TIREDNESS HIT HER in the form of a delirium. One light-time when she stole to the peephole in reply to a knock, there in the glass, wearing a tailored jacket and a neat, gray bob, was her own mother. Mary stared through the tiny round window. The street, fanned behind her improbable visitor, started to rock. Her knees quavered and she put a hand on the door to stem her sudden queasiness. The sickness was a kind of cabin fever, she decided, the result of being trapped inside. She was stuck on the lower deck with only this minuscule porthole to the outside while the world hammered at her door. No wonder her stomach rolled and spun with the turbulence.

She fixed her eye on her mother, hoping that a single point of focus would stop the motion sickness. The marvel was that her mother did not call or speak, not even to say Mary's name, which made Mary doubt that her mother was really there.

Tears spilled from her eyes and rolled down her nose, her cheeks, her chin, her neck, dissolving her mother's edges into a watery, navy splodge. With her wet eye stuck to the glass, Mary heard herself sniffle. It was a child's cry, a sorrowful little chirrup, the kind that heralds a long chain of similar chirrups, usually as the coda to a sustained hysteria when there are no words and hurt alone blurts small, pitiful hiccups. But this cry spurred no others. It came once, and Mary, trembling at the discovery, saw that once was all it took. She had done it! She had found the cry that expressed a need beyond tiredness or hunger, and her mother had listened. She knew this because her mother's hand was stretching toward her, growing larger and larger in the fish-eye. In a kind of ecstasy Mary shut her eyes and bowed her head, waiting to feel her mother's fingers close softly on her hair and begin to stroke. The rap of the knocker shattered her. Mary lifted her forehead from the juddering door and wiped her face fiercely with the back of her hand. Looking down, she saw that the top of her own navy dress—these days she lived in it—was sodden. It astounded her that she could weep a whole well with scarcely a murmur, but it did not occur to her for even a second to open the door. She went to curl up with Fox. She looped her arms around his tail, tucked her toes beneath his chest. His scent wrapped around her like a second skin, and when at last she woke, she went back to the peephole, her face itching with dried tears, and her mother had gone.

Dig in, Mary thought. We have to dig in. By now she had lost all track of days and told the time by sound. Once when the street was too quiet to be Saturday and too busy to be Sunday, the lounge sash began to rattle ferociously. Mary and Fox were sitting on the floor, eating—a chicken breast for her, three for him—but Fox jumped to the window, and Mary followed, unfastening the shutters far enough to glimpse the removal truck parked outside Michelle and Eric's. She had to grip the shutters firmly to stop Fox planting himself in full view of her neighbors. He seemed desperate to drink in the outside world.

"But the sign still says For Sale," she whimpered, and he pushed his head hard against her side. "They must have rented somewhere." Through the gap, they watched as two men and Eric went in and out of the house. Furniture scraped over floorboards, bashed into the back of their blue wall. Out came the sofa, the enormous refrigerator, and, she saw with a wince, Flora's cot.

When Fox heard her sigh, he dropped the firm underside of his muzzle to her hand. "All is not lost," she said. "They took everything, but they couldn't take you. Only you can take you."

A little later Eric emerged from the house with George. His wife followed, holding Flora. Mary raised a hand to the dark mop of hair that tasseled Michelle's shoulder. It occurred to her, then, that she too could be pregnant. Maybe because she had just eaten, her stomach made a small yelp, and she felt a flutter of shock. To think she might have taken that from Mark without him even knowing. She looked at Fox to see what he would make of this thought. Was it too soon? It didn't feel too soon. With her hand on her stomach, she watched her neighbors' final preparations. The business of putting the children in the car seemed to take forever. When the door shut, Michelle and Eric stood apart, looking back at the house.

Mary laid her other hand on Fox's head and said, "I think we might be in the clear." When she said "we," she let herself think, just for a moment, that they might be three.

SHE IGNORED THE next knock, ignored the way Fox leapt off the sofa, his fur elongating and thickening, as if he wore a winter coat.

She had thought he was getting used to the sounds of the house, even the interruptions, but he stood at the closed shutters, making a deep, throaty growl. Mary watched him from the sofa. Eight, nine, ten? sleeps had passed since Michelle and Eric moved out, but she slept in fits and starts, several times a day. At some point, her neighbors had canceled the milkman, and the soft electric whir of his float no longer heralded morning. Only the emptying fridge warned her that time was stretching further from the day Mark had left.

There was no second knock, and Mary turned another page. "Come and sit down," she said to Fox. She was on the sofa with her feet up, which she now tried to do between each nap. "I want to show you this." They had been looking at *A History of Western Art*. He liked to watch the pages flick, and then to slam a paw on anything interesting. "Ssshhh. Just ignore it," she told his wavering ears. She cared for nothing the postman could bring.

The painting open on her lap was by Constable, and she was curious to see Fox's reaction to the country scene. "You have cousins who live in places like this," she started, tilting the book to show him, for he had stuck where he was by the window. Then she faltered. She had not heard the postman leave. Fox gave a low guttural rumble. The black inside his ears widened. Mary wriggled to the edge of the sofa, just as footsteps slowed to a silence on the other side of the window. She reached out a hand to Fox's shoulder, trusting him to keep still, to let nothing of their lives leak through the sliver of light between the shutters. The glass in the lower sash flinched slightly as if absorbing pressure. Why didn't the postman knock again?

Even in her exhaustion, Mary felt elated when the gate eventually clicked shut, and she knew she had survived another scare. Sure, the nocturnal cooking sessions were taking their toll, but their enemies were weakening. "We can live like this," she rallied Fox, who had slumped beneath the table again. She felt perky. She had already had to loosen the tie on her dress. The scratches on her arms had healed. "We are making it work!" she told him. In her good moments, she believed it. In her worst, she feared she had shut them both in a trap, larger and more comfortable than the ones in the woods, but a trap just the same. Around her forehead and the back of her skull the sense of enclosure tightened.

She fell asleep and dreamt that she was at the zoo, on the animals' side of the glass. The keepers kept studying her oddly, as if she didn't belong. Whereas the weird thing was, the keepers were the ones who looked out of place. The parrots were chatting to her, and she sat in the shade of a tree, eating nuts while monkeys tidied her hair. All kinds of animals shared one big enclosure, but she felt no fear until the keeper's shadow darkened the glass. She cowered in her hideout, pulled a low branch over her face, and then the keeper with an almighty crash punched his fist through her letter box, breaking the seal of the Blu-Tack and tape, as he yelled her name. "Mary! Mary! I know you're there! Mary! I'm coming in!"

She screwed her eyelids tightly against Mark's shouts. "That's what he thinks," she whispered, thrilling as she heard the key jam against the new lock. Her conspiratorial tone must have sounded like permission to Fox because he lifted his shoulders and drew his tail from his haunch like a dagger. Mary pressed a hand to the place where a collar would be and felt the back of his neck thrum with a throaty growl. From the way he snapped his jaws over his shoulder, she supposed that he was desperate to run at Mark.

"Mary! Open up! You're not answering the phone. You taped up the letter box! For God's sake. Just tell me you're safe!" Mark must have held the whole door by the knocker, because the walls reverberated as he shook it. In the silence that followed, Mary heard him wipe his sweaty hands on his shorts, then let out a heavy sigh. Quietly and methodically—method, she knew, being his way of defusing himself—he dried his hands again and slipped the key into the lock. It slithered in but would not turn.

She had got rid of Michelle and Eric, and with them, she assumed, the Fox Fixer. But how was she going to get rid of Mark?

It was a moment of brilliant invention when she realized that the way to break this deadlock was to embrace the event she had been trying to avoid. All this time she had hidden Fox from Mark, when really she needed to show Mark that she had moved on. She turned to Fox with a grin. "Are you ready to go public?"

The second she lifted her hand from his neck, he bolted. His claws spilled across the floor. From the threshold between the lounge and the hall, Mary watched his rolling haunches obliterate the eyes that stared through the letter box. "There you are, Mary! Thank God for . . . What the—?" The letter box slapped shut and cut Mark off, and moments later her fox crashed his forepaws against the door, chewing Mark's shouts with his bark. When at last he hushed, Mary waited to hear Mark speak, but there was only pure, triumphant silence. She walked to the peephole, and the street was blank.

"We did it!" she cried, throwing her arms around Fox. "We did it! The siege is over!"

MARY TOOK OUT all the sausages that were left in the fridge. A dark, acrid smell arose when she peeled back the plastic wrapper. She checked the expiration label, but the numbers meant nothing to her. Well, he was happy feeding from people's bins, she reasoned, so the sausages would be fine. "Let's eat at the table again," she said. "A celebration feast!" He stood beside her, his tongue lolling on the worktop while she prepared the food. She loved the way the counter had flaked where he scraped it; each time she came out here she found a fresh scattering of sawdust or peeled paint from the door.

As the kitchen began to fill with rank steam, Mary darted out of the room. She had one more job to do. She paused on the half-landing: the place felt pleasantly unfamiliar, and it dawned on her that this was the first time since Fox moved in that she had been upstairs. In her bedroom she tipped up the cologne and shook the last drops onto her wrists. The bottle was empty.

"MICHELLE AND ERIC are gone. Mark has gone," she sang to Fox. He had eaten five sausages, two venison burgers, a raw egg, and she was now feeding him blackberries; he had a special fondness for them. "It's over. It's finally over." He licked the purple stains on her palm, and she thought his face looked sad. "Oh no, I mean the hiding," she said. "Not us, silly!" She opened the shutters at the front of the house and let in the light. The room speckled thickly with glittery dust, as if they lived inside a souvenir globe and had just been given a good shake. Mary lifted the rear sash, and air rushed in. The house sang with the voices of the day, the birds and the clapping of laurel leaves; children's cries volleyed from gardens down the street. It occurred to her as she re-took her seat that the summer holidays could have started; maybe this was how they sounded, in a family. She brimmed with hope.

Fox must have been thinking the same because when she turned to tell him how she felt, she realized, from the way his head cocked a quarter turn, that he already knew. He was looking down at her, and she met his gaze. Really stared into his eyes. She raised herself to her knees. His gleaming pupils distended as she peered in. She loved looking at him like this. There was always something about him she could not reach. She leant forward, until the whiskers that sprouted over one eye tickled her forehead, and her face warmed with his breath. It was like nearing the edge of a hole, she thought, staring at those dark slits, a place you want to know but can't go to. You think you're getting closer, but really it's the hole that's getting bigger. She had that hole in her too. It was OK. To be part of something you couldn't understand. To be unknown yourself.

Her heart tightened. Something was moving in both his pupils. With a feeling of vertigo, she squinted into the shiny black ovals, seeing with a pant that the other life that twitched in there, the thing leaning toward her in a hopeful, jealous, solicitous sort of way, was her own kneeling reflection. It was incredible how much of herself fitted in there. Within one narrow eye was a whole little Mary. Her right hand had instinctively advanced—it was what gave her the solicitous look—and before she sensed his move, Fox jerked his snout and snapped at her fingers.

She gasped, more in shock than in pain, for he had not closed his jaws completely. He had not wanted to hurt her, it was just a graze, he would never hurt her, he could hurt her if he wanted. It was only the trauma making her heave. She cupped her hands, and blood pooled in the upper palm. Two, maybe three fingers. She made to stand, meaning to go to the kitchen and take care of herself, but Fox dipped his snout and licked her hand. The surprise, the comfort, heat, nausea, made her sit back down, blow out sharp. More blood trickled into her hand, and he lapped that too.

"It's OK," she said. "It was an accident." She was sure it was an accident. And in any case, the truth was . . . the truth was that she had no right to blame him. She shut her eyes. At the thought of New Year's Day, her fingers began to throb, and despite the pain, and in memory of it, her hand curled again into a fist as she spooled back through their fight. Coffee streaming down the white paint. The crack of the mug. Mark hurling it at the bedroom wall instead of at her, a last-second swerve as reason gained the upper hand over anger. How she envied him that clever emotional feint, to muster control from shock, from the funny gurgling noise he'd made. To marshal the blood on his lip. It was Granny Joan's ring that had done it. Made the cut. Mark who had made her snap. Mary's hand slowly unclenched, and again Fox waggled his tongue into her palm as if she were holding out a bowl. It was very different. They hadn't argued, she and Fox. She hadn't made him, crushed him, pulled him apart limb by limb, boxed him in so he had nowhere else to go. It was only the exhilaration, the emotional exhaustion of having reached the end. She knew that, and in a funny way, the blood, in her hand, in his mouth, made them more kindred.

He gave a low bark that rose at the tail like a question. She had no idea what he was saying, so rather sadly she gave him the same bark back.

She left him in the lounge and went to run her fingers under cold water, but the pain made it feel hot, and her skin ached where the flow hit. Blood streamed into the sink. She needed to be sensible. Antiseptic, plasters. Fox would want her to take care of herself, especially in her possible condition, which was probably not a condition but anyhow seemed to create a new sense of responsibility to herself. It was really the possibility she was nurturing, the idea that she could. If she chose. And she had no idea if she would. She wrapped her injured hand in a tea towel and swung open the door to the cupboard under the sink—she was still getting used to how easy it was to do this—which made her think of Mark again. Mark checking on her, Mark punching through the letter box, Mark's ridiculous child lock, Mark rearranging her cupboards, Mark's ridiculous child lock . . .

She knelt on the lino with her stomach churning. All this time, there had been no lock. The poison sat in the cupboard, waiting for Fox to find it. Maybe it even smelt attractive to him. He could break the glass with his teeth . . . With her good hand, she began to shift bottles of washing-up liquid, carpet cleaner, ant killer, and scourers. Where had she put it? She moved more quickly. In panic she scooped the entire contents onto the lino and began to pick over them, splattering blood across canisters, packets, and spray guns. She checked in the cupboard, but the cupboard was empty. Slowly she replaced each item, waiting with a rising feeling of sickness to see the small vial she had somehow overlooked.

When there were only five things left on the floor, each so clear they left no scope for surprise or discovery, Mary gave a loud sob. Mark had taken it. Of course he had. He had gone through her cupboards. She knew that. But it hadn't occurred to her that he would have been thorough enough to find the poison. "Oh God, what have I done?" she said aloud. She was desperate to tell someone, but it was the one thing she couldn't share with Fox. What would he think of her then?

She was still sitting on the floor, bandaging her fingers, when he cleared his throat in the hall. "What's up?" she said. He had a gift for knowing when she was feeling down. One ear hid low, the other needled up. His fur shaded on his back as the muscles rippled: he was moving decisively and stealthily, his shoulders dipped, his white chest sloping toward the floor. Every limb pronounced its potency. "What is it?" she asked, feeling foolish that the sight of him scared her. But he continued his muscular swagger to the back door. "Oh yes!" she said, trying to regain their celebratory tone. "You're right. We've had our feast, and now . . . it's time for the grand opening! I think I might put the rug outside so we can doze in the garden for a change."

She drew back the bolt and gave the door a shove, expecting him to run outside. Instead he walked with a strange slow strut. His hips rolled thickly, giving him a broader appearance at the thighs, almost as if he wore chaps. She worried that the incident with her fingers had distressed him, so she followed him onto the patio and called out to ask if he felt OK. It was only when he failed to reply with any part of his body that she looked up and saw what he saw, that Mark had jumped from the top of the wall and landed in a puff of dust by the lime.

"I come in peace," he said.

"And you can leave in peace," she shouted, catching up with Fox, who had stopped in the middle of the lawn and was broadening his shoulders. "Go on, get out!"

"I am going," he said. "It's taken me the two and a half weeks since you dumped me to work it out, but that's exactly what I've come to tell you. I've sublet the flat. I'm moving south of the river. See?" He gestured to his rucksack. "I just wanted to say goodbye."

She nodded, feeling beside her for Fox. Not for the first time, she found herself wishing he had a collar. After today, it would be wise to order one. His back pulsed beneath her fingertips, and the beat calmed her.

"And also, Mary, I think I know you probably better than anyone else . . ."

She felt a growl form in her throat, and she balled her nose into a sneer.

". . . and you definitely know me better than anyone . . ."

Her eyes narrowed.

"That's why I'm here. I could have done this any day. You know that. But I didn't. I wouldn't have done it. Then this morning, when I saw through the letter box . . . Well, I realized how urgently you need help. I mean, look at you."

"You've made a mistake," she said, stroking the back of Fox's neck. "I've got all the help I need. Now get out!"

"I blame myself," he said. "For behaving like a jerk, for the way we broke up. But you can't live like this. You just can't. It's . . . it's madness. Look at you, Mary! You're filthy! What have you done to your hand? You can't live like . . . You can't befriend a fucking fox! You need to see someone. You need to stop this. You need help. You need to listen to me. You won't get better till you do."

Need, need, need. His old trick. He started to walk toward her, his ankles disappearing in the long grass. It seemed incredible that he had mown it on his last visit, but the garden, like her, had out-grown him.

"Someone's got to end it, Mary!"

"It's nothing to do with you! You're trespassing. You're harass-ing me. You're making out that you're looking after me to disguise the fact that you're a stalker!"

Mark took another few steps toward them, his arms outstretched warily.

"That's far enough," she said.

Beside her, Fox began to growl. His coat thickened, gleaming in the sun. He was big when she first saw him, but he had grown since then, and he shone with health and strength. He swiped his tail from his flank and held it high over his back. She could feel its load cutting through the air behind her. His shoulders rocked powerfully as he strode forward.

"All right, all right," Mark said, glancing nervously behind him to the wall. "Stop it, will you? Call it back!"

The truth was, Mary had no idea how to stop him. He was lis-tening to a voice in his head that was not hers, his tail stiff, his paws certain. "I can't," she said, following behind, excited by the sight of Mark's legs quickening their reversal, the panicked way he jabbed a foot in Fox's direction, only for Fox to part his jaws before continu-ing to advance.

"Wait!" Mark said. He had reached the wall, but when he saw Fox still in pursuit, he pulled himself up and scrambled over. "OK," he said, raising his hands in surrender. Fox stopped. It was one of the things she loved about him, that he was always ready to listen. He never lost his calm. "I'm out of here. Just let me say this. I did it for you, Mary. However much you hate me, I did it for you. And please, get some help. I know you don't want me, and you don't even want to hear it from me, but you really need to call someone. All right?"

"But you didn't do it!" she cried. "*We* did it. We stopped *you*! We won!"

Mark gave her a pitying look and shook his head. "Mary . . . Mary . . ."

"If I see you here again, I'll call the police," she said. "And I will. I'm not scared of you anymore." She felt riled by the scale of Mark's self-deception. Did it for me, she thought. What rubbish. "You did nothing for me!" she yelled at his back. She wasn't going to let him believe that he had been taking care of her all this time. "He has to make out that he's responsible for me," she said to Fox. She wanted to bury her face in his thick mantle of fur, but when she reached out a hand, he shrugged her off. He was listening beneath her words for the rustle and crunch of Mark's footsteps.

Eventually, Mary registered the lowering of his tail, and she knew they were safe. "I think that really is the end," she said when his ears still leant at the wall, though there was nothing more to be heard. "Let's go inside. I need a hug." A fly landed on his ear, and the ear flickered.

He tipped his snout at her, but his paws pointed at the back wall.

"What, now?" she said with a sigh. "Can't you go out later? Please?" She cupped a hand under his muzzle and tried to lift him round to face the house, but he arched his neck and shook her off. "OK," she said. "Just don't be too long or I'll worry."

IT TOOK MARY a while to check the woods, and when she returned, she glanced into the garden and was pleasantly surprised to see Fox already home. "The traps have gone!" she called. She had hauled herself to the top of the wall with one hand. "They've given up. It's over!" She steadied herself on the bricks, refastened the bandage around her bite, and began to lower herself. It was strange he hadn't replied. When her feet found the ground, she looked up. His body was making a shape it had never made before. His back oddly humped. Then snapped back down like a broken bridge. "Are you OK?" she said, feeling her neck flush.

Nothing about the way he moved was right.

He circled the lawn with alarming slowness. His snout grazed the floor, as if an underground hand pulled him down on a short rope. She ran to him, but his muzzle stayed low, his ears stuck flat to his head. He was oblivious to the movement, the sound, the scent of her. She touched his back, hot and clammy, feeling for a wound. There was no wound. His fur slid matted beneath her palm.

"Oh God!" she cried. She needed—what? The blanket. Water. She needed things. Indoors. Blanket from the sofa, looped over her arm. His bowl. She ran back outside, water slopping over her sandals, squeak-squeaking as she went, and her heart leapt because his hind legs were trying to unfold. "Oh, well done, darling," she said as he half stood. "That's great you feel well enough. But be still. You need to save your strength."

She tried to push him back down, but his snout was nailed to the ground, his ears fixed on something else, the belief in his own body that he could survive, or the iron claw in the earth that kept tugging him closer. She put the water in front of him, but he took no notice of the bowl or her. He was like a radio station that refused to tune, a fuzz of noise that would not unscramble. Try as she might, she could not hear his thoughts.

He lifted himself again, his shoulders low, his hind legs pushing up, and began to drag his body slowly forward. "Please rest!" she cried. At each step, his paws forgot whose turn it was and had to improvise their sequence. Round and round he went, just as that mouse she and Mark had caught years ago had gone round in the bucket. He was obeying orders from somewhere else, obeying the instinct of his hideous, circular patrol. Globules of spit slopped from his mouth, but he kept going. His body towed his heavy tail along the dusty lawn, muddying the white tip. He never refused the circle. It was as if a glass dome had been placed over him, and he could only hug its invisible walls.

"Why don't you rest?" she pleaded, when at last the circle delivered him to her, but his heavy lids, his jaws aghast, told her not to trouble him with questions. The white bandanna of fur that covered his lower face was smeared with saliva and dribbles of egg yolk. "Drink!" she said in despair. "Here!" She pushed the water in front of him, and his muzzle bobbed in and out. It bobbed faster and faster, as if the sound of the liquid slapping his snout was making him even thirstier, and he was nodding urgently, saying yes yes yes into the bottom of the dish.

The water clammed up the hairs on his chin, its dribbles drawing dark rivulets down his beautiful white chest fur. "There, there," she said, crawling toward him. "It's only me. Mary." With a pang, she realized it was the first time she had told him her name. "It's a bit late for introductions, isn't it?" she croaked through her tears. It was not what she had intended, and the slip, the stupid slip, seemed to overwrite all of the intimacy of the past few weeks with strangeness. She didn't need a name any more than he did. She was happy being Female. "And you, you are just you. Fox with no name. I'm going to look after you," she said. He made a sort of cackle. It was a noise of immense pain. She pitied him that he had to make it, and within the pity, she felt a fold of gratitude that he had come to her garden to make it. He had chosen to die at her side, and his choice validated everything the two of them had shared. She put her hand on the place where she thought his heart must be, and he keeled over in the long grass.

"Oh, darling," she sobbed.

She lay next to him, and he made a hoarse groan as her hand felt for his heart. She tried to count the seconds between each beat, like counting between lightning and thunder to measure the distance of a storm. She was counting to learn how far off death was. But the beats were erratic, and there was no telling the number.

She was crying when she said, "I love you." She kissed his snout and snuggled into him. His jaws closed lovingly around her ear, his teeth gently snagging her lobe. He was leaving her, turning off his thoughts, climbing back into whatever hidden world he had lived in before they met. He opened his jaws again, as if he would speak. But his tongue fell out sideways, and at least the grass was cool.

Mark did this. He took the poison. Did it for her, he said. Idiot Mary. She did this. She told Mark about the eggs, the hollow in the tree. She let him stay. If he hadn't been in the house, he wouldn't have found the vial. If she hadn't bought it in the first place . . . "Forgive me," she sobbed into the top of Fox's head. "I am so sorry." Her tears pasted his fur to her cheek.

He looked so pained. His spine juddered along every link of the chain. And then it started again at the top, as if every time he got the first few straight, the others knocked out of line, and he had to work over all the kinks. She leant on his spine to press it down to tell him to rest, and this time he stayed. His stomach sank into the grass, his legs stilled. He seemed to be shutting down limb by limb. She knelt at his head while he watched her out of one eye.

She had the sense that the range of his vision was narrowing, some vital channel between them closing. She wished she knew how to hurl herself into the shrinking gap and jam open the doors.

His eye snapped alert then, lucid amber outlined in ferocious black like a stained-glass window. The mist was gone, and his iris flared luminous and wild. "Oh, my love," she said and leant forward, catching sight of the Mary in his pupil. He blinked and blinked and blinked, and she cried because he seemed to want to wipe her from the lens. She lost sight of herself then. Light burnt through his pupil, as if it had just seen prey and was about to jump. But his body stayed prone, socks still on the floor. Only the eye jumped. This time, the lid stayed open and she knew he was leaving.

She buried herself in his side, pulled the blanket over them both. "Don't go. Or if you must go, take me with you," she begged, and dry tears heaved out of her, gulping and gagging until their two bodies lay still.

When she finally drew down the lid to close his poor stare—she had to be brave because it kept springing open—it was with the desperate thought that she was finally switching him off, that this whole summer of theirs had come and gone in the blink of an eye.

CHAPTER EIGHTEEN

Calm, calm. She had to stay calm. Think. The house phone—dead.
Mobile in the bedroom drawer—dead. Grab the charger. Back to
the hall. Mobile. Broadband. Landline. Plugged in a row. One, two,
three, she flicked their switches. A hum of electricity tickled her
fingertip. Something seemed to end—or was it begin?—right there
in the pinprick vibration that needled her like a pulse. There was
nothing she could do for him. A raucous cawing pecked into blue
pieces the sky behind her kitchen. The crows were beaking the news
from treetop to treetop, his death a squawk of black-winged gossip.
He was not coming back.

She needed an emergency vet. Or a fox rescuer. There was such
a person. She'd found his website once. She cocked an ear to the lino,
longing to hear the skitter of Fox's paws. But she knew. This plug-
ging in, recharging, phoning was just one thing after another thing
which would change nothing, and the realization nurtured her with
a furtive, creeping elation. The broadband blinked open its green
eyes. It must be the shock, she thought, making my feelings do the
opposite of what they should. The landline woke with an amplified
buzz. The message indicator on the base unit began to flash a red 0.

Its faint whir stirred her irresistibly. She felt . . . it was hard to believe what she felt. An overwhelming readiness. Her house was coming out of hibernation.

She stood watching all this, waiting for the battery bar on either phone to show enough charge to make a call. It was not unpleasant to wait. The last couple of weeks had been so . . . intense. She listened to the click and crackle, thinking.

He left me.

He left me yes. Because. He knew that he could.

It was the reciprocation of her faith in him.

A movement on her mobile drew her eye. The start-up animation had begun to play, a green world slowly turning. She pictured Fox on her lawn, the shape of him under Granny Joan's blanket. The hump of his haunches, the slope of his shoulders, as large in death as in life. The fabric had peaked over one pricked ear; listening to the last. She had drawn the rug right over him and then on second thought turned it back a fraction to leave his muzzle poking free—for air. It was a silly superstition, and she sobbed again to remember it. Who was she fooling? She just hadn't had the courage to cover him completely.

The base unit beeped, and Mary was glad of the interruption. She had the sense that not only the phone but something in her was being productively reset. As if to confirm this sensation, the red 0 flipped to 1, and she realized she was smiling. Maybe this was just a normal human reaction to grief—other than Granny Joan she had no experience of death—but she felt slightly embarrassed by how upbeat she felt. She willed poor Fox to mind, and this time the memory of his body under the blanket seemed to pulsate with fresh meaning.

Their shared life, the whole summer, played before her eyes. He had brought her everything he could bring. Boxers, nappies, glove, egg, shoe, rag doll, Flora, a loving relationship, a house full of hope, appetite, health . . . And finally, she could see this now, he had brought her himself. His body, out there in the garden, his ultimate gift. She thrilled at the discovery, just as the phone made another loud beep, and the red 1 leapt to 4, 5, 6, 7, slowly up to 9, then 12, 15. Mary watched in amazement as the answering machine loaded. It was oddly lifelike the way it jumped: 19, 20, 22. When the display finally settled at 27, she burst out laughing. It was the shock that made her. She didn't mind who the messages were from, or even if they were from the same few people. It was an extraordinary abundance of care.

She thought of her mother at the peephole, wondered how many were from her. Maybe even her dad. Saba, Charlotte . . . A welcome-home party seemed to begin right here in her hall.

With a start, she realized she had waited long enough for the battery indicator to light up. "Oh, Fox, I'm sorry!" she cried, kneeling to her mobile. A few weeks ago she had visited the rescue website, and now she waited for it to reload. The man answered on the third ring. He was based in Essex. If the traffic was kind, he'd be there inside an hour. Mary eyed the back door. She knew she should keep him company, but she didn't have the strength to go outside and sit with Fox. It was not for want of love. She just couldn't bear to face his lifeless body.

For a while she stood in the bathroom and watched the water fall into the basin till her unbandaged hand cupped and took the water to her face. Some old habit made her look up at the mirror, and she gaped, saw the fright arrive in the savage woman's eyes. It was her and not her. She dropped her head and splashed more quickly. Washing soaked her dress, so she whisked it off and climbed into the tub beneath the shower. When she was done, she put on clean shorts and top, pulled her wet hair into a ponytail, and ran to the front door. With a surge of energy, she leapt at the loose end of packing tape and ripped it from the frame with a loud unzipping.

Round and round the door she went. Five times. Then she balled up the giant, sticky brown snake on the floor and cracked back the bolts. Sunlight flooded over her, poured into the house, prompting an involuntary yawn, which made her feel again that she was waking up. She stepped onto her path, sensing the strangeness of being out front. The trees in the street had grown thick and green. The front of Frank's house opposite was a mass of hollyhocks. The dry air tingled with clarity: houses, windows, trees, every leaf hardened at the edges into crisp focus. She felt as if she had backed out of a dead end and was now facing the right way, approaching her home and all that it held with fresh hope.

An elderly woman was walking on the other side of the road, no one she knew, and Mary lifted a hand to wave. It was that sort of day.

THE RESCUE GUY pulled up. His window was wound down, and when Mary leant in to introduce herself she caught thick plumes of fox. It perturbed her that she found it indistinguishable from Fox's scent. Had she really known him as well as she could?

When the man climbed out, she tried not to look at his gloves or the burlap sacks folded over his arm. "He's in the back garden," she said. "Straight down the hall and out the kitchen. If it's all right with you, I'll wait here. I, I don't think I can watch." The edges of her mouth began to crimp, and she bit her lip. She didn't want to cry in front of this—Ethan, the website had said, though he hadn't introduced himself, and she didn't want to know.

She watched him go inside, then waited beside the palm in her little front garden, trying to distract herself with ideas of how she might spend the evening. A bath with rose oil, some TV—Fox hated TV—a takeout. It would do her good to have a break from cook-

ing. Then there were all the messages to listen to or save. She jig-
gled the mobile in her pocket. A surprisingly pleasant evening began
to unfold. At the sound of footsteps in the hall, she spun away from
the path, shielding her eyes.

"Hold on!" the man called over. "I haven't got him yet. Can you
come and show me where he is?"

"Well, it's pretty obvious," she said, trying not to sound rude.
Now she would have to endure the torment of seeing poor Fox again.

She reached the patio first, intending to steer the rescue man in
the right direction, then leave him to it. She looked around. The
grass was still yellowing, the trees still green, the shed still standing.
The garden was bafflingly the same as it was an hour before, in all
regards except one. Fox was gone.

"Where is he?" she said to the man accusingly.

She was staring at the place on the lawn where he had lain,
where they had lain together. But there was only Granny Joan's
blanket, almost entirely flat, as if he had slipped out with minimum
disturbance. Mary grabbed the near corner and whipped it in the air,
half expecting to see an escape hatch carved into the lawn, but
there was only dusty grass in a swirl of his scent. She dropped to her
knees. Her hands ran over the earth, feeling for something, a sign,
anything. A dribble, blood, vomit, scat, water, a clump of wounded
turf. She didn't care what. Any tangible proof. Her fingers dug into
the cracks in the hard earth.

"He was here, was he?" the rescue guy asked tentatively. "What,
on the blanket?"

The man's long shadow lay on the grass in front of her, and she
saw it scratch its head. "I covered him with it when he died," she said.
She knew what he was thinking. That she was one of those lonely
types who rang random rescue services just to have a visitor. No,
she told herself. She could prove this was real. The house was full

of Fox. What about Mark? Could he have taken him? He hated to leave a mess. But he wouldn't dare. Not so soon. Not after she had threatened to call the police.

The rescue guy was saying something, but Mary didn't hear what. She blinked, dizzy with the jolt of discovery. The garden spun around her. She felt misplaced, as if she herself had fallen through a trapdoor in the bottom of the world she knew and landed with a bump—where? This place looked the same but made her strange. Fox gone. Some weird bloke she'd never seen before, waggling on. She was unsure if she had escaped something or landed in a bigger trap. A procession of ants carrying boulders of food swerved her giant hand, and the perspective disoriented her. The garden was tipping up, the fences swaying, and she felt as if she too were a tiny creature, being lifted for inspection on a yellowing baize. She had watched him die. An hour couldn't change that.

"Are you OK?" The voice of the fox guy drifted down to where she kneeled.

Mary tried to turn toward him, but the movement accelerated the spinning. "I realize this sounds weird," she said, putting her good hand to her head. "But he definitely was dead, and he definitely isn't here now, and I don't know how to explain it. I am trying to grieve for him, and it is so much . . . so much harder if he's gone." She opened her mouth to speak again, and a loud sob came. "You see, I knew him. I really knew him. We are, were . . . friends. He loved being with me. He slept indoors."

The man crouched beside her and poked around in the grass. Mary's spirits lifted at the strong whiff of fox, before she realized it was coming off him. "Nah. Nothing strange about that," he said. "Little guy been coming to you for months, has he?"

"Not little. He was huge. But yes," she nodded. So what if "months" was an exaggeration? Some relationships moved faster than others.

The shed door swung open, and they both stared at it a moment, waiting for him to walk out. But it was only the wind getting up. That made the man, Ethan, laugh. She wished he would stop. There was nothing funny about it. She was staring in the face of an unmitigated tragedy.

"He's one smart guy," Ethan said, fetching the blanket and shaking off the grassy bits. He folded it carefully and handed it to Mary as if she were the next of kin taking receipt of the deceased's belongings. "He totally duped you."

"He did not! He was dead," she said. "I know he was. I shut his eyes for him. I'm not imagining it. As it happens, they were pretty hard to close." The heel of her hand went quickly to her own eye, to catch the tear. "And don't say 'duped.'" That wasn't his character! He had no need. He had everything he wanted. He was free to come and go. How could he be ill one minute, then get up and leave the next? There's nothing he needed to leave for."

"Come on," Ethan said gently. "Let's stand up, shall we?" She was only half-listening as he rattled on about how foxes were brilliant at playing dead. Did it to escape prey or catch birds, and if she wanted, he could show her on YouTube. It seemed unbelievable. It made no sense to Mary that he had wanted to escape. Her mind flitted to the occasions during the siege when he had stood pleadingly at the door. But she had explained, and he had understood. She still couldn't see that he might be alive and not be here. His disappearance, if that was what it was, felt so much more finite than death. In her grief, she had been able to console herself with the thought that he had given his life to free her. Barely an hour earlier, while she stood in the hall waiting for the phone to reboot, she had felt herself magically cured. But his disappearance stripped away all consolation. She was bereft, and he was more dead than before.

"But there was no prey to escape," she said, shrugging. By that point, Mark had gone. They were alone. Just Mary and . . . him. She felt less certain than ever what to call him. Fox sounded wrong. It was too intimate now. With this one act, he had cast their entire relationship into doubt. She wondered again whether she had really known him. She eyed the grass, looking for a flatter patch, the imprint of his body. But the bastard had not even left her that.

"Cheer up. This is good news," Ethan said. "He's had a happier ending than you thought."

This? A happy ending? "I don't think so," she said, trying to keep the hurt and fury out of her voice. Far from feeling pleased that he had somehow cheated death, she grieved at the thought that he had cheated her. Sweat trickled down her chest and stomach. She was drenched with disillusion. Mortification that he had abandoned her. That it took this "Ethan" to explain what had happened. Only his dead body here on the grass would soothe her, would prove that he had loved her, had chosen her, that they had enjoyed not only a shared life but a shared understanding of what that life meant. Mary stood and looked around the garden with a dawning disenchantment. His vanishing act had undone everything. To think she had called him, affectionately, an escape artist. It was the cheapest trick. So much for bringing her gifts. He had taken it all. Didn't he know it was impossible to leave without changing what was left? She gave a little shiver, for now what she felt was a cold and comprehensive dispossession.

Even in her turmoil she knew better than to say any of this to the rescue guy, who was discreetly looking at his watch.

"Well, there are other possibilities," she said, seizing at a hopeful thought. What if he hadn't wanted to deceive her? What if instead he'd tried to spare her the horror of dealing with his death? She pictured him, in a final act of consideration, dragging his carcass just beyond her garden. "Suppose you're right and he is alive," she said. "If he managed to get up, he couldn't have gone far. God, why didn't I think of that? I just sat outside waiting for you. If we find him and need to put him out of his misery, have you got something for that? If not, we could use a spade."

"Whoa there," the man said. He had stood up and was picking ants off his cargo shorts. "You were in shock. That's why you waited. You kept him warm. Left him water. You did all the right things. Maybe," he lifted a finger, "maybe you gave him the space to realize he could survive. Maybe your water saved him. Look. Now that I'm here I may as well have a quick scout about. And don't worry, if we find him and he's dying, I'll know what to do."

They walked down the garden. He whistled as they leant over the back wall. "Paradise! These woods are basically what a fox would design for his dream home. A perfect example of self-willed land in action."

Mary gave a rueful snort. "I always thought of it as woods. But it's a bit of a dump really. People chuck rubbish, furniture, any old crap out here."

"Still. It's pretty amazing for the city. A wilderness right next to civilization. You're basically living on the line between the two. No wonder he loved you. I'm guessing you saw loads of them, right?"

"Just him," she said. There was always, only, him.

"Really? It's a pretty massive territory for one fox," Ethan said doubtfully.

"You go that way and I'll go this," she said, suddenly anxious to be alone. She directed Ethan to the western end, the end where she had never seen . . . the fox. It gave her no consolation to take back his name. It was just another loss. As an afterthought, she called, "You'll know him if you see him. He has a white rib on his left foreleg."

When Ethan was out of sight, Mary fetched the spade from the shed. It was the perfect hour for finding foxes, when the day begins to lower its lids, and the air rearranges itself for the onset of evening.

She reached the clearing in moments, but this time the empty space seemed to expose her. A bramble rustled, and her heart leapt.

She eyed the scrubby undergrowth, feeling unguarded in her back and flanks. The fox's chewy tar smell thickened in her nostrils. Was he hiding in the bush? She banged the spade on the ground to rouse him, gasping at the loud flapping that rose from the bramble: incredible how much noise one blackbird could make. At the edge of her vision, something moved minimally, and Mary turned to see a snail pivot on a twig seesaw. He must have sensed her looking at him because he shrank back into his leopard-print shell. Surely leopard was the wrong pattern for a snail, but perhaps he had been one once, before a spell was cast.

Just then the leaves began to shake, and the rustling swelled from one end of the wasteland to the other, as if all the trees were filling their lungs and blowing out together. And then the branches stilled. When Mary looked down, the blackbird was eating the end of a worm, while the worm's front half seized its moment and slid under leaves.

She started to walk again. It seemed that everything was running away from her. The undergrowth teemed with creatures crawling, creeping, pattering out of her path. She was unsure if it would be worse to see or not see the fox. He was lost to her, so the worst had already happened. Actually, no, there was something worse . . . To find him out here with someone else. "Please, no," she murmured. She was thinking about what Ethan had said, about how they feigned death in order to attack, so she made her journey through the fern tunnel toward his other den with mounting nerves.

It was the sense that she was being watched that made her turn, half expecting to see Ethan behind her, with his raggy conservationist's beard. But there *he* was. Well, now. Was it him? He was appraising her as if she were a stranger, with that generic triangulated stare she had herself doodled all those weeks ago in the margin of Michelle's babysitting notes. His upper body rose out of the brambles fifteen feet away, his ears stiffly peaked, pinched along their creases. There was his powerful white chest. The commanding, if wary, expression. He appeared unharmed, though his lower half was obscured by thorny branches, and Mary realized with a crumple of relief that there was no hope of seeing or not seeing the white rib on his shin. Maybe it was owing to his distance or the fact that he was substantially obscured or just her disappointment making her think so, but he looked a shade shorter.

He did not move. He fixed her with the same stranger's regard. Because he saw her differently, or because she was gazing back at him differently? What had happened in the garden had changed everything. She had believed him to be a kind of cure, but he had taken what she supposed to be their moment of greatest intimacy and turned it inside out. Skinned it. He'd run out on them, and now there was no them. Didn't he know that without her, he was just a common garden fox? No name and no voice. "You need to come back," she said to his flickering ears. "I'll get more food, fresher food. You need to let me look after you. You need . . ." There it was again. The word rang in her head, and she stopped, openmouthed at what she had heard. The spade weighed heavy in her hand. No, she would not go there. Who was she to tell him what he needed, to presume to know? That was not what they had shared. He had brought her something different. All those weeks ago she had taken his first appearance in her garden as a sort of territorial theft, but it had turned out to be the opposite. He had given freely. Now he was going as he came. She could see he was about to go. She would let him, and she would take what he took. He thought he'd escaped, yes, and now she was escaping too. What was that expression this Ethan had used? Self-willed. He, her fox—*the* fox, she corrected herself—had never tried to control her, and she didn't want to control him. The sun glinted on the spade as she lowered it. She watched the tension in his forelegs tighten. He gazed at her, head tilted, and she knew that every hair was judging when to flee.

She clapped her hands once, like some old bit of wizardry, and he ran.

It seemed to her that she had freed them both.

"NOTHING?" ETHAN ASKED when she returned to the garden.

She shook her head.

"That's the beauty of a wild animal," he said, shrugging. "They keep their secrets. Living in their wilderness at the edge of our world . . . Or in the case of the fox, not even at the edge of it. Because the paths to their wild world lie right at our feet. Which is great. Cause we need that. We, humans," he clarified, seeing Mary's look of stupefaction. It was dissolving slowly. She had the sense that she was only now coming back to herself.

"What day is it?" she asked.

"Friday," he laughed. "The twenty-sixth." He glanced at her as they walked toward the house and added, "of July."

"See here," she said, rubbing the kitchen counter. "He made these grooves with his claws."

She listened to Ethan, telling her how privileged she was to have known such a guy, but her heart was in her fingertips, stroking the indentations in the wood. When his scent left the blanket, left the sofa, left her skin, when her fingers healed, and she'd straightened the house, they would be all she had of him. Those and the few tatty bits on the sill, the shoe, the glove, and that chewed old rag. She screwed up her nose; once Ethan was out of the way, she would drop them in the bin. But there was the magic egg, which was really just an empty shell. She lifted it for the final time, expecting to feel nothing because nothing was what it held, and nothing was the truth. And yet, even as she thought it, her heart quivered with a faint smile. She knew the egg's secret, but its surprise, its real magic, was that the wonder stayed intact. Well, there was no harm in keeping the egg. Mary followed Ethan down the hall, watching his shoes pick up a few stray polystyrene balls.

After she showed him out, she had no urge to go straight back inside, so she sat on the low wall beside her path, hot with a summer's heat wave. The truth was she had no idea what had happened. She could not say for sure if the fox was dead or alive. But then, he had always known things that she didn't, and in the past the not knowing, the not understanding, had given her comfort. He was beyond her. He had extended her world, tugged at its corners, let her lose sight of its edges and of herself. Just for a minute she allowed herself to imagine that she had never met the fox, that she had come home from work on an ordinary Tuesday and woken the next day to an ordinary Wednesday. But the contemplation gave out. It was too horrid to picture the state she would be in now. If he had never appeared, she would probably have had to invent him. Maybe humans—*people*, she corrected herself, she had to get used to thinking of them that way again, especially when she was in the office— maybe people needed to unwind every so often. Anyone could see how much stronger she had grown. Some part of her was made for a bigger, freer, wilder life. She would always have that now. A bit of that. Not too much. He had left her, but he had left her in a better place. She leant back and stretched out her legs, and let the sun warm her eyelids. The color inside was pure gold.

He crossed the wind so. No one would follow—

ACKNOWLEDGMENTS

Before writing came reading, so I would like to thank the people who taught me how to do it. Thank you to my parents and brothers for their support. Thank you, Ges Hartley, for showing me that liking books was no weird thing. And thank you, Ralph Pite, for asking the best questions and prescribing the best reading cures. I will always be thankful to Goring Library, for allowing me to grow up reading freely.

The first chapter of this story had its first listeners in a creative writing workshop at the University of East Anglia. I have benefited from the thoughts of many people who read a portion of this novel, but I'm especially thankful to those whose comments helped to encourage and steer it: Alice Falconer, Imogen Hermes Gowar, Rory Gleeson, Alex Goodwin, Sophia Veltfort, Poppy Sebag-Montefiore, Giles Foden, and Henry Sutton. David Higham Associates awarded me a bursary, and their generous early support was invaluable.

Thank you to those friends who read a full draft: Richard Beard, Ayobami Adebayo, Cathy Gould, and Joe Banfield. And special thanks to Joe Cocozza, who read every draft and has lived with the fox almost as long as I have.

Many books have been helpful in writing this one, especially David Macdonald's brilliant *Running with the Fox* and Roger Burrows's *Wild Fox*. Sally Charles and Trevor Allman kindly made time to talk to me about the foxes they knew. And my commute was easy thanks to the fox visitors who brought research to the back garden. (Though please note I'm finished now.) Malik Meer and Suzie Worroll made life workable with their flexibility and trust.

I will always be grateful to Natasha Fairweather for her enthusiasm and belief, to Jocasta Hamilton for the countless considerate nudges, and to Nicole Winstanley and Riva Hocherman for keeping me thinking to the end.

Thank you most of all to Ben, Elsa, and Gabriel: for the love, the encouragement, and the time.

ABOUT THE AUTHOR

PAULA COCOZZA is a staff feature writer at the *Guardian* and has covered everything from soccer to fashion to fourth-wave feminism. Her writing has also appeared in *Vogue*, the *Telegraph*, the *Independent*, and the *Times Literary Supplement*. She is a graduate of the University of East Anglia's creative writing program, where she won the David Higham Award. Paula lives in London. *How to Be Human* is her first novel.